Exit Kingdom

By Alden Bell

Exit Kingdom

The Reapers Are The Angels

Alden Bell

Exit Kingdom

TOR

First published 2012 by Tor
an imprint of Pan Macmillan, a division of Macmillan Publishers Limited
Pan Macmillan, 20 New Wharf Road, London N1 9RR
Basingstoke and Oxford
Associated companies throughout the world
www.panmacmillan.com

ISBN 978-0-230-76674-7 HB

1 3 5 7 9 8 6 4 2

A CIP catalogue record for this book is available from
the British Library.

Typeset by Ellipsis Digital Ltd, Glasgow
Printed and bound by CPI Group (UK) Ltd, Croydon, CR0 4YY

Visit **www.panmacmillan.com** to read more about all our books
and to buy them. You will also find features, author interviews and
news of any author events, and you can sign up for e-newsletters
so that you're always first to hear about our new releases.

This book is dedicated to

Matt Miller, Benita Jackson, Jerry Wong,
Kelly Maglia, Keith Weilmeunster, Tom Atwell, Hunter Stern,
Kara Duckworth, Eric Feinstein, Brian Maytorena,
Chrissy De Luca, Sonny Singhania.

We built each other – and what goddamn subtle architects!

He was very little more than a voice. And I heard – him – it – this voice – other voices – all of them were so little more than voices – and the memory of that time itself lingers around me, impalpable, like a dying vibration of one immense jabber, silly, atrocious, sordid, savage, or simply mean, without any kind of sense.

Joseph Conrad, *Heart of Darkness*

Little pyramids of truth he erected and after erecting knocked them down again that he might have the truths to erect other pyramids.

Sherwood Anderson, *Winesburg, Ohio*

Part One

MISSION

One

A Caravan » *Two Strangers* » *A Story on the Topic of God*

And so the living persist, stubbornly, and the memories, and the crumbling road, and the stories. And so the caravan moves east, its people all a-marvel that the bridges, some, still arch mighty across the Mississippi. The men clap each other on their backs, they puff out their chests, they feel a moment's shelter beneath the girders of their own ensteeled history.

The sun rises and sets, and they move on, huddled together, five vehicles in a row – a school bus in the middle holding the young, the old, the sick, the frail, the weak. They collect others as they move towards Florida. People are not lost, there are no more lost, not this long into the new world, thirty years gone into the wastage. The people they collect are not lost; they are simply wanderers. And if their vectors of travel happen to coincide, then they will share the road for a while.

One such wanderer is a large man with a beard, ursine and spectacular. They discover him somewhere east of the river. He is simply there, one evening, on the margin of the bonfire, as though he were a distillation of the damp night air itself – heavy water, a coalescence of air and earth and ice and dark. He wears an eyepatch, and the children, fascinated, inch closer to him until they are snatched back by their mothers.

He sups with them, holding a tin plate close under his chin. Some of the men approach him, their hands twitchy on their weapons, and enquire about his business.

I ain't a brigand, he says and scoops a spoonful of beans into his mouth, nor any other kind of threat to you. How you can tell is my guns are in that duffel over there. You can hold them if you're inclined, but make no mistake I'll have em back when I depart. Meantime, I'll help you keep your meatskins down.

He refers to the dead who share the landscape with the living, who wander in unhurried strides of ownership across the earth as though it were – by proper claim, by title and right – their own bleak purgatory. The one-eyed man promises to keep them at bay while the company stops in the evenings.

And he does, wandering the perimeter of the circled vehicles after the others are abed, putting down roaming slugs with nothing but a long curved blade.

He has a companion with him, another man almost as large as he, except this one is slow and mute. The one-eyed man speaks almost nothing to him, but he makes sure the mute is fed and washed and kept from harm.

The two men travel with the caravan for three days, and the one-eyed man says little more than the mute himself. He is not accustomed to company. When queried by some of the men or even the women, he brooks the attention as bones brook the sun that bleaches them white over the span of dusty years. He answers questions cursorily and looks behind him over the dark, empty plains, as though weighing, with minute fineness, the value of this coterie compared to his own lonesome desolation. He seems to find them comparable, the contradictory enticements of humanity and wilderness, and perhaps the only thing that keeps him by the bonfire is the warm inertia of indecision.

On the third evening, someone declares it to be a Sunday, and since no one knows otherwise the talk around the bonfire turns to holy matters.

Some words are read from out an old Bible, and if they are not prayers they string together to sound prayer-like enough for the delectation of this assemblage.

All eyes lowered, lips mumbling, one of the children clambers over to the one-eyed man before anyone can grab him back.

Hey mister, the kid says. Mister, do you believe in God?

The man licks his lips as though considering whether to consume the child whole, a wolf in a grandmother's bonnet. But his gaze is not on the boy. Instead, it stays fixed on the void, as though magnetized by darkness.

I ain't got to believe in him, the one-eyed man says. I see him everywhere I look.

The boy glances behind him, as though expecting to see God himself emerge from the dark like a vaudevillian from behind a curtain.

No one speaks. He is a man who would be listened to, for his voice contains grand and grimy oratory, and they wonder at this curious preacher who seems to utter passages from some Bible scripts lost centuries before.

He wipes his mouth on his sleeve, the bristles of his beard loud as the cicadas. He is quiet for a while longer, as though his speech were a byproduct of silence, requiring effort to form itself out of that drear material. Then he does speak.

More'n a half-century old, he says. For the hire and salary of a few hearers, I could remember you some things on the topic of God.

No one says a word, and their silence is a contract, an acquiescence.

And then are they all mute, and all slow. And then are they all his companions in journey.

And this is the story he tells.

Two

Brothers » Las Cruces » A Contract and
Its Fulfilment » Two Beatings

It is a time of vision, a time before the loss of his other
eye. Any cyclopean will tell you: there is a clarity even
in broken things – the way things fall is governed by
laws so immutable they could be inscribed on the earth
by the ink of rivers and streams. So too the way people
fall.

It is a time ten years before this telling of it, twenty
years since society itself fell down, forty years after the
birth of the bear-like man himself. These measures of
time, they eddy and flow, capricious. In truth, there are
only two states: before and after – and even those only
relative to arbitrary points. Pick one point and call it
zero – you might as well count the motes of dust in an
abandoned room.

Moses Todd, for that is his name, has a travelling
companion. Not the mute – who he doesn't yet know
and won't even meet until five years later – but his

younger brother, Abraham, his only remaining family, runted and greasy and dangerous of appetite. They travel the wide open spaces, and though they are brothers, they seek very different things.

They move during the day and hole up after the sun sets. In whatever bastions of civilization they come across they remain strangers, sometimes welcomed, sometimes suspicioned, sometimes reviled.

Moses Todd has been many things in his life – father, warrior, thief, wastrel. Abraham Todd has been one thing only: degenerate. Moses watches his brother as a man who keeps a rabid dog penned in his own back-yard.

*

Once in the course of their vagabondage they stop at a small gated community in Las Cruces. The struggling residents are in need of supplies, and they speak to the brothers of employment. If the brothers bring food, medical items, guns, ammunition, then they will be compensated with a feast and comfortable beds for as long as they would like to remain.

Sure is difficult, Abraham Todd says and shakes his head, to settle on coin of value these days. But there's other specie than food and lodging.

And his eyes cross a low-lit room to a girl in a blue nightdress.

Moses Todd walks out. His brother emerges soon after, having agreed on terms.

We're in business, Abraham says.

It don't have to be that way, Moses says. You don't always have to take the most they're willin to give.

They agreed to it, didn't they?

So they collect the supplies for the community and return. The people are pleased, and the brothers are fed. Moses watches as the girl in the blue nightdress is instructed by three older men to go and sit by Abraham. She does so, and Abraham puts an arm around her shoulders as though to reassure her. He takes a slice of tomato from the table and tries to feed it to her, but when she doesn't open her mouth he slides it across her lips as though he were applying a stick of lip rouge.

You and me, Abraham says to her, we got time to kill.

A highball of whiskey is brought for Moses, and when he gulps it down they fill it back up again. He drinks and smokes his cigar down to an ugly stump and feels all his muscles go slack. They are gathered in one of those big cardboard mansions built in clusters on cul-de-sac roads, and there is a blazing fire on the hearth that casts lovely shadows on the thin eggshell walls.

He sits on the couch and drinks more and talks to the elder men about all the places of the country they have been, and he can hear his brother's hyena laugh behind him but he can't bear to cast his eyes backwards. Instead, he lets his eyes fall closed and is soon asleep.

It is still before dawn when he is awoken, though the fire has burned down to embers. All is quiet, and he is quiet in himself, when a sudden shrill cry sounds through the mansion. He is up, quick, a blade readied in his hand, despite the woozy, thunderous tides going back and forth in his head.

A figure bounds down the stairs, a frail white shape. The girl from the night before who was wearing the blue nightdress, except now she's naked. She notices Moses at once, screams again, and runs out the front door. Now others appear, men and women commoted from sleep.

And his brother, Abraham, at the top of the steps, naked also, his filthy unwashed hands and face like gloves and mask on a pale, chalky skeleton.

We had a deal, Abraham says.

Get in your clothes, Moses says.

It was bought and paid for with services, Abraham says.

Get in your goddamned clothes.

Abraham disappears and returns a moment later. Half wrappered in his pants and shirt, he stumbles down the staircase as the men of the community begin to circle, looking angry.

What's going on? they say.

We're leaving, Moses says.

And the two brothers open the front door to find a man with a shotgun aimed directly at them. He is a skinny old man with white hair and red-rimmed eyes. He is decrepit, and the shotgun shakes in his hands.

What did you do to my granddaughter? the old man says.

It was bought—, Abraham begins, but then Moses

seizes his brother by the back of the neck as you would pluck a kitten from a litter. Abraham winces with pain and hushes.

We're leaving, Moses says to the old man.

My granddaughter, you filthied her.

I got no truck with you, old man, Moses says.

Others from the community gather round. They wonder what devils they have invited into their midst for the price of a few supplies.

You got truck with this, the old man says, gesturing to the shotgun with shaky hands.

Moses quickly unsheathes his knife and thrusts it at the man's face, the point of the blade an inch from the old man's nose. The old man quakes and shrinks away but keeps the gun pointed at Moses.

Stand down, Moses says. I ain't so sure you can pull that trigger. But I'm damn sure I can use this knife. I am repentant about the agitation we caused, but we're gonna be on our way now. Understood?

The old man hesitates a moment longer then lowers the gun and steps aside miserably.

Filth, he says as Moses passes by dragging his brother along by the neck.

The brothers climb into their car. Most of the residents of the community watch quietly as they leave. And a few gather around the old man to hold him back as he starts to run after the car, crying, You go to hell! You go straight to hell!

Some fun, eh? Abraham says.

Shut up, Moses says, and his voice must be a gavel of

some sort, because it works to keep his brother hushed for the next half-hour.

*

And when they are out in the desert, Moses pulls the car to the shoulder of the road and brings it to a stop. In the far distance there are two slugs walking slowly, knocking together clownishly as they move. When they see the car, they begin to amble towards it – but they are desiccated and slow.

What are we stoppin for? Abraham asks.

Moses climbs out of the car and walks around to open the passenger-side door. Then he reaches in, grabs his brother by the upper arm, drags him out of the seat and tosses him to the hard pebbled earth.

What did you do to that girl? Moses says.

It was bought and paid for, Abraham says.

Say it again. Just say it again. Now what did you do to her?

Nothin. I didn't do nothin. I barely touched her, her just laying there like a stinkin mackerel.

Moses wants to strike him, but he turns and brings his heavy fist down on the hood of the car instead. The metal warbles with the violence.

You better get right, Moses tells his brother.

Get right? Mose, we're fuckin mercenaries.

Who is?

We all are. Everybody is. Ain't you noticed?

Get right or you're gonna get made right.

Get made right by who? You?

Not me.

How come not you?

I'm your brother. You got one fate by me but another fate by the world.

Don't get mystical, Mose. Ain't but one man could stop me doin anything, and that's you. You don't stop me, that makes you complicit.

That ain't how it works.

According to whose laws? Theirs?

Abraham points to the two slugs drawing closer.

There's plenty in the world to stop you, Moses says, but only one to stand beside you. Whether I like it or not.

Abraham stands and brushes off the seat of his pants.

That's a touching thing you just said, big brother. Now I'm all filled with grief and contrition. Come on, that girl, it was just a little fun I was havin is all.

Moses looks at him, his younger brother. There are forces working on forces, there must be, and so they must converge on every moment, every place, every person – even his brother. There must be born somewhere the force to take care of the problem of his brother – just as his brother was born an antidote to so many strains of goodness. These things converge. They must.

Moses walks past his brother into the desert.

Get in the car, he says as he passes.

Where you goin?

I'll be back.

He walks towards the two slugs ambling towards

them. He seems as though he would greet them, except in his outstretched hand is the blade. He topples one of them with a kick and drives the blade deep into the eye socket of the other. He twists the blade in the eye and shoves it as deep as he can with no leverage. A clear jelly runs down the cheek like congealed tears, and the slug falls backwards.

They are weak, these. They might have been wandering the desert together for years, brothers too, bonded in twitchy recognition of the barest humanity.

With one down he toys with the other, kicking it in its stomach and chest. He can feel the fragile bones breaking with each blow.

Without knowing what he means, he says under his breath: You ain't one of me. You ain't one of me. Then: I'm sorry. I'm sorry.

He is soon out of breath, and the slug barely moves, opening and shutting its jaw with the hope that some meaty part of Moses Todd himself will find its way between those teeth.

Finally, Moses kicks the slug to turn it over on its belly, puts the point of the blade at the base of the skull and drives it upwards into the brain.

Then everything is still. And Moses can feel his own heart. And everything is still – as with waiting.

Later in the afternoon, driving slow along the desert road, just about at the crest of a faint hill, Moses pulls the car over again and gets out.

What are we doin now? Abraham asks. You gonna whip my ass again?

But Moses just stands by the side of the car, his hand shading his eyes, looking down on over the road behind them.

We're bein followed, he says.

Abraham gets out and follows his brother's gaze.

I don't see anything.

Your vision is of a different sort. Get in.

So what are we gonna do?

Moses shrugs.

*

They drive further, making headway through the cactus-lands, passing quiet and slow through the rusted-out ghost towns, looking for aught of interest.

That night, they set up camp out in the open where they will be able to see trouble coming from a distance. They will sleep in shifts, so one can hold vigil while the other rests. But not long after dark, they see the head-lights of a car approaching from the direction they came.

The car slows and stops on the road near their camp-fire. A lone figure emerges and walks towards them.

You best announce yourself, Abraham says and reaches for a pistol.

I'm not carrying any weapons, the man says. He gets closer, and his face resolves itself in the firelight. He is a tall man, gaunt but still strong, the fortitude of a steamroller succumbing to rust and waste. A fortitude that *will* succumb but has not *yet* succumbed.

Evenin, Moses says.

Which one of you defiled that girl? the man says.

You're from them? Abraham asks. It was bought and paid for.

The tall man looks at Abraham. He has his answer. Moses can see his jaw clamp down, as though all his muscle were behind those teeth and he would gnaw his way through the world. Then the man reaches into his pocket and pulls something out – a small brown cylinder. Moses can see it by the firelight, a prescription-medication bottle.

You did us a service, the man says, and you have the right to compensation.

He tosses the bottle to Moses, who catches it. It is full to the top with pills.

Amoxicillin, the man goes on. It's the one thing we have more of than we need. It should be of some value wherever you're going.

Who are you, Abraham asks, her daddy?

I'm a concerned citizen, he says to Abraham. They shouldn't have offered her in the first place. You took her, that's on us. But you didn't have to defile her.

Abraham looks at his brother and chuckles, as though to share in the quaint pedantry of this character before them. Moses says nothing and keeps his eyes on the man.

That's to pay you, the man says and points to the bottle in Moses' hand.

We already been paid, Moses says.

No, the man says. It's to compensate you for the renege of our deal.

What renege? Abraham says. What's he talkin about?

This renege, the man says and strikes suddenly, punching Abraham hard on the jaw. Abraham goes down with an expression of stunned disbelief that quickly turns to animal fury. Then he's back up and flailing his arms at the man. The two clobber at each other, and Moses watches. He watches while the tall man beats his brother to the ground and then kicks him twice in the stomach. That's when he steps in, pushing the man back.

That's enough, Moses says.

The man puts up his hands and begins to back away.

Like I said, that's payment I've given you.

Like I said, Moses counters and tosses the bottle back to the man, we already been paid.

When the man has driven away, Moses carries his brother to a spot away from the fire where the cool desert breezes can succour his wounds. One eye is bruised shut, and his upper lip is busted open. Bruises cover his torso, but Moses can feel that no ribs are broken. Abraham will mend.

He coughs once, painfully, and takes deep breaths, his one good eye cast up at the sprent of stars overhead.

Hey, brother, Abraham says. Is that the divine justice you were lookin for?

That was it, Moses nods.

Was it enough?

Moses uses his fingers to brush away the dirt from his brother's cheek. It is a light touch, delicate and studied. Then he says:

Get some sleep.

Three

The next day they come across a massive derelict airport.

Where are we? Abraham asks.

Tucson, says Moses. The international airport.

Let's hop us a jetliner to gay Paree.

Moses wanders the runways and the hangars, admiring the monolithic machines. The fences are mostly intact so there are almost no slugs to interrupt his constitutional, and he wonders at what a vast museum the world has become.

The paint on most of the planes has been bleached to dull fade by the desert sun. Many are docked at their gates, long hollow gantries connecting them to the body of the terminal itself. Others are abandoned at random places on the tarmac, their doors gaped wide, some with their deflated yellow emergency slides spilled flaccidly on the ground. Moses raises his palms and feels the long, smooth underbellies of the aircraft.

When he was young, and the world was not as it is today, there was a great deal he took for granted. He was a young man when things went sour, only two decades old – and for all the seeing he did, he might as well have been blind. He does not allow himself to think frequently of those times – and not out of fear or cheap lament, but rather because that gone world exists for him in faint outline like a childhood storybook that remains in memory as patches of colour, or deceptive fragments of images that are shuffled so by time you can't seem to reassemble them into any coherent picture.

There were people everywhere you looked. So many of them – you wouldn't believe how many. And all full to stinking of life and sin. Boundaries were murky, borders were crossed willy-nilly, the abundance of riches and luck so overflowing that parsing it out was a fool's game.

Even the dead seemed not quite so dead. People died, and they were hidden away from the eyes of man – enclosed in boxes or burned to subtle ash, kept present in the form of photographs on mantelpieces, home videos that denied death, counteracted it. Technology a contraindication of death. To swim in radiant pools of life, death made abstract and commercial. A notion of the mind, Moses recalls. A pretty little idea spawned in goddamn kid dreams.

But now the dead are everywhere as the living were

before – and now can be observed all the fleshly moods of death, the tearing skin, the bluish hue of rot, the muddy eyes, the crustiness of dried sputum, the salty white of chancre and peel, the acrid, biting smell of organic decay. Now, even though the dead walk as the living do, the lines are clearer between death and life. You may know little, you may know next to goddamn nothing, but at least now you can see what you are and what you are most definitely not. Moses is intimate with death – he lives in its company every day, and what he knows is that death ain't a floating up to cloudy heaven, no angel wings and toiletpaper-soft robes and dulcet harp-playing. No, instead it's a slow crawl of atrophied muscle and the vestigial instincts of our most piss-poor appetites. That's the face of death.

But still and all – now there is meaning in the goodness of things. Now does order signify, because now it matters. Now you can see with clear vision the difference between good and bad, between life and death, between should and shouldn't. And there are forces, ambling armies on the earth, that are there to take a bite out of your soul at your electing to transgress.

And it's true – the right has never been more beautiful, has never been bolder in the colour of sunrises over the blasted plains.

Moses was blind to it before, but now he runs his palms along the underbellies of the aeroplanes, like an honest supplicant to the altar of righteous ingenuity. People didn't use to be able to fly, and so they built wings. And now those wings are clipped, people gone to ground – but the artifacts of majesty remain, all the more beautiful for their inutile splendour.

Now there is much to appreciate in the perfectly curved surfaces of human architecture. And so he wishes he were an artist or a craftsman – someone to build things and name them names.

What're you doin? Abraham asks.

Nothin, Moses says, startled. Come on. Let's collect what there is to collect.

*

At the end of one runway is an overturned plane, its fuselage bent and cracked in the middle. There are bodies, long ago dried up, but they have been taken care of. Every one of them has a gunshot wound in the skull. They hunch over, some still buckled in, even though they and their clothes have become indistinguishable from the upholstery upon which they sit.

A breeze blows through the massive metal straw, and Moses can see the filaments of hair on these dead skulls whipping to and fro like blades of summer grass.

Bleak pastoral.

But the broken plane has been picked through before. Abraham finds some packets of ibuprofen in one of the seat-back pockets and a set of dried-up water-colour paints in the pink backpack of one of the little girl corpses.

What're you gonna do with those? Moses asks.

I don't know. Maybe take up paintin. Maybe it's an artist's eye I got.

You mean the one eye that ain't beat shut from your debauchery?

But Abraham remains unfazed.

That's the one, he says.

Emerging again from the fuselage onto the tarmac, Abraham runs a hand over his scruffy chin and considers the massive terminal in the near distance.

I bet there are some treasures to be found in there, he says. All shut up tight away from prying hands other than ours.

Moses too looks at the terminal.

Look at all those windows, he says.

So? his brother asks.

We're off the grid here. You notice any lights last night?

No.

Me neither.

Moses knows that where the population is dense enough to be strategic, there are people barricaded in power stations, keeping segments of the power grid alive. There are even a few who have managed to recapture and run refineries. Corpus Christi is one Moses has seen with his own eyes. Gas and electric. Infrastructure. Humanity clawing back some of what was taken from it.

But between those oases of civilization, there are vast wastelands of dark – and it is in these places that the settlers have reverted to primal frontier living.

If you were gonna take up residence in this area, Moses continues, wouldn't you want to do it in a stronghold that's got unbreakable glass walls and all the light you need?

Oh, Abraham responds. You think there's people in there? People who don't care for the scavenging likes of us?

What do you think, little brother? You feelin watched?

Always, Abraham says. But usually by you. Anyway, if it ain't been co-opted, that makes it prime co-opting for us.

So they find a way in, bashing in one of the maintenance doors and climbing their way up an unlit concrete stair until they come through a door and into the terminal building proper. Inside, there are very few signs of disturbance – almost as if the place were shut up and made relic before the chaos of the dead had a chance to crumble it.

The light coming through the tinted panes of glass all around is dimmed to a faint blue that's almost like sweetness, and over everything is a thin coating of dust, the settling of the air itself as though time makes all things – even breath – palpable and falling.

They pass a number of gates until they arrive in an open area that Moses recognizes as what used to be a food court. Above is a mezzanine level, but both escalators leading up to the balcony are barricaded with heavy chairs, tables, vending machines, barbed wire and other debris.

What's all that for? Abraham wonders.

Don't know, Moses replies. Ain't no other signs of

skirmish. Could be this was a last stand. But if it was, then where's the bodies?

Et up?

You ever seen a slug eat someone so clean and mannerly they leave no trace? They ain't the napkin-usin type.

So what's all this then? Abraham asks again.

This time he's answered not by his brother, but by a megaphone voice from the balcony above.

I'll tell you what it is, the screeching voice says. It's a couple of addlepates tryin to elbow in on what's mine.

*

The brothers cast their gazes upwards through the grimy light filtering in through the windows. But there's nothing to be seen behind barricades of airport furniture. The voice comes first from one place and then another – and the megaphone projects it loud, even though they could have heard the man easily without it.

We ain't here to pillage, Moses calls out. We'll work for food and shelter – if you have a mind for it. Otherwise we'll take our leave.

You'll take nothing! the voice says from above. Now it seems to be coming from the far left, and there are clanking sounds, as of bolts being drawn and chains unwound. You'll take nothing! I gave no permission!

What's that sound? Abraham asks his brother in a low voice, pointing to the left where, on their level, is a double set of maintenance doors. As they watch, the doors shudder slightly, and then there's a sound like rat's feet on cold stone.

How many of you are there? Moses calls up to the man with the megaphone.

How many? the voice calls back. He wants to know how many! I been here three years. I got a big marble floor. All I use it for is a calendar. You count the days, don't you? That's how you know.

Do you think he's the only one? Abraham says to Moses.

Could be.

More activity comes from behind the double doors, and another metallic sound, like a metal bar being shifted aside and clanging to the ground – like a barrier being drawn.

We better get, Abraham says.

What's your name? Moses calls up to the balcony.

My name? comes the voice. Then Moses can see some movement behind the furniture barricades. The small shape of a man dressed in colourful clothes moving back and forth in a frenetic way. He catches glimpses of the man through the niches in the stacked furniture.

My name? the man continues. He wants to know my name now. If you guess it right I'll let you live.

Let us live? Abraham calls up. Man, you best learn some manners or you're gonna—

We'll just leave, Moses calls up, not liking the sound of what's behind that door. We're leaving now.

He moves in the direction of the corridor down

which they originally came. But before they get there, a demented laugh comes from above, and a steel gate comes smashing down over their only exit from the food court. Abraham runs to lift it, but the gate is solid.

All right, listen, Moses calls up to the shape moving back and forth above them. We ain't here to cause any fuss. We'll just go peaceful.

Now the voice comes from directly above, in the middle of the balcony.

It's the work of months behind those doors, the man says. Rounding them up, one at a time. Using myself as bait. Months of work. And when you two are dead – well, then, the work starts all over. But that's just the nature of time, ain't it? It goes on ahead, and we follow. Now guess! Guess my name!

Jesus Christ, Abraham says.

No, it ain't Jesus Christ, says the man.

Then the doors open. There is no drama, no bursting. They sway open slowly, inch at a time, because what's behind them is in no hurry. Instinct can afford to move slow, because it moves with a surety of purpose foreign to most things.

Slugs. A lot of them. They push through the door, stumbling over each other. The first few fall to the ground and climb back to their feet slowly. The ones behind begin to lumber in the direction of the brothers.

Okay, Abraham calls upwards. Okay. How about James? Robert? Michael? Frank? Richard?

Abe, get straight, Moses says and brings a pistol out from his satchel.

Goddamnit, Abraham says. How many of em do you reckon?

Fifteen, twenty. Don't shoot wild, we're low on ammo.

Abraham drops his satchel on the ground and unzips it. From it he pulls a blunted shotgun, the barrel sawn off just beyond the stock.

The first few they take out with quick head shots to thin the herd. Then Abraham circles around the side of the group and begins tossing obstacles in their way – tables and light aluminium chairs, artificial plants in clay pots, light-weight kiosks. Anything that will stumble them up and make them easier to deal with one at a time. As he does this, Abraham continues to cry derision upwards to the man on the balcony.

We're gonna get you, you asshole. Billy, Fred, Simon, Lee, Gary, Paul, Albert, Roger, Carl, Michael.

You already said Michael, the man above says through squealing laughter.

Prick.

Abraham grapples with one slug that's got behind him somehow. The dead man is dressed in grey overalls with his name embroidered on them. He has a stringy beard and milky eyes – and when Abraham turns, the slug's mouth is already open and ready to bite. Abraham takes aim with the shotgun and pulls the trigger, but he has miscounted the shells and realizes he's out. Stumbling back against a metal counter, he reaches behind him to a canister filled with plastic utensils, grabs a handful of plastic knives and shoves them into the dead man's open maw. Then he uses the palm of his other hand to ram the knives in deep, where they lodge with thick wetness in the back of the slug's throat.

Unable to bite down, the slug claws at Abraham with his useless cold hands, and Abraham pushes him backwards, sending him tumbling along the floor.

On the other side of the food court, Moses has taken an iron adze from his satchel and backed himself against the metal gate. There are four slugs shambling towards him. He looks in their eyes. Humans made animal. He, too, has been animal on the earth. He feels no hatred towards these things, nor pity neither. They – the slugs and Moses himself – are objects in contention for space. That is all. And which object ultimately holds sway, he knows, is more a matter of nature's hazard and caprice than the will of any bearded Overseer with a mission for humankind.

Still and all, there's got to be an order. There's got to be.

All right, he says. All right.

He rushes forwards, raises the adze and, putting all his weight behind the swing, buries the curved blade of the instrument in the skull of one of the slugs. It is a woman, and her head hinges apart as though made to do so. Then Moses wrenches the adze out of her head and, in the same motion, swings it across the face of the next slug, whose jaw shatters. Fragments of teeth and bone fall to the cold tile floor like a smattering of summer hail. Another woman already has her teeth on Moses' forearm, but he wears a leather jacket for just such a reason, and she has trouble gaining purchase. Instead, she leaves a long smear of rancid drool on his sleeve. He pushes her back and cleaves the side of her skull with the adze. Instantly, the life goes out of her, and she collapses to the ground.

Where does it go? Moses wonders. All that motion, all that force. It must be released, invisible, into the world. If you could only catch it – then we would be as a civilization again instead of lost, lonely children wandering a wreckage of man.

He takes care of the other two slugs, first an old man with spectacles and then the one without teeth.

There is no grace in his motions, he knows. No elegance. It is not a dance. It is a labour, a hewing of wood, a digging of stone. He is a labourer, has always been. His hands have no delicacy. They are rough from use, prone to clumsiness, but also forceful. There are sniper hands and shotgun hands, and his are shotgun hands. If you give them an approximate mark, they are bound to do big and unsubtle damage.

Across the way, he sees his brother Abraham rising from a pile of inanimate corpses. They have survived again – and it is no victory.

There is one remaining slug, a man in overalls, stumbling to and fro, choking on a fistful of plastic knives jammed into the back of his throat. As Moses watches, Abraham moves slowly, as though exhausted, to where the last slug stands. With a thoughtfully tilted head, Abraham considers the dead man for an extended space of seconds, pushing aside the slug's grasping fingers.

Then he seems to glance around him, searching for a tool to finish the job.

Moses steps over the pile of slugs before him and walks to where his brother is. He reaches out and offers Abraham the adze. His brother takes it, looks wearily once more at the slug with the mouthful of plastic, and then uses the adze to get shut of the business.

Then the world comes back, the sound of their own deafening heartbeats fading into the background. And above them they hear the cackle of the man.

Couple of gladiators, ain't they? his voice says, half through the megaphone and half not as he is distracted from its use. It's my own personal coliseum. You could get to be a rich man in the wasteland, couldn't you? Games of chance – you ante up your life. So it goes, ain't it?

That way, Moses says to his brother, pointing to the collection of debris piled on the escalator to the mezzanine. Abraham goes first, delicately beginning the climb upwards, balancing against the shifting objects on the escalator. It is a slow climb, one they could not have accomplished with a passel of the dead behind them. But they will make it.

Hey, says the little man on the balcony. Hey! It is not permitted! You ain't guessed my name yet!

They ignore him and continue to climb. Moses, a heavy bull of a man, makes a misstep and sends a deckful of chairs crashing down below, and for a second the whole assemblage threatens to collapse beneath them. But it holds, and they continue up. When Abraham gets to the top, he reaches a hand for his brother and helps him the rest of the way.

Then they see the man himself. He is dressed like a harlequin in an outfit of patches sewn together from a hundred different items of clothing. It is a wonder to behold because of its purposeless grandeur. There are clothes everywhere – the world full of clothes to be had whole and for free to anyone who wants to claim them. There is no need to construct new ones – sewing a science for times of luxury that are long past. But here, on this man, is an outfit of loving craftsmanship – a bricolage of textiles in a spectrum of colours. He wears a hat, too, stitched together in the same way – a triangular cap with a brim that comes to a point in front and makes him look like a degraded Robin Hood.

The little man does not retreat as they move towards him, so distracted is he by the intrusion into his kingdom. He drops the megaphone to the ground and shakes his fists at the brothers, stomping his feet against the hard tile.

I gave no permission! he cries. It is mine, ain't it? All of it is mine. Rounded them up, I did, and set them as a trap for those who would assail me. It ain't yours to take. You ain't guessed my name yet!

Rumple fuckin stiltskin, Moses says to the little man and uses one big hand to push him backwards.

The little man goes flying as though he has no weight at all, collapsing to the ground and rising instantly to a seated position, supporting his upper body on one hand and using the other to wipe the spittle

from his mouth. Suddenly he is quiet and looks at
Moses askance as though reconsidering the nature of
his adversary. Then he smiles and cackles again, picking
himself up and raising his hands to show he is no combatant worthy of beating. Then he says:

Man of erudition, ain't he? Man of book learning or
just memories of mama stories? Who can tell? Bear
with the voice of a man, at least. The sideshow's come
to town.

*

Where do you domicile? Moses asks. Tell us, or it'll go
hard with you.

The little harlequin raises his hands again.

I'll tell, won't I? Take you there myself. Spoils to the
victor. No harm done. Nothing that can't be rebuilt.

Then the little man turns and walks down the long
wide corridor of the terminal without turning to see if
the brothers follow. Moses and Abraham look briefly
at each other and then go after him. The sun comes
through the tall windows to their left, and it is a majes-
tical fortress indeed. Fortress of glass and silence. Plenty
of space to feel your aloneness, Moses thinks. Plenty of
room for madness to seed itself and grow. A stadium
of space, he knows from experience, invites grief to fill
it in every corner and niche. This little man has been
here on his own for five years, according to his own
word. And alone who knows how long before that. As
Moses walks through the terminal, his heels resound-
ing echoes to the vast ceilings above, he feels like he is

wandering through the caverns of a mind dizzied by castaway isolation.

Eventually, the harlequin turns to the right and passes through a smaller corridor to a door marked VIP Lounge.

Very important person, ain't I?

Then he opens the door and they enter the little man's sanctum. It is no longer recognizable as a lounge, having more in common, instead, with an elf's workshop. Along all the walls are tables covered with bits of detritus from all over the airport. Pieces of planes, unrecognizable splinters of metal bent and repurposed to some other function, motors from vacuum cleaners, computer circuit boards, aluminium chair legs, kitchen utensils, monitor screens unseated from their plastic shells, fasteners of all sorts culled from a world falling to pieces anyway.

In one small corner of the room there is a bare mattress and an oil lamp sitting on the floor – as though sleep were the least worthy of the projects that take place here.

The harlequin, seeming no longer bothered by the presence of his visitors, marches purposefully over to a stool, sits down, takes up an object that looks like a mechanical spider and begins to tinker with it, gazing at it every now and then through a big magnifying glass suspended on a metal arm over the workbench.

Moses looks from table to table. There are things here they can use, including ammunition.

You tried to kill us, Moses says. We mean to take

your property as forfeit, leaving you your hide – and you should count yourself lucky.

Take what you want, replies the harlequin, for anyway the value's in the building of a thing, not in the possessing of what's been built.

Maybe we'll stay the night, Moses goes on. Save us the work of a campsite for once.

He's a proclaimer, ain't he? Do what you want.

So the brothers bed down in the terminal for the night.

Well after midnight Moses is unable to sleep, and he can hear his brother's snores echoing through the wide corridors of the terminal. He rises and goes to the harlequin's workshop, where he finds the little man still diligently at work by the light of an oil lamp.

You don't sleep much, Moses says.

Sleep's a fool's game, ain't it? The more you take it, the more you gotta have it.

Fair enough. I never took to it much anyway.

So they talk, the two men. The harlequin speaks mostly to himself – which is how, Moses guesses, he has kept his voice alive for so many years. Moses himself is simply the incident – an accidental audience for the man's soliloquy. But there is something to admire in the harlequin's speech. He employs big notions everywhere, a tinkerer of ideas as well as machines. The world to him is a world of toys. He must have been something back before everything happened. A genius of something – maybe a scientist or an artist or a philosopher.

They talk, and the terminal sleeps around them, and the harlequin's hands are always moving. Moses lights a cigar and tells of the places he has been, the things he has seen.

The world's a wide place, he says. Wider than you think. Even tiny places have got wide histories. Do you believe it?

Oh I believe it, says the harlequin, tapping his ear as though that is where his belief were contained.

Then Moses goes on to talk about his brother, Abraham, and the evil things he has done. The man goes on tinkering as Moses speaks, and Moses is grateful for not having to meet his eyes. And he is pleased to see that craft and creation can continue even in the hearing of such monstrous deeds. He is no good man himself, he explains to the little artisan hunched over the workbench, but he does believe in certain things: order and obligation, conduct and code. There has to be a logic to such things. There's got to be. Because otherwise everything is a goddamn shambles – and the dead getting up and walking'll be the least of it. Life comes and goes, and what it's contingent upon is a mystery even to the wisest man – but order, that's something else altogether. Maybe just a creation of man, but still and all maybe his most beautiful one.

Moses explains to the harlequin that it is his contract – his duty – to protect his brother, but that it ain't the world's duty to do so. The world has been, Moses says, a pretty fair arbiter of things so far as he can tell. So how come it goes so light on Abraham Todd?

The mind's a puny machine, ain't it? the harlequin says. Most of em are rust and fissure all through. What's the oil that keeps em running smooth? Anyone's guess. Some people think machines are built to follow expectation, that a machine not performing to expectation ain't no machine at all. Me, I think different, ain't I? Every machine its own miniature god circling its own miniature earth.

Meanin what?

Meaning, the harlequin says and turns on his stool to look Moses in the eye for the first time in the conversation, your code is your soul – don't expect em all to look alike.

They talk more, and the insomniac night wears on. You would think the world could get no emptier – but in the hours before dawn, you might as well be alone on the earth. Even over the palaver by the oil lamp, the two consorting figures are only accidental and temporary mates. They speak, truth be told, not to each other but to some haunted version of themselves.

*

In the morning, Moses wakes his brother and tells him it's time to go. They gather what ammo and supplies they can carry from the harlequin's room.

You tried to kill us, Moses explains.

You've got a right to it, ain't you? So take it. People abide.

What they take isn't much, since they are accustomed to travelling light. When they have zipped up their satchels, the harlequin stands gazing at them with a sly smile.

There's what you took, and then there's what you should of taken, he says. You overlooked the biggest prizes.

What prizes? Abraham asks petulantly.

Something for each of you, the harlequin says and moves to the opposite side of the room where he shoves aside piles of blueprints and diagrams to reveal a massive metal chest. Moses recognizes it as a deep freeze, like a refrigerator toppled over onto its back – but since there is no electricity, the thing has become simple storage.

The harlequin lifts the lid and shuffles around in the contents of the chest until he finds what he's looking for. He tugs at it for a moment until he manages to pull it free with both hands. He has trouble lifting it, and as soon as it clears the edge of the chest, he lets it fall with a heavy clank to the ground.

Made it with my own hands, the harlequin says, but I weren't mighty enough to lift it, were I? He's a big one, though.

He indicates with a nod of the head that he is referring to Moses, so Moses goes and takes the object from him.

It is a brutal-looking weapon – a twisted and carnivalesque instrument of destruction. Constructed on the base of an iron pipe about the length of a great sword, there are blades welded on every which way. Dagger blades and hatchet blades. Kitchen-knife blades bent at spidery angles. There are blades all the way up and down the shaft of the iron pipe, but an increasing number towards the end, where a vicious iron spike protrudes from the tip. The grip is simple and inelegant – layers of duct tape wrapped around the base of the pipe.

It can be used to swipe or cudgel or pierce. But any way it moves, Moses can tell, it will whistle sticky death through its path. He lifts it, feels the tremendous heft of it. A slow weapon, graceless and nasty. It's not surprising that the harlequin cannot use it – Moses is barely able to hold it aloft comfortably with all the strength of both arms.

But he looks closely at it – the colours of the welded metal where the blades come together, the elemental blues and blacks and greens and browns. The distilling of metal into liquid and then the cohering of liquid into strength.

There is an awesome ugliness to the thing, and Moses admires it.

He does not thank the harlequin, for such a gift is beyond the formalities of words. Instead, he accepts it in silence.

Then the little man is digging around again in the chest and comes up with a smaller object – a cigar box. He places the box on the workbench near by, lifts the lid and sifts through the objects until he finds what he's looking for. This he hands to Abraham.

What is it? Abraham asks. He holds the thing up to the light. Moses recognizes the object, dimly. He has never been one for computers, neither in the new world nor in the old, but this thing he recognizes as a something you plug into a computer port. It looks like nothing to speak of – a rectangle of plastic, smaller than a matchbox, with a sliver of metal poking out of it.

It's magic, ain't it? the harlequin says in response to Abraham's question. Here there ain't no grid, no spark, no electric. So it ain't no use to me. But find you a working machine to plug that doohickey into, and it'll journey you whole new places, won't it?

Uh-huh, Abraham says, unenthused. Hey, you don't happen to have another of them killer swords, do you?

This strikes the harlequin as funny, and he laughs his cackling laugh, shaking his head and waving his finger in the air as though to indicate that he needs a moment.

Killer swords, he says under his breath, smiling.

Hey, buddy, Abraham says, slipping the plastic object into his pocket, you're all right, you know that? What's your proper name anyway?

The harlequin straightens up and puffs out his chest, announcing himself with military seriousness.

My name is Albert Wilson Jacks, ain't it?

Moses observes the expression on his brother's face collapse.

Albert? Abraham says. Albert? Your name's Albert?

Albert Wilson Jacks, the little man repeats.

I guessed that name. Albert – that's one of the god-damn names I guessed back there.

Is it? says Albert Wilson Jacks with a bashful smile.

It goddamn well is, Abraham confirms.

That's a lesson to you, ain't it? Justice and hearts – they're naught but busted machines.

*

So Moses and Abraham Todd leave Albert Wilson Jacks the harlequin there in his solitary fortress – and when they will think of him in the future, they will think of his hands that never stop tinkering and of his words that are spoken only to himself and to the myriad crevices of madness that mark any lost space.

Back outside in the desert sun they cross the vast runways between the rusted corpses of the massive airplanes. If technology has a life, and from what they've seen of the harlequin's workshop the brothers believe now that it has, then this is a place of lost souls. A graveyard of machine corpses. Their stillness is a beautiful betrayal.

They arrive at the car and climb in. They roll down the windows to release the hot air baked stale and stifling by the sun. But Moses does not turn the key in the ignition. He keeps his hands, unmoving, on the wheel.

What is it? Abraham asks.

Where are we goin?

What do you mean? We're goin west.

That ain't what I meant.

What'd you mean then?

I mean what are we doin just wanderin hither and thither across the globe?

We're surviving. We're warrioring our way through

life. We're doin the best we can. Doin better than most if you ask me.

It ain't enough, Moses says and looks grimly through the windshield. In front of them is a road that leads only two directions: the nowhere they came from and the nowhere they haven't yet been.

Well, what're you lookin for then? Abraham asks his brother.

I don't know. How bout a direction? A destination. How bout a purpose? It ain't quite livin without a purpose to shape the action. Even the slugs've got that.

Abraham considers for a moment. He is fifteen years Moses' junior. An accidental birth given way to an accidental life. Five years old when everything went to hell, he only barely remembers the time before. He grew wrong somehow – Moses doesn't know how. But the only thing he seems to respect in this world is his fraternal bond with Moses. And that's worth something. It counts.

Okay, Abraham says finally.

Okay what?

Okay, then, let's find ourselves a purpose.

Four

Purpose is sometimes a building. The architecture of order.

Two miles from the graveyard of the Tucson airport, they discover the Mission San Xavier del Bac. Long ago, someone built a high stone wall around the whole place, but there is a painted sign on the arching gate doors:

TRAVELLER
YOU ARE WELCOME
RING THE BELL

High up on the wall, a rope has been tied around a cleat in the adobe. Moses gives the rope a tug, and above them a copper bell sounds its tinny note through the desert heat. A few minutes later, they are greeted by a woman who without speaking bows to them, her hands folded in prayer to her lips, then beckons with her hand for them to enter and shuts the big gate behind them, securing it with a whole series of iron bars slid through huge hasps.

The mission itself is a wash of whiteness towering against the cloudless blue of the sky. Two octagonal towers rise up on either side of the façade, and between them is an ornately carved stone entrance that looks to Moses like a massive holy book with a door in it – as though you were being asked to step into the very illuminated manuscript of faith. Three wrought-iron balconies protrude from the front of the structure, and in one of them sits a young girl, maybe seven years of age, her legs dangling over the edge, her hands gripping the bars. She watches the Todd brothers enter below, and in her expression is there more manuscript than in all the building façades in the country.

In the front courtyard are planted many varieties of cactus and, at their bases, herb gardens in thick verdant patches. There is a full community here, and as the two men enter, they are greeted with serene nods by the residents: plainly dressed men and women who are carrying baskets of tomatoes or digging in the earth with hoes or stitching up child-sized overalls.

How many are you? Moses asks the woman.

But the woman doesn't answer. Instead, she puts her fingers to her lips and shakes her head apologetically.

You don't talk, Moses says. That's all right. Mostly palaver'll just get you in trouble. That's been my experience anyhow.

Then Moses comprehends the weighty silence of the place. He realizes that no one is saying anything.

Hold on a minute. It ain't just you, is it? It's everybody here? You *could* speak if you wanted to, but you opt not to. Is that the thing?

Again the woman holds up her hands apologetically and invites the two brothers to follow her through the huge, arching mesquite doors and into the church itself.

White dove of the desert. Just beyond the threshold into the Narthex, the air cools considerably, as though God were a force of balance where all things hot become cool, all things cold become warm, and good and evil are meted out as on a swaying balance that always finds itself, eventually, level. Rows of wooden pews with arching backs line the nave, and some silent supplicants sit in individual prayer with heads bowed on folded hands. Were there whispers of devotion, they would reach high into the octagonal domes painted with robed angels – but instead there are only shuffling echoes and the aching sound of wood creaking beneath faithful bodies.

At the cross aisle, the woman gestures at them to wait, and they do, casting their gazes upwards to the dome and all around. Candles being scarce, homemade torches illuminate the interior with flickering movement like breathing. Could you read human circumstances like a living tarot, you might make something of the arrangement: Moses on the right, Abraham on the left, fixed like soiled anchors holding true to their resolution. There they are, epistle and gospel, parallel at the transept. At Moses' side the alcove contains a white-gowned Virgin Mary, haloed and glorious, encircled by figures who would admire her – force of the distinctly feminine – and, yes, Moses would pay homage at her feet. The phoenix exquisiteness of girls. And then, in the opposite alcove, Abraham's side, is the supine statue of an entombed man, San Xavier himself, shrouded in blue robes. A figure of recumbent death, made holy by slaughter and sacrifice.

And so would death and purity enclose Moses' journeys like cards from a mystical deck laid on either side of his seeker.

As they wait, the woman moves towards the front of the church where, in the apse, an emaciated bald man kneels in a brown robe. She does not interrupt him but instead stands where he will see her when he looks up from his prayers. He smiles gently at her, and when she nods her head in their direction, the man turns and his sad eyes fall on the brothers Abraham and Moses Todd. The smile persists on his face, faltering only slightly as Moses perceives it.

The thin monk walks down the steps, leaving the woman behind him at the altar, and gestures for the brothers to follow him. He leads them through a door and past a large courtyard where other residents of the mission are tending to a large vegetable garden. A smell of cooking herbs wafts through the desert air from a long low adobe structure on the other side of the court-yard.

Abraham and Moses follow him to a small domicile separate from the other buildings in the complex. Inside there is a simple cot and a table with two chairs. The monk closes the door behind them and gestures for them to sit in the chairs.

Please, sit, he says.

You talk? Moses asks.

I do. As an order we've taken a vow of silence, but the times warrant exception in the case of welcoming guests.

Much appreciated, Moses replies.

Yeah, Abraham says, I ain't much for miming.

I'm Moses Todd, and this is my brother Abraham.

My name is Ignatius, says the monk. If you mean us no harm, you are welcome to stay.

Moses notices that the monk is looking at Abraham's busted lip, bruised face and half-shut eye from when he got beat up on in the desert two nights before.

I know we look somewhat raggedy, friar, Moses says, putting on a formal voice. But we're just travellin through. We ain't in the business of needless harm.

Ignatius smiles gently, and all the suspicion leaves his glance.

I'm sorry if I've offended you, he says. We've had unfortunate encounters in the past with brigands. How-ever, what I've found is that most respond truthfully to a questioning of motives. It is indeed a time of honesty.

I suppose lying has become, comparatively, so minor a sin that most don't see the percentage in it.

My brother and I, Moses says, we're hard to offend, friar. You likely couldn't stumble by accident upon the offence to us – you'd have to give it your full effort and strategy. So don't fret yourself on that account. We're happy to get whatever you feel like offerin. And we're happy to offer services in exchange.

Very kind of you, Ignatius says.

Kind ain't exactly hittin the nail on the head, Moses says, glancing at his brother. But we'll try to be of little bother to you.

There are not many of us here. Fifteen, and three children. The vow of silence is hardest on them, the children. But the quiet seems an appropriate devotion when the world itself has lost its tongue. And there is a practical purpose as well – it keeps from attracting the dead.

It's as true an act as any, Moses says. We're all of us become our actions – and any act done in sincerity is as good as we can hope for.

Well spoken, Ignatius says and nods his head in approval.

So the brothers are given permission to visit freely the compound, and they do, giving friendly nods to the residents. Moses keeps close to his brother to watch him. There are girls here, young and younger, and Moses does not like to think about what kind of temptation they give to Abraham.

*

Just before the sun sets, everyone gathers at two long wooden picnic tables behind the church itself. Food is served – a stew of vegetables and beans, brick-oven-baked bread, water sweetened with cactus nectar. During the meal Moses notices two things, one that distracts him from the other. First, he notices a young woman who is escorted to the table by two other women and seated at the end as though with great honour. Moses has not seen her around the compound before this moment, and she wears a white gown that looks like the one worn by the Virgin Mary statue in the epistle alcove of the church. Treated like a queen, Moses expects the girl will behave in a queenly fashion. Instead, though, she eats her stew with a spoon gripped in her fist like a child would grip it – and her eyes are darting and sly rather than peaceful like the eyes of the other parishioners present. And when she sees newcomers Moses and Abraham at the table, she stares hard at them for a few minutes – a look with more gut than glory, more gravel than grace.

Moses would like to watch this young woman and read the meaning of her presence at the table, but he sees his brother Abraham's attention caught by the little blonde-headed girl who greeted them from the balcony when they first arrived. The girl wears a pair of sunflower shorts and a white tank top, and she slurps loudly at her stew. It is impossible to interpret Abraham's gaze on the girl, but Moses fears it. His brother, he knows, is abominable – and where but in a place of God is abomination more apt to quench its awful appetites?

What will Moses do if his brother looses his demons in this place? You suffer your loyalties as you suffer any burden.

So Moses watches his brother, a searing ember growing in the pit of his stomach. After the meal is over and the gentlefolk once again scatter to their routine business, he sees Abraham, his eyes still on the little blonde girl, rise from the table and go to his satchel. Moses rises as well and feels the action warming in his hands. Something is happening.

But when Abraham moves towards the girl, it is because he has a gift in his hands – the set of watercolour paints he salvaged from the broken fuselage at the airport. Abraham kneels down in front of the girl, puts the plastic palette in her hands and uses the brush that comes with it to show her what to do.

Look, he says to her. They're paints.

He takes the brush, draws it across his tongue to moisten it, dips it into the red oval of dried colour and then paints a red streak across the back of his hand.

But you don't gotta use spit, he says to the girl. They'll refresh with a little water.

The girl clutches the paint to her and smiles up at him.

I know you ain't supposed to talk, Abraham says. So don't worry about thankin me or anything.

But the girl leans over and whispers in Abraham's ear. Moses has crept close enough that he can hear the words himself.

The girl says, I don't always hush like I'm supposed to.

Abraham laughs out loud, pats the girl on the head and stands up again.

Atta girl, he says. Obeying too much'll make you soft-headed.

The girl scurries away, and Abraham turns to find his brother just behind him. He must notice something untrusting in Moses' expression, because his own grows dark and spiteful.

It ain't blood in everything you see, Abraham says. How about trying to wipe your eyes clean?

Moses says nothing, and he watches his brother walk off around to the front of the church.

*

And so, long after the sun sets and the residents of the Mission San Xavier del Bac have gone to sleep and the snakes have emerged from their nests to warm themselves on the stones that still hold the heat of the day, then does Moses, who has trouble sleeping, wander the compound and find the monk Ignatius kneeling in prayer at the altar of the church. He tries to retreat quietly, but his unwieldy body crashes into a wooden pew and sends screeching disharmony to all corners of the cruciform structure.

Sorry, friar, Moses says and continues to back away.

Don't apologize, says Ignatius, rising from his knees and standing with his hands folded. At this hour it's only you and me and God. Please don't look so stricken. Stay if you like. Sinner though I am, I look forward to the times when I can exchange words.

The harlequin Albert Wilson Jacks – he too was a man of observance and faith. And so Moses finds himself again, for the second night in a row, engaged in late and lonely palaver with a man of holy demeanour. He sits down gently on the wooden pew, and Ignatius sits near him, the two men facing forwards, gazing at the ornate golden interior of the apse.

When you pray, Moses asks, you pray without words?

I do. In prayer, speech is simply a byproduct.

What were you praying? I mean when I came in.

I was reciting a passage from Daniel. Would you like to hear it?

I reckon I could listen to it.

And the fourth kingdom shall be strong as iron. For as much as iron breaketh in pieces and subdueth all things, and as iron that breaketh all these, shall it break in pieces and bruise.

Break in pieces and bruise, Moses repeats barely audible.

And whereas thou sawest the feet and toes, part of potters' clay and part of iron, the kingdom shall be divided. But there shall be in it the strength of iron, for as much as thou sawest the iron mixed with miry clay. And as the toes of the feet were part of iron and part of clay, so the kingdom shall be partly strong and partly broken.

It's a good prayer, Moses says, nodding his head and stroking his black beard. A fine prayer.

It's apt, Ignatius agrees.

We're all of us partly strong, partly broken, ain't we?

I would say so. But Ignatius must see something in Moses' flinching expression, because he goes on to ask: What happened to your brother?

Abraham?

For a moment, Moses is confused. What is it that the monk is asking? But Ignatius clarifies with a hand gesture circling his face. What he's asking is how Abraham came to be so damaged of physique.

Oh, Moses says, that. He got into a tussle a few days back. The other man got him pretty good. It was out in the desert. He walked away – the other guy, I mean. I didn't kill him or nothin.

Ignatius nods but says nothing. Moses supposes he's waiting because he hasn't heard the real answer to what he was asking.

The big man shifts in the pew, and the wood creaks uncomfortably beneath his weight.

There was a town, Moses goes on. Abraham, he got – he got too close to one of the girls. I mean, it was agreed upon. Consensual, I mean. But still and all – there was something about him she didn't cotton to. He must of done something – I don't know what—

I think I understand, Ignatius says.

Moses looks at him, wondering if the man truly does understand. A man of God after all – but also one of pretty phrases and toy silences.

He was born wrong, Moses says.

But you watch out for him.

Watch out for him, Moses repeats as though the

phrase has two meanings, which it does, and he is juggling between them in his mind. I got a brother's duty, he says at last.

And what does that duty tell you?

It tells me I'm his blooden kin and that even the worst of us has got at least one person in the world to honour them.

Ignatius says nothing.

I try to keep him from doing things, Moses says miserably.

Ignatius again says nothing – just continues to stare piously at all that baroque gold artistry above the altar. Maybe God speaks directly to him through statues.

What I would know is this, Moses says, raising his voice suddenly so that it echoes through the empty hall. If I'm the one man whose duty it is to honour my brother, how many others are out there – not blood to him, mind you – whose duty it is to hold him true accountable for the things he does? How many? What would your reckon on that number be?

Moses points angrily, first at the statue of the Virgin Mary in the alcove on the right and then to the entombed statue of Saint Xavier in the alcove on the left.

A man ain't built like a church to hold divided loyalties. How can a man do honour to both a man and the man's victims? You tell me that. Where is the order that would punish this man? What about all this?

Again Moses gestures to the church – all the statues of saints and angels and martyrs looking down upon them.

I brung him here, and I lay him down before you – and where is the arbiter to set him true or make him pay? You command tongues to hold themselves for the name of God – and now there's a sinner, nay two, in sore need of redemption or condemnation – either one'll do. So redeem or condemn. I keep to my order, so why ain't you keepin to yours?

Moses, having spilled forth this liturgy of frustration, looks again to the monk Ignatius, who sits benignant with his head bowed and his hands folded in his lap – as though his were a peace that becomes stronger the more you assail it.

Finally, Moses sits back in the pew and breathes deep.

I apologize, friar, he says quietly. I'm a coarse lout who sometimes talks out of turn.

Ignatius shakes his head, as though forgiveness were too bulky a thing for two such puny beings to trade between them.

You are looking for an order, the monk says, some structure beyond your own contrivance. It may be that there is no such order.

This strikes Moses as funny, and he gives a brief, aborted chuckle.

You're not much of a friar, friar, he says.

The laws we create for ourselves are beautiful, says the smiling Ignatius, but don't expect the world to conform to them. You'd be lucky to find one single other person who shares your code. If you do find that person, cleave to him with ferocity. But otherwise . . .

Order's a dancin megrim, eh?

Now Ignatius chuckles.

You have a poetry that makes me miss the words I so infrequently use.

That's a kindness, friar, assuming you're not makin fun.

Rest assured. Friars don't make fun.

They sit in silence for a while, listening to the crackle of the single torch left burning in the church. The shadows move long and panicked in the orange flicker, and the statues cast phantasmagoric shadows across the frescoed walls – and the effect is of two different artforms in combat.

It's a beautiful place you've got here, friar, Moses says.

It was built by the Papago in the eighteenth century under the direction of a man named Juan Bautista Velderrain.

Moses nods.

There's been a lot of history between then and now, Moses says. The memory of a man's name – what does it get you?

Not much, I suppose. Just a thing to collect. Like stamps or currency – things whose values used to be accepted as common. Still, not all the magics of the past have gone away. There are still some in the desert. Still some even here at the mission.

Like what magics?

Ignatius breathes in deep and narrows his eyes as though looking past the very walls of the structure.

Interesting thing about the Papago, he says. Apparently their customs lacked much of the pageantry of other tribes'. Their dances were shuffling barefoot on the earth. Their music was drumming on overturned baskets – which makes almost no noise. Everything they did was aimed downward, as though life were something that came from above and were meant to be spilled into the earth. Now everything's backwards. You plant life in the earth – call it death if you like – but it gets spit back up. Maybe we've fed the earth too much. Maybe it's lost a taste for us.

Maybe, Moses says. He's thinking about the sound of dry palms pounding on overturned baskets in the middle of the desert. Dry, skeletal rattle, man shaking his bones.

I have a job for you, Ignatius says, if you could find terms on which to take it.

What's the job?

Tomorrow we'll talk. I want to show you something. But tomorrow.

*

Talk, Moses says to the caravaners. All we've got is talk.

He pauses in his story as if to show how great a vacuum is left in the world by the absence of speech. He gazes into the bonfire, and the others gaze with him. It is late, and the sky overhead is lightless, the stars hidden behind the blinding screen of smoke from the fire.

Talk, Moses says again. There ain't nothin good or bad in the universe that can't be turned the other way by talkin it around. The world, it's all palaver. You might think different – I did too, then. But break bone and tear flesh, those are just actions that a man might do, just ways of killing time between the questions we ask ourselves in the dark. Me, I've built and broken in equal share – and the earth ain't any more or any less, on the balance, as a result of my doings. But you could just sit still like we're all doin right here and talk your way the entire journey from heaven to hell and whatever purgatory's between.

He pauses again. No one speaks. Miles are travelled, perhaps, in their minds.

I've wielded thousands of weapons in my half-century of livin, Moses continues. Everything from rifle to tree branch. And I'm tellin you there's no artillery more powerful than words. Those spoken and those un – it makes no difference.

The mute who travels with him, the one he calls Maury, suddenly howls up at the sky, an extended, inchoate keen like that of a coyote – representing not hunger nor loneliness nor anything else but some arcane and inscrutable desire cried to the unanswering heavens. One-eyed Moses turns to look at his companion with brief but solicitous care. But the mute hushes again and begins to play with his fingers quietly.

Words, Moses goes on, spoken or un, comprehensible or in, it makes no difference. I used to be one kind of man, and then I became another. And then another. And still another after that. Moses Todd, the painted man. Maybe all of us are painted, all of us circus clowns – and the act moves from ring to ring. I used to be one kind of man, and then I spoke to a monk and I became someone else. And then there was a girl, and the two of us talked, and I became someone else.

He goes silent for a moment, his eyes lost in contempla-
tion of his own past, but then he shakes himself back into the
present.

But no, that's something else – the girl, I mean – that's a dif-
ferent story. See, words are dangerous for how they proliferate.
The plague of the dead ain't nothin to the plague of language,
for it works insidious at your memory and your perception of
all things. This story – the one I'm speaking to you right now –
it's about holy things. But the tellin of what's holy and what's
not – well, that's a beautiful magic of parlance, ain't it?

He pauses again, lowering a stick into the fire until it
catches and then bringing the flaming end up to his cigar. He
puffs three times to bring the weed alight, lets the smoke spill
out between his lips and over his beard, and then continues his
story.

*

The brothers sleep in a crib of the horse stables on
mounds of dry hay. It looks as though there have not
been any horses in the stable for many years. Instead,
much of the space is taken with the storage of provi-
sions – barrels of water in anticipation of the dry
months, jars of food in anticipation of famine.

They were offered beds in one of the bunkhouses,
but Moses declined for the both of them. They have
slept in worse than a stable crib, and there is a sour
pleasure in sleeping as beasts among these good and
righteous people. Moses bites down upon the self-
subjugation, as you would upon a rotten tooth to feel
the flare of pious pain.

In the morning when Moses wakes, coughing the dust from his lungs and picking dry hay from his beard, he discovers that his brother Abraham is gone from the crib. He rushes from the stable and through the courtyard where the faces of the acolytes question him without words. Ignoring their expressions, he continues the search for his brother near the picnic tables, by the kitchen house, in the vegetable garden.

He eventually discovers Abraham in the church itself. He holds in his hands a fragment of cloth that has painted on it in watercolours a house and a sunset and a smiling girl. The girl herself stands next to him and beams up happily at his admiration.

This is quite a picture now, he says to her, holding it out away from him in an exaggerated performance of appreciation. You got a deft touch with the brush. I'll tell you something, this is about as pretty a picture as I've seen in years. They should hang this up in a museum somewhere. You know what a museum is?

The girl shakes her head no.

It's a place where they put all the greatest paintings in the world. And this one here could hold its own against any of those.

He hands it back to her with great delicacy.

You best hold tight to that, he says. Keep it safe. It's so pretty, someone's gonna want to steal that away from you.

The girl takes the watercolour back and scurries away.

Behind Moses the monk Ignatius appears. He has been observing the interaction as well.

Your brother doesn't seem like the man you make him out to be, Ignatius says quietly.

You missed the point, friar, the lesson he was teachin that girl. It was to watch out because pretty things get plucked.

Then Abraham notices the two standing in the wide doorway of the church.

Mornin, he says. Moses can see him bristling under his brother's suspicious gaze.

Good morning, Ignatius says. I trust you both slept well. I hope you'll reconsider your arrangements for tonight and take one of the bunkhouses. We have plenty of room.

I think we may be movin along today, friar, says Moses. You been very kind, and we don't want to take undue advantage of your hospitality.

Leaving so soon? Ignatius says. All the more reason to show you what I need to show you and make you my proposition. You have weapons, I take it?

So Ignatius instructs them to get a couple guns from their car and to meet him at the front gate of the compound.

What do you suppose the holy man has in mind for us? Abraham asks Moses as they dig through the satchels of weapons in the trunk of the car. You think it's a trap?

It ain't a trap, Moses says.

Then what?

Moses shrugs.

We'll know when we know. It ain't these people who are a danger to *us*.

What's that mean?

But Moses doesn't respond. He hands his brother a rifle and takes a pistol for himself and walks to the front gate of the mission, hearing Abraham slam the car trunk closed and follow behind him.

At the gate, they find the monk Ignatius waiting for them – and next to him the young woman in white robes that Moses noticed at dinner the night before. She has long red hair brushed straight out over the back of the robes, and there's a quality to her expression that Moses can't make sense of – as though there were springs in the corners of her mouth that naturally want to draw her face into a sneer were it not for the constant exhausting effort to keep it serene. He estimates her age to be just over two decades – though a pair of decades rich with hazard and life.

Ignatius gestures for them all to follow him out the front gate – and once outside he glances around nervously, but there are no slugs to be seen. In the distance, there are desiccated, sand-blown corpses like features of the desert – and some of them might rouse themselves to action if you were to come near them – but the place is too barren for much life, even the life of the dead.

As they walk around the perimeter of the mission, Ignatius introduces the woman.

Abraham and Moses, I am honoured to introduce you to the canoness, the Vestal Amata.

The which now? Abraham says.

Pleased to meet you, Moses says.

May God grant you life, the robed woman says and gives the brothers an expansive smile.

You talk? Moses says, and the woman glances quickly at Ignatius, who nods forgivingly.

She has had trouble taking to the vow, Ignatius explains. She does her best – especially around the others – but it's possible that silence is anathema to her nature.

We are all bound to fall in some way, the woman says. Otherwise how would we know rising? My particular dereliction is the spoken word.

It's okay, Abraham says. We've seen worse derelictions, haven't we, Mose?

Moses ignores his brother and turns to the woman.

What title was that the friar gave you?

She is a canoness, Ignatius explains before the woman has a chance to speak. She serves the church, though she has taken no vow.

The woman lowers her eyes to the ground she walks upon, as though in deference or shame. Still, Moses knows shame, knows regret, and what he reads in the woman's movements is something different entirely.

Not that title, Moses says. You called her something else.

Vestal, says Ignatius.

Like in vestal virgin?

What kind of virgin's a vestal virgin? Abraham asks.

Come this way, Ignatius says. Right up here.

They are climbing a small hill behind the mission, and near the top they arrive at a flat area bordered by high jagged rock formations that create an unclimbable wall. At the base of the rock wall is a grotto where the rock recedes under a half-moon overhang creating a low, shallow dell like the mouth of a troll. In the shallow cavern is something that looks like a white marble sarcophagus – and across the mouth of the opening is a long iron gate held in place by two marble columns on either end. Strung between the bars of the gate and along the filigreed wrought iron at the top, there are garlands of flowers gone dead and dry long ago.

What is it? Moses asks.

It was built as a shrine to the Blessed Virgin, Ignatius explains. Look.

He points up to a cavity higher in the rockface, and inside there's a small statue of the Virgin Mary like the one in the mission church below.

As they approach the grotto, Moses sees two other recumbent figures behind the gate. One is another virgin statue – this one broken at the base and knocked to the ground. The other is the body of a man, prostrate and half hidden by the marble shrine. It is only when they are at the gate, Abraham gripping the bars, that the body of the man begins to move, slowly and with great effort using the shrine to hoist itself first to its knees and then to its feet.

Who is that? Moses asks.

His name is Perry. Douglas Perry. He died five months ago.

What're you keepin him penned up for? Abraham asks.

We're not keeping him. When he got sick and knew his end was near, he came out here to die. We didn't think it was our right to question his final resting place.

As they watch, the dead man lumbers over to the gates and reaches his arm through to the watchers, who back away just out of his grasp. His skin is dark and leathered, burned from the sun, his eyes milky white, his hair pebbly with blown dirt. Otherwise his body is intact – as though he will simply shrivel up and blow away as a dried husk or as the petals of the dead flowers wound through the gate.

Maybe he has obligated himself as the custodian of our shrine, Ignatius says. I like to think so.

What do you want to show us? Moses asks. He is made uneasy by the odd assortment of things – the broken Virgin, the raisin-headed slug, the maw-like cavern, the redheaded Vestal. He wishes to be away from this place.

Without responding, the monk Ignatius moves to the right end of the gate, where there is a hinged door shut with a chain and lock. He uses a key to undo the lock and slides the chain away.

Both Todd brothers ready their weapons and aim them at Douglas Perry, who begins to move slowly towards the door in the gate, clutching at each metal bar as he goes.

What're you doin? Abraham says.

But Ignatius ignores him and turns instead to the Vestal.

Amata, if you please, he says and gestures with an open palm for her to step into the gated grotto.

No, huh-uh, Abraham says. I ain't here for no perverted sacrifices.

Moses rushes forwards and gets between the girl and the door in the gate. Meanwhile, Douglas Perry moves closer.

Wait, Ignatius says.

I'm gonna kill this thing, Abraham says and aims his rifle at the slug's head.

Please wait, Ignatius says. He won't hurt her.

That thing ain't your parishioner any more, friar, Moses says. It don't discriminate between holy and un.

I promise you, he says. He won't hurt her. Amata, please.

He turns to the redhead with a look of longing.

Then she, the Vestal, produces a look of utmost peacefulness and brilliance – like a stage angel backlit with spotlights.

It's all right, she says to Moses, putting her hand on the hand that holds the pistol and lowering it for him. He won't hurt me. It's all right. I'll show you.

Moses does not trust her – trust isn't what's behind it. But the strange woman has a desire to prove herself at the mouth of death, and that's something Moses respects. He will come between her and him who would make her a victim, but he is not one to come between any woman and the mode of life or of death she chooses for herself. He will not be held arbiter of such things, and he steps aside.

What're you doin, Mose? Abraham asks, the rifle still aimed at the slug's head.

Let it happen, Moses says. It's her own say-so.

So Abraham follows his brother's lead. The Vestal Amata steps into the grotto, and Ignatius closes the door behind her and locks it again.

And that's when Moses Todd sees something he has never seen before in all his travels across the wide and fissured country.

*

The Vestal Amata steps towards the dead man Douglas Perry. She comes within two feet of him and offers herself to him, spreading her arms wide, palms up to the sky, head lowered in submission. The slug turns his gaze upon her, and for a moment everything stops. The two stand together, a wretched tableau, ancient beast and virgin sacrifice, devil and canoness, displayed behind black bars strung through with dead flowers, under the stony proscenium of the grotto. There they stand, like statues in a museum diorama – or a new station of the cross: holy horror rendered paralysed and dumb.

The slug looks at the Vestal, his eyes cloudy and curious. He seems confused by her presence, by the aggression with which she offers herself up to him. An embarrassment of riches for the cannibal dead. But his confusion quickly transforms to something else – and something else besides hunger too. For a moment it looks like deference – Moses believes for a second that he sees obeisance in the way Douglas Perry's eyes drop to the hard-packed earth at the feet of the redheaded woman. But then Moses realizes it's not even that, not even awed respect or fear but rather just indifference. The slug loses interest. The dead man Douglas Perry looks at the woman as he would with faint curiosity at empty clothes fluttering their sleeves on a clothesline in the middle of an abandoned yard. A momentary distraction before the resumption of a purposeless wandering.

And so the slug drops his eyes, turns away from the Vestal and takes a few shambling steps in the opposite direction.

What in the holy hell, Abraham exclaims.

What's the matter with him? Moses asks Ignatius. You trained him? Is that what you did?

Moses has never heard of such a thing being done, but maybe the monk Ignatius has found a way.

Did you blind him? Moses asks of Ignatius, who stands, smiling proudly. He can't see her? What did you do?

It isn't him, Ignatius says finally.

What? What do you mean it ain't him?

And then, as if illustrating the friar's point, the slug Douglas Perry takes an interest in Moses himself, reaching at him with clawing fingers, stretching out one arm in desperate hunger through the bars.

It isn't him, Ignatius says again. It's her.

*

It was in a travelling sideshow that Ignatius discovered her. It was a mangy troupe of men who passed from place to place, seeking shelter and services in exchange for an opportunity to view their menagerie of freaks. The troupe travelled in a convoy of caged vans. They would park the vans in a row and open the back doors of each to reveal a slug or two behind welded metal bars. These slugs were monstrously transformed – some just remnants of animated bodies, and others surgically altered as if by a mad Frankenstein. There was one creature that was just a head, suspended in a large fish-bowl and swaying back and forth from a harness made of belts, its mouth opening and closing like a Venus fly-trap waiting for something edible to fly into it. There was a dead woman whose body was gone just below her shoulders, just a head, neck and a pair of arms to drag herself about. Another had an additional head stitched on the shoulder of a body that had had its arms removed. The two heads gnawed at each other, chewing away the flesh of the cheeks not in animosity so much as boredom. The arms had been removed, presumably so that the creature couldn't simply rip off the added head. One playful van contained a dead child, a young boy dressed in a sailor suit. His cage was filled with severed hands which he chewed like a dog or gathered into piles or tossed about. One dead woman had multiple rotting breasts sewn all over her torso in imitation of a nursing sow and, in the same cage, there was a man with multiple penis lengths sewn together in a row so that he dragged around his penis like a tail, tripping over it with cartoon absurdity.

A bizarre and horrible exhibition of distorted humanity indeed – an antic and fleshy rococo delivered in metal boxes roving across the country. And she was one of them, the redhead, shut up in one of the vans with an emaciated slug who showed no interest at all in eating her. They had been wretched cohabitants for nine weeks before the troupe stopped at the mission and Ignatius found there his holy woman.

It was immediately clear to me, he says, that she is an offering from God Himself. The incarnation of His grace. A breathing, walking end to our suffering.

So he attempted to barter for her, trying to convince the leader of the troupe, a man named Fletcher, to trade her for supplies, shelter, meals, blessings, even some of his congregation willing to sacrifice themselves for the exchange of this imprisoned seraph. But Fletcher would not have it. The redhead was his prime attraction.

He was a greasy, spotted man with scabs and scars all over his body. He chewed on his own fingers as though he were himself part slug. But even though he smelled of foulness and pestilence, and even though he was oozing with abomination, he was among the horrid crew of the living.

She ain't for sale, padre, Fletcher said. But you can take another glance at her on the house. Or for a sift through your medicine cabinet, I could arrange you a quick wick-dip in her. I know you're a holy man and whatnot, but holy bangin holy's gotta be a lawful act, don't it?

So Ignatius cast them out of the mission and told them to move on. But he followed them and, three nights later, when Fletcher and his men were drunk and whoring in a compound near Yuma, he stole the woman away and brought her back here to stay in the mission with them.

Three days I waited, Ignatius says. Three days I followed. And when I acted, I left it to look as if she had managed to escape herself. I even had her run for a mile in the opposite direction in case they followed her tracks, though I don't think they are hunters by nature. I didn't want them to trace her back here.

They'll come back, Moses says. Sooner or later. She's too valuable to them. Even if they believe she's run off, they'll try this as a place for her to run to.

It's been four weeks, Ignatius says, and they haven't come back yet.

Could be they're tryin other places first. Could be they know that if she's here she'll be easy to get. But they'll be back.

It makes no difference. She won't be here.

Where's she gonna be?

With you.

What Ignatius wants is for Moses to take the Vestal to someone he knows, someone who will know what to do with her, a high priest who oversees the largest citadel still operating in the country – a haven for the devout, and the devout are populous in these times.

I ain't an escort by trade, Moses says. You don't got enough to endow my bounty for that kind of work.

I'm not offering to pay you, Ignatius says.

Then what?

I'm asking for your service.

A favour?

Not a favour. A duty. An obligation has befallen you. These are the things a man of honour does, and I know you to be a man of honour.

You got it wrong. A man of honour I ain't.

A man with a code then. They are much the same thing when there's no one around to say which creed is honourable and which isn't.

It occurs to Moses that just two days before he was seeking some purpose, some direction to their travel – a simple reason to be going one place as another. In these times, when all places and people seem distinguished only by the most ephemeral and muzzy of boundaries, when the peaceful walking dead begin to look like the salvationed and the huddled living the damned – then does a man seek for something beyond pills and shelter and woman comfort, then does he seek for objective, for vocation.

But my brother, Moses says, holding up the last weak barrier to what he already sees as his given mission.

Your brother isn't taking her, Ignatius says. You are. You have the capacity to protect her – even from your own blood.

Moses felt himself steeped in blood, all kinds of blood, the family kind and otherwise.

Where is this citadel? he asks.

And the monk Ignatius responds:

Colorado.

That night, lodged in the stable crib, Moses sees his brother Abraham lying back on his straw bed, scraping at his teeth with a wood splinter. Abraham hums a tune Moses doesn't recognize, and Moses wonders how much of his brother's music is just the creeping harmonic wastage of his own poxy mind.

We're leavin tomorrow, Moses says.

That's fine by me, Abraham says. I had just about enough of the silent life.

You seemed to get along just fine.

I been on my best behaviour.

You done all right.

Anyway, I don't much care for the witchy shit they got goin on. I ain't in all my life seen a slug pass up a meal. That girl's cursed.

Cursed? Moses says. The friar thinks she's blessed.

These religious types think everything's blessed. Dump a bucket of shit on their head, and they'll thank God for it not being two buckets. But I'll tell you something.

Abraham points the toothpick at his brother to make his point.

I'll tell you this, he goes on. Whatever hell those walking dead came out of, I ain't interested in gettin cozy with the girl they're afraid of.

You got a vision, Abe. There's no denyin it. The way

you see the world – those eyes of yours ought to be enshrined somewhere important.

Abraham casts a suspicious gaze at his brother, as if unsure of the true thrust of the remark – but he grins proudly despite himself.

But it don't make any difference, Moses says. Because tomorrow when we leave, we're takin her with us.

Who?

The Vestal.

What in the hell would we do that for? If you want to steal some holy bride, why not go for one of the other ones? Maybe one that knows how to cook.

We ain't stealin her.

That Ignatius ain't gonna be very happy with you stealing his cannongirl.

I said we ain't stealing her. The friar asked us to take her somewhere, and we're gonna take her.

Where?

North.

How far north?

Colorado Springs.

Colorado? Shit. Is it gonna be snow on the ground?

It's a likelihood.

You know I ain't good with the inclement weather. I got bad circulation in my legs.

You'll endure.

What's in Colorado anyway?

A citadel.

A what now?

A church.

Another church?

That's right.

Jesus, we're spendin a lot of time with the gospel. What happens if I come out the other end all godified and priesty? What happens if I want to take the vow?

Moses chuckles.

I wouldn't worry about it.

Abraham is quiet for a while. He picks his teeth with the wood splinter and looks thoughtfully at the beams running across the roof of the stable.

What're we doin this for, Mose? he asks. Really now.

It's a mission, Moses says. We wanted a mission and we got one.

Abraham nods.

But let's be clear on this, Abraham says. You were the one that wanted a mission. It was never me.

Moses nods.

Fair enough, he says. My mission, then.

Abraham considers a while longer.

All right then, he says finally. I'll come along with you on your mission. It's a brother's duty, ain't it?

*

And later, well past midnight when Moses cannot sleep, he rises from the crib and steals out of the stable to stand under the coal-black sky and listen to the shrill cricket-song stretched taut and incontrovertible over the desert.

He sits heavily on one of the picnic tables and folds his hands as though waiting politely for someone to bring him sustenance. His beard is dark and heavy.

Soon someone does come. It is the Vestal Amata, still dressed in her white robes, and she sits down across from him and looks into his eyes.

He has not been, for many years, the kind of man whom a woman approaches. It used to be different, long ago, before things changed. Then he was clean-shaven, tall but still lithe. He knew how to be playful. He knew how to juggle oranges found underneath a laden orange tree. Now he has forgotten much of who he was before. Now he stomps and rages and draws lines he dares people not to cross. He is a man of hard laws and hard action, a man sharpened on the grit of constant violence. He is a barbarian, he knows.

So he does not know what to make of a woman who approaches him alone in the middle of the night. He suspects again this Vestal – her slightly sneering mouth, her red hair, her eyes that do not look away in fright at the world and its barbaric things.

We're taking you, he says to her. My brother and me. We're settin out tomorrow.

Ignatius told me, says the Vestal.

She confronts him with her obstinate silence. He does not know whether he seeks refusal or gratefulness, but he finds that he has no gambit against the woman who does not reveal her game.

Sunrise, he says. Just after sunrise.

That's fine, she says.

Colorado, he says. That's where we're goin. I don't know if the friar told you. It's a citadel.

He told me.

It's in the mountains. It'll be cold. Bring what you have. We'll make room.

Fine.

We'll keep you out of harm.

That's fine.

She deflects his words easily and looks at him as though she is the one trying to unlock his secrets, as opposed to the other way around.

He stands and begins to walk away, but he can feel her eyes on his back – and large as he is, he feels delicate and frail.

Hey, she calls to him.

He stops and turns to face her but says nothing.

You and your brother, she says. Are you holy men too? Or just hired guns?

He is no expert of locution, but her words seem different now than they were earlier in the day. Perhaps she is a phantasm – her night form and her day form not the same.

But her question unsettles him. He does not know how to answer it. So he replies in kind.

How bout you? he asks. You an authentic miracle of God's holy grace – or just a hoax?

She smiles at him now – and now all pretence of purity is gone. What replaces it in her expression is something conspiring and downright lascivious.

All right, Mosey, she says. Let's get out of here and

play for a while on the big checkerboard. Maybe we'll both find out what's what.

So he leaves her there, clad in her white robes, her red hair spilling lurid on her shoulders, her eyes like false gemstones – and, too, like a fluid and perverse treachery, her curving lips.

*

Though the sun is not yet risen before the commotion begins.

There is a man's voice, loud – spitting and thick, as though the tongue were too big for the mouth.

We'll burn it! the voice calls. We'll burn the whole goddamn place to the ground!

Moses rises, kicks his brother awake and moves to the stable door to look out. There's nothing to see except the parishioners gathering in fearful huddles around the courtyard. The voice, he realizes when he hears it again, is coming from outside the perimeter wall – at the front gate.

Open the goddamn doors! If she's in there, we're takin her. If she ain't, we got no truck with you all. It can go quiet, or it can go rough. Your choice.

Then Ignatius is there, dashing around the corner of the building with the Vestal Amata in tow. The expression on the woman's face is equal parts fear and anger.

I ain't goin back with them, she says under her breath. Ignatius doesn't seem to hear her, and the words are directed to no one in particular. It is a personal vow to herself and nothing more.

It's the man Fletcher, Ignatius says to Moses. He's back. The whole carnival of them. You have to go now. Leave by the back.

Abe, let's go, Moses says, gathering his satchel and weapons. Show us where to go, he says to Ignatius.

The monk gestures for them to follow and leads them around the chapel itself to a place where barrels are stacked against the back wall and can be climbed upon. Moses goes up first until he can see over the top of the wall. It's clear.

Don't worry about us, Ignatius says to reassure them. They won't bother us if she's not here.

It did not occur to him, until the monk Ignatius uttered this last, that he should be concerned about defending the residents of the mission. He did not think of it at all.

And so it is that he is no hero by nature. And for what cause, then, is he a warrior?

Hand her up, Moses says to his brother. His brother lifts the Vestal Amata into his arms, and Moses hoists her to the top of the wall. Then he tosses his satchel over the back and turns to leap down himself. But before he goes, he looks back over the mission. On the opposite side there's a glow against the sky, the front of the structure illuminated by the headlights of Fletcher's convoy. It is eerie, the blaze and fracas at the intersection of people's lives.

He turns and looks down on Ignatius.

I'll protect her, he says to the monk. But I ain't a good man. You understand that?

It doesn't matter, the monk replies. Partly strong, partly broken. It's the same with everything. Just go.

And they do.

*

Moses drops down on the other side of the wall then helps the Vestal Amata to the ground. Abraham comes last, leaping down with a yee-ha like a cowboy and tumbling in the weeds. He wears a mad smile on his face, as though there is no difference in his economy between fear and frolic. He stands and dusts off his hands.

The Moses realizes something.

The car, he says.

What about it? Abraham asks.

It's around front with them.

So what? We'll find us another one.

It's got our things in it.

Nothin we can't replace.

Moses thinks about the weapon in the trunk, the bladed mace made for him by the tinkerer Albert Wilson Jacks. Abraham is right – most things in the world are replaceable, but that is not one of them. And this is a time of cherishing unique things.

We ain't leaving without our things, Moses says.

Abraham looks off into the distance, as though he would rush headlong into it were he unleashed to do so.

All right, he says. So what's your suggestion?

Then, suddenly, there's another voice behind them, a

man. He has crept around the corner of the wall while they were talking, and now he aims a gun at them.

If it's any help, he says to the three of them now, here's my suggestion.

The gun in his hand fires, and Moses' brother Abraham cries out and falls to the ground.

Five

Aw, fuck! Abraham yelps. He lies on his back on the
ground and clenches his thigh with both hands.

Before Moses can determine his next action, he sees
the Vestal already running towards the man with the
gun. The man wears jeans and a pair of boots and a
baseball cap, but no shirt. His bare chest is gaunt and
taut against his ribs, his skin tattooed with homemade
designs. The Vestal runs straight at him, in spite of the
fact that the gun is pointed directly at her chest. This is
something Moses will remember about the girl. It's not
bravery – he wouldn't call it bravery. Nor is it fury or
daring or hard mettle. Not exactly those things. In fact,
it is nothing she possesses in the positive but rather

something she lacks. There is a blankness in her action – an absence that allows her to move rapidly and without hesitation. Yes, that is it. It is not bravery but instead the absence of fear.

Whoa, says the bare-chested man to her. Hold it there. I'll shoot you, I swear to—

But he doesn't shoot. Instead he begins to back away, and he can't even complete his sentence before she is on him. She seems to pass right by the gun, as though he were merely holding his finger out to her in playful mimic of warfare. She moves past it, leaping at him, her small form still dressed in the white robes tossed absurdly against the larger man, her body itself a weapon, her thin elbow cracking him across the face, something snapping in his jaw, a jet of blood, black in the night, spitting from his nose.

Her movements are not beautiful or elegant – she is no graceful spectre or lithe athlete. Her violence is not art but simply the act of a weary and brutal practitioner.

The man drops the gun, and screams loudly. When he stands upright again, Moses can see that his jaw is dislocated, his lower teeth jammed at an oddly angled underbite, the bony hinge protruding at the side of his face, tenting out the flesh of his cheek and giving an inhuman droop to his eyelid. The man has been made immediately monstrous, and he is suffering – his hands up around his jaw as if wanting to put it back in place but at the same time afraid to touch it lest it pop off completely.

Moses sees the Vestal retrieve the man's pistol from

the ground, and before he can call to her to stop, she has aimed it at the man's head and pulled the trigger.

A charred hole appears in the man's cheek, and a thick soup sprays from the exit wound at the back of his head. He collapses first to his knees, his hands still held up near his skewed jaw, and then falls forwards on his face. There is an absolute stillness to him now, and the bullet through the brain means he won't come back.

What'd you do? Moses calls to the girl.

She turns to him, still holding the gun, looking confused.

He rushes to her and seizes the pistol away from her.

What? she asks. He shot your brother.

In the leg, Moses says, pointing to Abraham who sits up in the distance, gritting his teeth and grasping his thigh.

I know him, the girl says about the corpse at her feet. He would of killed all of us give him the chance.

And besides that, Moses goes on, the racket's gonna bring em all—

But it's too late, because beyond the girl's shoulder he can see them coming around the perimeter of the wall, a group of men with rifles and baseball bats. There's one man in front, wearing a wide sombrero. He would seem ridiculous if he weren't so putrid with evident corruption. There are tears all over his flesh, wounds kept open by picking fingers. Some are scabbed over and some are dripping blood or pus. Others are sealed closed but still fresh. It seems as though, riddled with plague and offence, he cannot keep it all contained behind the walls of his thin, translucent skin. The sombrero, with a neck strap that hangs down like a disembodied grin below his chin, is a horrific joke. The displaced laughter of a man cursed by hell to giddy misfortune.

It's Fletcher, Moses knows, recognizing him from the description Ignatius gave. And it's not surprising, such a torn and bloodied little man. A relay of brutality – inflicting on the world the same mundane suffering he feels daily.

Moses hesitates not a second. He rushes forwards while the men are still startled and confused by the corpse of their companion lying on the ground, gets one big arm around Fletcher's neck and spins him to hold him from behind, the gun in his hand shoved against Fletcher's temple.

What Moses hopes for is some loyalty on the part of Fletcher's men – and it's a risk, because loyalty is a quaint and toylike notion in this ravaged place.

But there must be some impulse that touches on loyalty, because when Moses tells them to drop their weapons, they lower them at least.

Moses pressed the barrel of the pistol harder against Fletcher's head, and it feels like it will slip away on the greasy film that covers the man's skin.

Goddamnit! Fletcher says to his own men. Do it! Drop the guns, you pricks, or I'll kill you myself!

So it's not loyalty so much as fear. But it works in any case. They drop their weapons.

Now who the fuck are you? Fletcher asks Moses,

trying to angle his head to see the man who has him by the neck. And what do you want? You might as well wish big, cause you're gonna be dead by dawn, you cocksucker.

Moses looks out over the horizon, the sky diffuse with brilliant umber.

It's already dawn, he says close to the man's ear.

Fuck you, you literal prick.

Now Moses can see Ignatius and the other congregants carefully peeking over the edge of the wall, watching the exchange with solemn interest.

Moses backs away, dragging Fletcher with him.

I'm taking my brother and the girl, Moses says loud enough for everyone to hear. That's our Chevy in the front. We're taking it. Understand?

Fletcher's men look uneasy about what to do, so Fletcher gives them commands.

Let's just hold off on takin action at the moment, he tells them. Let's all just wait till I don't got this goddamn pistol on my brain. How's that sound? This asshole can't keep huggin me all day.

Moses pulls Fletcher back to where his brother sits on the ground.

Can you stand? Moses says.

Just barely, Abraham says.

Lean on the girl, he says. Then he says to the Vestal Amata, Help him up.

So the four of them hobble their way around to the front of the mission, Fletcher's men following at a respectful distance. But when they turn the last corner to the front gate, there are more of Fletcher's crew waiting. A caravan of eight or ten trucks and vans, lined up in a neat row, and figures posed around each with rifles and pistols aimed at Moses and his small, stumbling group.

Now what, smokey joe? Fletcher says to Moses. You gotta let go of me at some point.

Yeah, Moses says. About ten miles up the road.

The fuck you are.

Moses moves them to the Chevy and then calls out to Fletcher's crew surrounding them.

Now look here, he says. We're gettin in this car. First the girl and my brother. Then your bossman. He's gonna sit in the front seat with me. I'm driving away, but my brother's gonna have a gun pointed at his head the whole time.

He hesitates. The snarling faces of the men suggest that he is relying too heavily on their love of Fletcher. He wonders if they would mow them all down where they stand if it weren't for the loss of profit from the girl herself.

I'll tell you like you told the padre and the people inside, Moses calls out. I got no truck with you or with your boss. You stay back, you let us get out of here – and if I don't see you behind me, I'll drop him by the side of the road ten miles down the freeway. Then you can chase us down all you want if you got the time and inclination.

How do I know you'll let me go? Fletcher says.

I don't like lookin at you, Moses says. And I won't kill you cause I ain't a killer of wretched things.

There are about thirty of them, the caravan's crew, and they all wait on Fletcher's word. For a moment, the little scabbed man is silent. His sombrero is tilted to the side in goofy asymmetry so Moses can fit under it too.

Everything is quiet, and Moses can hear the metallic thudding of the slugs inside the caravan trucks – no doubt moving back and forth in their miniature black cells.

All right, goddamnit, Fletcher finally says to his people. Wait fifteen minutes and then come after me. I don't wanna be sitting by the side of the road all goddamn day.

*

Watch your hands, Abraham says to Fletcher, pushing the barrel of the pistol against the back of the man's head.

But Fletcher isn't going for any weapon – he's just reaching up to pick nervously at the scabs on his neck and the side of his face.

Ugh, Abraham says. Why don't you just leave yourself alone?

Fletcher ignores him and speaks instead to the girl.

Who's your friends, Tillie?

You won't let him harm me, will you? the Vestal says to the brothers.

Listen at her talkin now! Fletcher says, laughing heartily. Ain't we graced to carry a little princess in our motor carriage!

Hush up, Moses says to the man.

But Fletcher doesn't hush.

She was *my* hire and salary, he says to Moses. And she was took from me unlawful. You want to pay for her release, we can talk terms. I ain't an unreasonable man. But she was my main event, so she don't come cheap, and she certainly don't come free.

I ain't payin you, Moses says. I got nothing to pay you with.

Fletcher looks around the car, sneering.

No, he says. I don't guess you do. This is sure enough a sorry little band of rescuers. You realize we're gonna kill you, right? And we're gonna kill you sloppy.

Hush up, Moses says again.

They drive west along the highway, Moses glancing every few seconds into the rearview mirror. No one is following them yet. One of the advantages of desert travel – you can see miles of where you're going and miles of where you've been.

She's more fuss than she's worth, you know, Fletcher continues. Trouble with a capital T. But I guess you ain't seen that side of her yet. I don't know what kind of show they had her doing there at the mission, but she was never dressed in no white robes for our performances. Seems like she picked up some airs these past couple weeks.

Moses can see the girl in the rearview mirror. Her head is turned sharply away from Fletcher, and she is gazing out the window as though pretending not to be present at all. But Moses can see her jaw shut tight, the muscles in her face clenched rock-like.

When they have been driving fifteen minutes, Moses pulls the car to the side of the road at the base of a stony outcropping. He leaves the motor running and gets out and goes around to the passenger side where he opens the door.

Get out, he says to Fletcher.

Happily, Fletcher says. It's a lovely day for a nice sit.

The greasy man climbs out of the car and leans down to say farewell to the girl.

See you soon, fancy lady.

Come on, Moses says and leads him away to the shaded base of the outcropping where he tells him to sit.

Now you listen up, Moses says. We're takin the girl. She ain't part of your show any more. She don't belong to you. You understand that?

You think she belongs to you? Fletcher says.

She don't belong to anybody.

You got that part right, at least. Hell, take her. She can make you some money, but she's bad business in the long run. I mean, Jesus, even the dead don't want her. It's a bad sign when those that'll eat anything won't even take a nibble from you. She's a curse I'm glad to be got rid of.

Moses is staring at the man, considering these words, when he hears the car door open and close behind him. Then the girl herself is at his shoulder, and they both gaze down at the ridiculous oily man in the sombrero.

What's going on? she asks.

We're just havin a little palaver, Moses says.

What's there to talk about? she says.

All manner of things.

You're killing him, aren't you? You swore to protect me.

See? Fletcher says. You see the bitterness in her heart?

I ain't killing him, Moses says.

How come?

You see it now, sure, Fletcher says. Get shut of her while you can.

There was a bargain, Moses says to the girl. A bargain between us and them – and it's gonna get upheld.

Respectable, Fletcher says. A man of his word. Let's all be men of our words.

I never made any bargain, says the Vestal Amata.

There is something hard in her, something angry. Moses wonders what exactly he has sworn to protect, and he wishes to know it for what it is. He wishes to sound the depths of it so as not to get drowned in its tides or ripped to pieces on its shoals.

No, Moses says to her. You're right. You never made any bargain. So you kill him.

The two gaze upon each other. She realizes she's being tested. Their eyes lock, and Moses feels as though he is being watched by a giant caged animal – a panther pacing back and forth waiting for its moment to strike.

Give me the gun, she says, holding her hand out-stretched.

But he doesn't give her the gun. Instead, he kicks

around the base of the outcropping until he finds what he's looking for. A loose stone roughly the size of a bowling ball. He hefts it up and holds it out to her.

The shot'll signal to them something's gone wrong. You want to kill him, you gotta do it this way.

Hey, Fletcher says. Hey, wait a minute.

He rises to his knees, but Moses points the gun at his head.

Stay down, Moses commands.

We had a deal, Fletcher says to Moses. You can't just let her do it. That's akin to doin it yourself.

Akin to it, but not exactly the same, Moses says.

He can see the sudden fear in the man's eyes. There is no doubt in Fletcher's mind that she'll kill him.

And, indeed, she takes the rock from Moses. The weight of it nearly topples her, small as she is, but she steadies it against her chest.

Jesus Christ, Fletcher says, raising one hand over his head and knocking the sombrero off to protect him from the stone and another palm towards the pistol to protect him from the bullet. He is, at the moment, a truly pathetic thing. Jesus Christ, he says again. Tillie, don't.

The Vestal Amata uses all the strength in her small arms to raise the rock over her own head. She pauses for just a moment. Moses looks to see what's in her eyes, and resolution is what he finds there. Deep, unquestioning resolution.

At the last moment, Moses reaches out, seizes the rock from her hands and tosses it to the ground where it gives a deep, earthy thud that makes Fletcher fall forward into a foetal position as though he has actually been struck.

What happened? he says.

What happened is you got a stay of execution, Moses says. Now sit tight till your people come for you.

Moses takes the girl by the arm and heads back to the car.

This is your last chance, Fletcher calls out to Moses as they walk away. He has regained his confidence now that there is no rock hanging over his head waiting to bash his brains in. You give her back now, and we won't even charge you to take her off your hands.

And he laughs.

*

Before they reach the car, Moses seizes the Vestal Amata by the shoulders and looks down into her un-flinching face.

You were gonna do it, he says. You were gonna kill him in cold blood.

That's right, she says. And you weren't.

He wasn't no threat to you – not then.

He shot your brother.

Is that what you were gonna do it for? On behalf of Abraham?

No. I was going to do it on behalf of myself. And on behalf of decency.

Decency, Moses repeats and guffaws. That's a mighty big concept for such a little redheaded thing like your-self.

Little nothing – I'm the Vestal. Or haven't you heard?

Your name ain't Amata. He called you something different. Tillie.

Amata's the name that monk gave me. Tillie the Vestal just didn't sound right to him. I didn't use to always wear white robes either.

I guess you didn't.

What's that supposed to mean?

That trick back there with the slug. How'd you do it?

Her voice suddenly takes on a deep southern twang, as though in imitation of Moses himself. Though Moses can't decipher the shifts in her dialect – can't determine which voice is performance and which is real.

It ain't no trick, brother Moses, she says. I'm special-like.

You ain't a holy woman.

Do you know what's holy and what ain't? You sure bout that?

I got a few ideas on the topic.

Well, don't expect a deep dissertation on the matter from me. Let's you and I visit a slug town together and see which one gets along better with the locals.

You also got a trick to save you from throttling by living men who just get tired of your talkin?

Ladies and gentlemen, she addresses the desert around them, my sworn protector. Take a bow, Mosey.

Moses turns and walks the rest of the way back to the car. The Vestal follows a little behind.

Everything taken care of? Abraham asks from the back seat.

Everything's fine, Moses says.

Good, Abraham says. Cause someone better fish me the whiskey out of the back. The next time we stop you're gonna have to dig a bullet out of my leg.

*

The Vestal is convinced that Fletcher is still after her, and Moses has suspicions in the same direction. So to disguise their trail, they drive west along the highway for two hours, then double back ten minutes and take the road north.

They move slowly, she says, Fletcher and his people – because there are so many of them. But they've got an Indian with them. A Zuni. He's a good tracker.

What do you recommend? Moses asks.

I don't recommend, says the girl. I'm just supplying information.

The road north is a small two-lane black-top crumbled to dust in some places, piled high with the shells of abandoned cars in others. They frequently have to slow to a crawl and navigate the sandy verge of the road, being wary about getting stuck since Abraham is useless to help at the moment. Moses looks intermittently in the rearview mirror, and so far he has seen no sign of Fletcher's caravan. The one advantage of the slow road is that it will be even slower for Fletcher and his large, heavy vans.

Soon they see signs for what seems to be a cluster of

large towns: Phoenix, Scottsdale, Tempe, Mesa. The slug population, too, grows denser as they approach the city centre.

Do we go around it or through it? Abraham asks.

It's up to you, brother. What do you feel like?

The sun is getting low on the horizon. The day has been a long one. They have been driving non-stop. Abraham has been drinking from a bottle of whiskey for hours, readying himself for the surgery he will have to undergo. He is sleepy and sputtering.

Hell, he says. Let's stay in the big city for the night.

So they follow the road into the city, which is uninhabited by the living and dark as pitch when the sun falls. It is possible that the entire state is off the grid, all the survivors having moved on years ago to other, safer areas. Phoenix is a place gone to rust and ruin – massive buildings collapsed on themselves, weeds growing up through the cracked pavement, everything etched to a pale, colourless grey by the sandstorms that whip around the corners of buildings season by season.

The firebird city rises again only in the dead who wander its streets. It is a mystery what they are feeding on, these shambling slugs, for there are no signs of life. It is only when they arrive in the city's downtown that Moses sees the soot and ash everywhere settled like new snow, the black char on the sides of many structures – and he realizes something. This place is not among the cities abandoned a decade ago or longer. No, this place is newly dead. There were people here not long before.

The gutters are stained with dried blood, and he knows what that means.

He knows from experience how to age blood – how, upon leaving the body and splashing on a brick wall, for example, blood will go from red to brown to black to grey, how it will flake off, eventually, in the desert heat, or how it will rehydrate and run in the rain, how it will eventually disappear altogether, leaving only a stain like the dirt of the earth – and how, long after that, even the stain itself will evaporate, because the elixirs of human life are unstable – because human life itself wants to merge again with the elemental world it was born out of and is kept separate only by the puny will of individual fancies.

This blood, the blood in the gutters downtown, is less than a year old. This place is among the recently fallen, and there is a grim sombreness in the air.

But it explains why there are so many slugs, and why they are so active.

There were survivors here, Moses says. Till not so long ago.

How can you tell? the girl says.

I can tell.

Could there be some left?

Moses shrugs.

There could be, he says. We'll keep an eye out.

Is it too dangerous? she says. Should we go back?

Moses shrugs again.

Everywhere's dangerous. Just different kinds is all.

Abraham and me, we've been through most varietals. Six of one, half-dozen of the other.

They drive until Moses finds what he's looking for: a hospital. But the place is blasted through, burned down to its empty metal skeleton, unsalvageable. So he looks for the next best thing, a drugstore, but those too seem to have been looted clean a long time since. Yes, this place was a thriving bastion for a long while.

No luck, Moses says to his brother. We may have to do it on pure nerve.

We done it before, Abraham says, taking another gulp of whiskey. I got lots of nerve left, I reckon.

So they find a place that looks shut up tight, a hotel, and they climb up on a dumpster and bust through a second-storey window and hoist themselves in. Then they kick the dumpster away so that they won't be followed.

Inside, the building is deserted. They sit Abraham down in the big dusty lobby, on a green upholstered couch with a filigreed back, and then Moses and the girl light candles to search the dark back rooms.

In the abandoned bar, they find two whole bottles of Jameson's.

It's Abraham's lucky day, Moses says. He can drink himself straight into anaesthesia.

You think they have any canned food? the Vestal asks. All I've been eating is beans and garden fruit for weeks. That's probably the kitchen back there.

And she pushes through a swinging door into the next room.

Be careful, Moses calls out after her. Don't get et.

He peruses the bar some more, but many of the bottles are gone or smashed. There's a register with a drawer full of money – bills that he remembers people coveting in his long-ago childhood – but now they are the last thing the survivors are interested in lugging around. They make good kindling, but that's about it.

When he pushes through the swinging doors into the kitchen, he spots the Vestal on one end, leaning deep into a cupboard and sifting through its contents. On the other end of the kitchen, on his hands and knees, is a slug. It's an ancient man, hairless and dressed in an apron. His skin is grey and shrivelled and flaking as though he were made of papier mâché, a crawling stuffed mannequin, a mocking imitation of humanity.

The first thing Moses notices when he steps into the kitchen is that the slug is not making his way hungrily towards the Vestal. It seems he has climbed to his hands and feet with only a vague interest in the sudden movement around him. He stares after her as Moses has seen some slugs stare at night-time stars or at television screens that have not yet burned out or even at each other – simple, animal curiosity.

So it is no trick. The girl is somehow, impossibly, outrageously, beyond their appetite.

And it is just her, because when the slug sees Moses, he immediately begins a jaw-clamping crawl towards him, reaching out his grey bony fingers with the little strength he has left in his desiccated muscles. The thing would consume Moses if it could, would eat him right up. And yet it has no interest in the redhead wearing the white robes.

Moses takes an iron skillet from a hook hanging above him and bashes in the slug's skull. The head caves in easily, the slug collapses on his stomach, and whatever small amount of blood there is slowly oozes out of its ears and nose.

Startled, the girl emerges from the cabinet.

What was that?

Slug, Moses says, pointing.

Oh, I didn't see it.

You should be more careful.

I'll be all right, she says and shrugs. Look what I found.

She holds out a jar of olives in oil.

When was the last time you had an olive? she asks.

I don't care for olives, he says.

Look at you! she says. Some high and mighty mister with tastes! Well, some of us can't afford to have picky palates.

She tries to pry the lid off the jar, but it's on tight. She holds the jar between her knees and leans over, getting her whole back into the project, but the lid won't budge. Then she knocks the lid against an aluminium tabletop, and all the discarded utensils on the table shudder and rattle like bones. But when she tries again, there's still no movement.

Moses watches the entire process until she looks up

at him, holding the big jar in front of her like an infant baby.

Will you open it for me? she asks. Please?

Come on, Moses says. Let's go get that bullet out of my brother.

*

Abraham drinks until he can no longer keep his head from lolling around on the loose hinge of his neck. Then they lay him out on a bed in one of the guest rooms on the first floor, and Moses removes his pants.

Do you wish me to avert my gaze? says the Vestal Amata, but Moses can tell it is said in jest. She has rested the big jar of olives, still unopened, on the night stand.

Moses puts towels under his brother's legs and uses a steak knife from the kitchen and a claw-like instrument from an ice bucket to dig the bullet out. At the first thrust of the knife into the bloody hole, Abraham screams loudly then passes out. The rest of the operation takes place in silence, the Vestal compressing the wound firmly so he won't bleed out. Then they wrap the thigh tight in ripped towels and let Abraham sleep it off.

He'll be hurting when he wakes up, the girl says. Do you have anything for the pain?

Aspirin, Moses says, but not much.

It'll be bad.

We've been through worse.

Then Moses goes to the olive jar on the night stand and uses the pressure of his thick paws to wrench the lid free.

There, he says. Thanks for the help with him.

My pleasure, says the Vestal, her eyes going wide at the green oblongs floating in oil. She plucks one up between her thumb and forefinger and pops it in her mouth. Scrumptious, she says.

You take the other bed, Moses says. I'll sit here in this chair tonight. I ain't used to sleepin much anyway.

Are you kidding? she says. We're in a hotel. There are beds everywhere.

Safer to stick together, says Moses. Don't worry, I ain't gonna touch you or make any untoward advances. That's more Abe's thing, and he's down for the count tonight.

So she settles onto the bed and leans back against the headboard and eats olives from the jar.

You did good with him, she says to Moses after a silent while. What were you before? You know, before all this happened.

Me? Moses replies. I was a no-good. I didn't do much of anything. I think maybe I was just waitin on the apocalypse so I would have something to occupy me.

So are you occupied now?

More or less. What about you? What were you?

I was just a little girl. I don't remember much. Just a lot of people everywhere.

What about after? What were you before you were part of Fletcher's sideshow?

Lots of things, she answers in a sleepy voice. Lots of things. Many lives. I wasn't even always a redhead.

But she doesn't want to talk any more and falls asleep on top of the blankets. Moses goes over to the bed and takes the jar of olives out from between her embracing arms, sets it on the night stand and puts the lid back on. Then he returns to his chair and lets his mind wander wide – though his thoughts don't get very far before he, too, is lost to sleep.

*

When Moses wakes again, it is because his brother is calling to him from where he is sitting up in the bed.

Mose – up and at em, big brother!

Bright light floods the room, and Moses pinches his eyes closed. He turns in the chair he has slept in all night, and his bones creak, his muscles complain. He realizes it frequently these days: after four decades on the earth, he is getting to be one of the aged things.

The nun's gone, Abraham says.

What?

The red nun. She's gone.

His brother points to the other bed in the room, which is empty save for a pad of paper with something written on it

She's not a nun, Moses says and rises to take the note from the bed. The paper has the hotel's logo on the top of it, and her note is scratched onto it with pencil in the curlicue handwriting of a young girl.

> *Thanks for the lift.*
> *You are two souls lit by heaven.*
> *Bon voyage!*
> *Peace and love,*
> *The True Vestal, Canoness Amata*

What's it say? Abraham asks.

She left, Moses says.

Left where? Out there? Slugland? Without any protection?

I reckon she don't need protection from the dead.

You really believe it's real?

Moses looks away from his brother to the window where the sun feels hot and good on his face.

It ain't an issue of belief, he says. She's took off. Whether she's gonna be et or not, she ain't here any more.

So what now?

Now we try to find her.

Goddamnit, Abraham says. Seems like we're settin up to spend an inordinate lot of time pursuing a girl we ain't allowed to bang when we find her.

Moses looks at his brother's leg, stretched out straight on the bed with a towel wrapped around it.

Can you walk?

It hurts like straight damnation, Abraham says. What'd you do, gnaw the bullet out of there with your teeth?

Are you able to walk on it?

If you ain't in the mood to carry me, I could hobble. Fine. Let's go.

*

Outside, in the car, they drive slowly, looking for traces of the Vestal Amata. The dead are dense and easily riled, but there are no signs of a wake – a tide of dead all moving in one direction, at the head of which you usually find some poor fool running for his life. It seems that they are so uninterested in her they don't even pay much attention to her passing. She's an invisible – a ghost even among the dead.

They do not know which way to drive even, and Moses makes widening concentric squares in the car – a series of right turns, each one a block further than the previous. But the dead accumulate, drawn by the sound of the car – and their density makes it increasingly difficult to push through.

We're collecting quite a crowd here, Mose, says Abraham.

Moses drives on in silence, the dead becoming so thick that their clawing hands on the car sound like driving rain, their nails ripping away on the painted metal, their skin, sometimes, sloughing off in sheets that stick and will harden in the sun if they are left untended, fleshy tattoos of the dead past plastered on the decaying machines of a promised future that will now never arrive.

Moses leans forward to gaze out the windshield with grim seriousness.

It seems impossible that they will ever find her. The world is wide, and she, blessed or cursed as it may be with freedom beyond the common share, has the impunity to go anywhere in it.

Hours pass and the sun starts a descent on the far side of its meridian. She is an invisible, and she could be anywhere, and the world is wide, and Moses is near to giving up when he sees something in the road.

There, he says.

What? says his brother.

Moses stops the car but doesn't get out. There are too many slugs around. He points through the windshield to a broken jar on the side of a main drag that leads to the freeway ahead.

She's been took, Moses says.

Took by who? Slugs?

No. Not slugs. Took by other people. Maybe Fletcher, maybe others.

What're you talkin about?

That olive jar. She was feastin from it last night.

How do you know it's the same one?

It's recently busted. There's juice still in it.

Okay. So why does that mean she's been took?

She ain't the kind to go bustin jars just for the jollies of it. Plus, she knows we're after her, and she wouldn't of left any clues behind on purpose. No, she's been took.

If it's Fletcher, that's bad news for her.

Mostly likely it's bad news for her any which way. No kind soul givin somebody a lift would begrudge them the luggage of a jar of olives. A conflict took place here.

So they know they are headed in the right direction anyhow, and they drive with an eye on the horizon, looking to find some sign of the Vestal.

They drive slow, and soon the city is behind them. Just before evening falls, they see something else caught up on the bramble bushes by the side of the road. The vestments of the ghost herself, like a disregarded bed-sheet left over from a child's Halloween costume: the Vestal's white robes.

At least we know they went this way, says Abraham Todd grimly. He massages his knee below the gunshot thigh, wincing.

When night falls, they stop, afraid to miss the clues of the Vestal's path, and barricade themselves in a dusty second-floor room of an old motel. The dead have a difficult time climbing steps. They can do it, eventually, but it costs them time and fuss – and by the time they have reached the top, they have usually forgotten what brought them there in the first place.

That night Moses lies awake listening to his brother turn fitfully in the bed next to his. The room has heavy curtains blocking out the moonlight and so is straight-up blind dark. He has grown accustomed to it over the years of roaming the deadlands of the country – but it was not always like that. When he was a child, there was light everywhere. It seeped in under doors and through blinds. Nothing was ever entirely dark. You had daylight, and then you had dimness – and it seemed as though the world was a glowworm of a place, a thing that produced its own bioluminescence –

and you would never have thought how dead a place it could be.

Abraham shifts again in the dark.

How's the leg? Moses asks.

Guy must of shot me with a poison bullet, says Abraham.

You want to take a look?

Tomorrow.

Again silence permeates the dark, and Moses feels what it must be like to be buried alive. Then he listens harder, and he can hear the dead outside, bristling along against each other like a nest of rodents.

Then Abraham speaks again.

Why do you think she ran away?

Don't know, Moses says. Likely she's the kind who eschews too much company on her travels.

But a holy girl. How's she got the guts to . . .

She ain't so holy.

What do you mean?

It occurs to Moses that his brother has never seen the other side of the Vestal Amata. He was tending his leg when she shot the man who injured him. He was waiting in the car when she nearly bashed Fletcher's brain in.

She can take care of herself, Moses says. You haven't seen it. She's got a little bit of killer in her. Who knows what else.

That girl?

You didn't see.

So she ain't immune to them? That was just a trick? I knew it.

No, it ain't a trick. I don't know what it is. Maybe she's holy in some ways and unholy in others. Or maybe holiness wears a new aspect these days. I don't know. But all I know is that she ain't no damsel in distress.

Abraham is quiet for a moment. Then he says:

If she ain't no holy girl, does that mean I can bang her when we find her?

He chuckles in the dark, and Moses replies with simple silence.

Sometimes Moses feels he is more at home among the wandering dead – for while he does not share their appetites, he can understand them. Now he finds himself in the company of reprobate brothers and unholy Vestals. The dead may refuse to rest, but it's the world of the living that's gone asunder.

No, but serious now, Abraham says again in the dark. If she ain't a holy girl like we thought before, what are we huntin her for? We ain't getting paid, and we ain't on a mission for God – so then what?

She's still a lost girl – holy or not.

But it seems like she don't want to be found.

Moses says nothing for a moment. Then he turns over on his side and blinks his eyes. The dark is the same no matter whether his eyes are open or closed.

I don't got the answers for everything, he says. Sometimes you do things just cause they need to be done by someone and there ain't nobody else around. Is that answer enough for you?

Abraham shifts again in his bed, grunting.

Sure, he says. Me, I'm easy. Free and easy. Abraham Todd is like a delicate autumn leaf, brother. He goes where the wind blows.

*

The next day they find her in a little town called Fountain Hills at the edge of a vast scrub desert. They follow the tides of the dead, who are stirred up, presumably, not by the Vestal herself but by whoever took her. There is a park in the middle of the town, and that's where the bandits have set up camp. There are not many of them – maybe ten – just enough to travel light but protected. Their cars are parked in a huddle, the bandits are guarding the camp from the slow but steady onslaught of the dead while at the same time they hoot and holler at the redheaded girl dancing naked in the centre of the camp.

The exchange is a quick one. The bandits see the Todd brothers approach and attack. It is no matter to them who the Todds are or what they want: this group of travellers moves from place to place exercising their desires with a violence inherited from the very land over which they travel. They are scarred and ugly and brutal in their actions. They speak the language of death with accents muddy and coarse.

But the Todds have travelled the same ragged roads, and violence is a language that flows from their tongues as well. There are a couple with rifles, and Abraham dispatches those quickly, cutting off their range. The others scrabble to melee – but they are all distracted, caught unaware in their leisure.

Moses uses Albert Wilson Jacks's horrible blade for the first time. It is grotesquely heavy, and once put in motion it seems to swing through arcs of destruction all of its own accord. Moses finds himself merely trying to finesse the direction of centrifugal rage in the weapon. It rips and tears and leaves slews of rooster-tail blood behind its swing. Moses flails it across one bandit's middle and sees the man's guts spill out of the multiple gashes opened up in his abdomen. There is no grace in the weapon, no art. Brought down on another bandit's head, the skull simply pops like a frail coconut, the mess of grey brain splashing every which way and the cudgel digging itself well down through the man's throat and lodging between his shoulder blades. Moses has to let the body fall and put his foot against it to pry the weapon out again. Graceless and resolute, the thing moves through flesh without recourse or order or reason or precision. It is the opposite of surgery – it is senseless and animal.

Many of the bandits dead and the others fled, Moses Todd wipes his face on the sleeve of his shirt, getting the blood out of his eyes but smearing it across his cheeks and forehead like a successful hunter wallowing in the sloppy viscera of his prey.

The Vestal Amata stands amid the wastes of carnage, still naked, her white skin spattered with blood and white splinters of bone. There is a leaf of scalp adhered to one breast, and she plucks it away by the hair and lets it drop on the ground. Her eyes are wide, fixated on the mush of a body at her feet.

Abe, Moses says. Find the girl some clothes.

Then he turns to the Vestal Amata herself.

Come on, he says. We'll get you cleaned up, but not here. We gotta go. All this commotion – there'll be more slugs than we know what to do with.

So Abraham finds the girl some clothes belonging to one of the smaller bandits – men's pants and a shirt that fits her ill but covers her nakedness.

What Moses expects in her face is the blank trauma of horror – but the expression is different altogether. It is something of weariness, something even of irritation. In the back seat of the car, droplets of blood crusted in her red hair, she looks at Moses in the rearview mirror.

Who called in the cavalry? she said. Damn inelegant is what that was. I had the situation under control.

Is that right? Moses says. What was your plan? To tarantella them to death?

It was a distraction, she says. They were lettin down their guard. The slugs were coming. They would of been overrun in another fifteen minutes.

And what about you? Abraham says. Where would that leave you?

The Vestal shrugs.

Slugs don't bother me none. You've seen it yourself. I would of gone along my merry way.

What's with the talk anyway? Abraham asks. How come you keep changin the way you talk?

Why, sir, she replies with a sly smile, I can't possibly imagine what you mean.

They drive north, and the road takes them through an empty desert dotted with dense copses of brushwood. They put Fountain Hills behind them, and the bandits, and the accumulated dead. The Todds made sure, as they always do, that those they killed are killed for good. They will not swell the rout of walking dead on the surface of the earth.

Soon they are in a town called Sunflower, which is a nothing of a place. They take an off-ramp from the highway to find a few untouched buildings, some corpses, long dead, littering the street. Some of the corpses try to pick themselves up when they hear the noise of the engine drive by – but so old are they that their flesh has burned itself to the very tarmac, and when they rise, they pull half their faces off. Then they sit, their energy wasted in the simple act of rising, and poke curiously at their own faces, the exposed skull and the dry eye, now lidless, which will never shut again.

But there is a women's discount store on the main drag of the tiny town, and the Vestal Amata scrounges for clothes better fitting than those Abraham found for her in the bandits' inventory. They do not trust her not to run away again, so the Todd brothers go into the store with her. They stay at the front, spreading out a map on the counter and trying to figure out the best way to reach Colorado Springs. The largest freeways are not always ideal, travelling as they do through cities most densely populated with the dead.

As they consult the map, Moses notices that his brother keeps looking away, distracted. It's the Vestal. She's walking up and down the aisles pure naked. She tries on garments and slings them over her arm if she likes them or drops them to a pile on the ground if she doesn't. Her face and hair are still spattered with dried blood, but the rest of her body is a pale white thing like something just crawled out from under a rock and feeling the sunlight for the first time in years. She is freckled all over her chest, and her bosoms are small and pointed. Unselfconsciously, she scratches at her crotch and the bush of red pubic hair until she finds a pair of red underpants that suit her. Moses does not know what kind of textile those underpants are made from, but they are shiny and not at all modest.

She wears a necklace, Moses sees. It's a small wooden pendant in the shape of a cross.

Stop gawking, Moses says to Abraham to make his own leer feel less criminal.

What's she gotta walk around like that for? Abraham whispers. She's testin me, Mose. That nun is testin my mettle.

I told you she ain't a nun.

Then what is she? She think she's immune to the appetites of live men like she is to those of the dead?

I don't know what she thinks. Let's just take her where she's gotta go and get our leave of her. That's all.

*

They continue north, and the road climbs into the evergreen mountains where the slug population is sparse. Where there were very few living, there are very few dead. They come to a small bridge and see a stream running underneath. Moses pulls the car over, and they clamber down the verge, Moses helping his brother, to where the water runs cold and clear.

Thank God, says the Vestal. I'm crusty all over.

She strips off the impractical outfit she got in the last town – a leather skirt and a corset-type top – and wades into the river naked, splashing the water on her skin.

It's bracing! she cries. You boys have a nose for the good life. Maybe I'll think twice before running off again. Hey, what's the matter with Abraham?

Moses looks at his brother. There is an expression on his face of outraged desire – as though he is furious at the girl for making him want so much. Moses has seen that expression before, and it does not bode well.

Moses says, I reckon you best try to keep yourself covered up around us, Vestal. A desperate man's a sore creature to deal with.

The redhead laughs and splashes water at them.

Silly boys, she says. The world's gone dead everywhere you look, we're livin on the opposite side of grand apocalypse, and they're still Adam-and-Eve-ing it through the corridors of their own shame. They're just bodies is all. I bet you seen countless dead pussies, but a living one gives you quivers all over. Puzzle that one through for me.

She stands there in the river, the water up to her thighs, her arms akimbo, hands on her hips as though she were some kind of perverse schoolteacher. Her language has by now lost all of its polish and elegance. The Todd brothers say nothing in response. They have been scolded by a naked earth mother in a flowing river. Nature is a curious thing indeed.

All right, she relents finally. I don't like to cause a fuss. I'll go secret myself behind that bush to conclude my ablutions.

She moves down the riverbank a little way until she is just out of sight. But they can still hear her singing happily while she washes herself.

> *Oh, Mademoiselle from Armentare, parlay voo.*
> *Oh, Mademoiselle from Armentare, parlay voo.*
> *She got the Palm and the Craw de Gare,*
> *For washing soldiers' underwear.*
> *Hinky, dinky, parlay voo.*
>
> *You didn't have to know her long, parlay voo.*
> *You didn't have to know her long, parlay voo.*
> *You didn't have to know her long,*
> *To know the reason men go wrong.*
> *Hinky, dinky, parlay voo.*
>
> *She's the hardest working girl in town, parlay voo.*
> *She's the hardest-working girl in town, parlay voo.*
> *She's the hardest-working girl in town,*
> *But she makes her living upside down.*
> *Hinky, dinky, parlay voo.*

She'll do it for wine, she'll do it for rum, parlay voo.
She'll do it for wine, she'll do it for rum, parlay voo.
She'll do it for wine, she'll do it for rum,
And sometimes for chocolate or chewing gum.
Hinky, dinky, parlay voo.

The cooties rambled through her hair, parlay voo.
The cooties rambled through her hair, parlay voo.
The cooties rambled through her hair –
She whispered sweetly, 'Say la gare.'
Hinky, dinky, parlay voo.

She never could hold the love of man, parlay voo.
She never could hold the love of man, parlay voo.
She never could hold the love of man,
Cause she took her baths in a talcum can.
Hinky, dinky, parlay voo.

My froggy girl was true to me, parley voo.
My froggy girl was true to me, parley voo.
She was true to me, she was true to you,
She was true to the whole damn army too.
Hinky, dinky, parlay voo.

You might forget the gas and shells, parlay voo.
You might forget the gas and shells, parlay voo.
You might forget the groans and yells,
But you'll never forget the mademoiselles.
Hinky, dinky, parlay voo.

They can hear a big splash at the conclusion of the last verse, and a high cheerful laugh following – as though the girl were having the gayest time of her life bathing there in the river in the middle of a deserted mountain range in the middle of a vast corpsedom.

Abraham looks as though his muscles, beneath his skin, are all knotted taut around each other. He picks up a stone from the grassy verge and hurls it into the river, where it makes only the most pathetic little splash.

I swear to God, Mose, says Abraham. Things are gonna start gettin rapey around here if that girl don't leash herself somehow.

Moses kneels down and splashes water in his face. It is cold, like melted ice, and the sound of it running over its rocky riverbed is peaceful.

Stow it, he says to his brother. Come on, let's take a look at that leg of yours.

So Abraham strips off his pants, and they wash the wound in the river – but his thigh is still swollen and painful, and there's an ugly brownish-grey colour in the skin around the hole where the bullet went in.

Hm, Moses says.

What is it? asks his brother.

I ain't sure about this.

Forget it, Abraham says, grabbing his leg back and splashing some more water over it. I had worse. Everything heals give it enough time.

Not everything.

Never mind.

So Moses strips naked too and submerges himself in the icy water of the river. When he rises, the water streams out of his beard. He sits in the shallows and plucks the nits from the coarse hair all over his torso, squeezing them between his fingers and then drowning them in the river and letting them wash away on the current. He must look, he realizes, like a massive infant – a big hairy baby or a corrupted orangutan or something else not quite right. It's one of the happy things about a world gone so wrong: your personal freakishness don't stand out so much.

When the Vestal Amata wades back from around the bend to where the Todd brothers are, her lower half is sunk in the water and she is wearing a brassiere on her top half – which is something in the direction of decency.

Hey, she says and points to Abraham's wound drying in the sun, that's not lookin so good. Is it going rotten?

We'll find somethin for it on the way, Moses replies.

It ain't anything, Abraham says and begins wrapping it up again to keep it from solicitous eyes.

The three of them stay for a while longer, wading in the small river. They should be travelling, they know, and yet they are reluctant to leave. Overhead, a breeze rustles the leaves of the trees, and they shiver in the cold – and still they do not wish to go, as though dozing under some spell of nature, the classical form of the earth itself that they sometimes think of as lost and gone.

After a while, they emerge from the river and let the air dry them. The Vestal Amata peruses her companions as they sit in the sun.

Are you sure you two are brothers? she asks. One's a big hairy bear and the other's a skinny, runty little thing.

We had different mothers, Moses says.

I guess you did, the girl replies. Maybe not even from the same species. So what were you two up to before you embraced the duties of holy protectorate?

We wandered around a lot, Moses says.

Seein the world, huh? she says.

There's a lot of it to see, Abraham says.

One thing a plague of death does, Moses says, is rip down a lot of borders that people used to put up to keep the likes of us out. Now there's no place that's off limits to us.

True enough, the Vestal says, nodding her head. The world is wide open now. All those builders and maintainers of society – they're dead and gone. So who rushes in? I guess us. The rules are gone. Is that happy-making or sad-making?

It ain't either one nor the other, Moses says, rising to his feet and beginning to dress. And the rules ain't gone – they've just took up a new home on the inside of your brain rather than the outside of it.

He walks back to the car and smokes a cigar while waiting for the others. It's peaceful here, all right. So peaceful it makes you long for things you don't know the names of.

*

She was beautiful, Moses says, addressing those members of the caravan still awake to hear his story. Some have slunk off and some have fallen asleep on their own arms by the fire. The sky is deep dark now and no one has spoken for a long while save the large one-eyed man himself. The fire is lowering. A few listeners toss twigs and brush into the flames, but more for the brief flashes of consuming light than to keep the fire alive. The face of the large man is becoming difficult to see – but by the momentary light of a handful of burning weeds, it is possible to make out his features, his grizzled beard, his downturned mouth, his liquid staring eye.

Beautiful, he says again. That's what you ain't able to see. Her face. Her hair. Her body. These things, too, these images – they're the prisoners of language, and I ain't speaker artistic enough to set them free.

He is silent for a while. A coyote howls somewhere on the plain, and it is a reminder of the wild things that roam everywhere around them. But the man seems not to hear the creature – in fact, seems to hear nothing save the voice of his own speaking, constant, inexhaustible, evened to a single level as if it were a thing forged in fire and hammered over time into something long and flat and unbendable. It is a voice that continues even when he has stopped speaking – for him and for the listeners too – a voice of mortar and steel, like the framework that remains when a building crumbles. It is a structural element that endures, even though it holds up nothing at all.

Don't get me wrong, he continues finally. I knew women in my time. Them and their flowery effulgence dropping like pollen on all the world. It's a powerful dust – like fairies – it gets in your eyes and blinds you from things. And why have we always got to see anyway? Aren't there times where we shut our eyes full willingly? The truth. They used to say that beauty and truth were the same thing. But from what I seen, the two are at deep odds. You try for the truth, try to fill your heart up with it. It's the action of an honourable man, ain't it?

He is quiet again for a moment, and no one moves.

But this other woman, he says, this redhead, this priestess, this Vestal, whatever she was – she was beautiful in a different way, like she lived in that beauty the way other people live in houses. Did the beauty belong to her or did she belong to it? You can't tell such things. She was all of a beauty, and there was no name invented by human tongue could check her. But she was other things too.

He pauses as if to line up his words in proper order.

It ain't exactly right to say she was a trickster, ain't exactly right to say she wore masks. Instead it was like one single mask handed off to a whole host of people for each of them to wear it for a little while. You spoke to her, and you weren't never sure who it was behind that face. Not that it mattered none. The face itself was the thing. The face was the thing in the end. It made you love it – and whatever shams it perpetrated, well, you loved them too.

*

They drive on. In a place called Shiprock, they see signs for the Four Corners Monument where the miracle is that four states meet at a single point.

Let's go there, says the Vestal Amata.

You're just tryin to delay our trip, Moses says.

Maybe I am and maybe I ain't, but don't you want to see it?

Moses considers. Eventually, he says:

I reckon I do.

So they drive fifteen miles west and find the monument, which is just a big granite platform in the middle of the desert covered over almost entirely by years of collected dirt and weed. There's a corpse half buried in the dirt, in the middle of the platform, its skin mummified black and leathery by the sun. Moses drags the corpse away.

At first they aren't sure what they're looking for, and then Moses kicks away the layers of dirt on the platform where the corpse was until he finds a bronze disc the size of a saucer embedded in the middle of it. What the disc says is:

US DEPARTMENT OF THE INTERIOR

CADASTRAL SURVEY

BUREAU OF LAND MANAGEMENT

1992

And in the middle of the disc is something that looks like an addition sign with the names of the four states in each of the quadrants: Utah, Colorado, Arizona, New Mexico.

Here we are, says Moses Todd.

Yep, says his brother.

Sort of makes you feel like you're at the centre of things, doesn't it? says the Vestal Amata.

It does at that, says Moses Todd.

Someone went to all that trouble, says the Vestal, to locate that exact point in the dirt.

And for what? says Abraham. Now it don't mean anything.

But Moses thinks differently.

It never meant anything, Moses says. Not to the god above it and not to the earth below it. It never did. Not even when they first did it. But it's the doin it that counts. It's something. You draw imaginary lines. That's what you do.

The Vestal looks at him kindly, a smile on her lips that seems affectionate – even maybe admiring.

Then what do you do with the lines? she asks.

And Moses looks at her straight and true. He says:

Then you pick one side or the other and you stand there.

Part Two

SANCTUARY

Six

The air grows colder, and soon they begin to see snow on the ground.

I'll be damned, Abraham says. I ain't been north in ages. Does that mean it's winter then?

January, Moses confirms.

We missed Christmas?

I guess we did.

Abraham looks sincerely disappointed.

Don't worry, Moses says. It'll come around again. It always does.

A snow flurry stirs up, and the flakes whip around them as they drive. Moses pulls the car over, and they all get out. Abraham opens his palms to catch the flakes as they fall. He watches them melt immediately into his hands, fascinated, perhaps, by the ephemera of nature that shimmer away on contact with humanity.

The Vestal Amata opens her mouth wide to catch the flakes on her tongue, as though she would consume greedily the falling sky itself.

Moses himself remembers the snow from his youth, when he travelled many places. He is and has always been a traveller, for longing rather than necessity – even before things changed. With the agitation of the dead the world changed, and what it became suited Moses even more than what it was before. But he does recall a year he spent in the mountains of California, the heavy blades hitched to the fronts of trucks to push the snow out of the way, the mounds of sooty ice collected by the sides of the road. Back then, snow was a nuisance, an obstacle, something to be got around or over. Now the world has slowed down, there is no hurry. You watch the snowflakes fall lazily on their way, and you are reminded of your own floating, your own speedless descent through life.

From a ditch by the roadside, they see a dead man stir. He, too, is blanketed with snow, which fissures and sloughs off as he rises slowly. He moves with exquisite languor, as though his very joints are frozen stiff. It takes him many minutes just to climb to his hands and knees and then to his feet. Then, for a moment, he simply stands there and looks around, his head turning on the creaky hinge of his neck. Who knows how long he has been lying in the ditch, and now what a wonder the world must look from this new altitude.

Then the dead man seems to regain his purpose and shuffle slowly to where the three stand by the car. He scrapes his feet across the frozen tarmac and tries to lift his arms in a pathetic attempt at grasping. His skin is completely grey with blue undertones – death gone to pallid ash. The dead don't take naturally to temperatures such as this. They don't move well to begin with, and the cold slows them down considerably more. For this reason, there are more communities of survivors in the north where the seasons make it safer for many months of the year.

The dead man reaches for them, his fingers immobile on the stumps of his hands.

Poor thing, says the Vestal Amata. Do you have to kill it?

It ain't doing him any favours to keep him alive, Moses says.

He walks over to the dead man and pulls a small folding knife from his pocket.

The dead man reaches for Moses, opening his mouth. There is no smell to the man, dried up and frozen as he is, and Moses can see the shrivelled tongue in the well of his mouth, the cracked grey palate, the teeth turned to chalky stone.

The arms grasp for him, but Moses gets to the man's side and reaches one arm around the back of his torso to keep the arms lowered. It is a gentle gesture, almost like a brother's embrace. The dead man looks confused.

He tries to rotate his head to a position where he might get a bite out of Moses, but the neck doesn't allow such range.

Be still now, Moses says quietly.

Then he takes the knife in his free hand, unfolds it, and raises it in front of the dead man's face.

Close your eyes, Moses says to him. It is tender, the process, like a surgery or a baptism or a sudden kindness. Close your eyes now, he says.

He raises the knife to within an inch of one of the eyes, and the dead man instinctively closes them. He is peaceful now, his mouth still open but more by muscle slack than appetite. And then, with quick precision, Moses thrusts the knife deep into the man's eye socket. A little dribble of fluid, neither pus nor blood, spills from the burst orb of the eyeball – and then the man's whole body goes limp.

Moses lets the body down gently onto the ground and removes the knife from the eye socket. Then he sweeps up a handful of frozen dirt from the verge to clean the blade with.

Poor thing, says the Vestal again.

You want to say something over him? Moses asks.

Vestals must have blessings, she says. Don't you think?

But neither of the Todd brothers responds, and after a while of standing shivering over the dead man, they all return to the car.

*

They drive. They snow abates, having left a thin dusting over everything. Moses looks behind them in the rearview mirror and sees the two parallel tracks of his tyres marking their progress over the whited earth.

There's a town called Dolores, but there's not much in it – just a few blocks of houses north and south of the main drag, which is called Railroad Avenue. But it must be on the edge of some active grid, because they see the lights miles before they reach it. It's the first electricity they've seen in weeks, travelling the deserts of the south-west as they have, and their minds get filled with visions.

But what the town of Dolores is is an outpost at the base of a mountain range – a last stop of civilization before the rangy wild. And it is an outlaw's town, a bawd's town. The Todd brothers have seen many assemblages such as this – pirates congregated at a pit stop for travellers. They provide safety and services for a fair exchange of goods – and they steal what they want above and beyond that fair exchange.

It is night when they arrive, and snowing again – the streetlamps illuminating the flakes in smoky circles as they fall. They drive slowly, stared at by men whose gesture of welcome is that they hold their rifles casually at their sides. But in the middle of town they arrive at a large inn with twin gabled roofs, and a woman comes out to greet them.

Welcome to the Historic Rio Grande Southern Hotel, she says.

She is thick around the bosom and waist, and her

flesh is pushed and pulled every which way by a bustier that cinches her middle, and squeezes her breasts up into a shelf of flesh. Her face is rouged, and her tinted hair piled in a gaudy stack on top of her head.

She smiles invitingly to the Todd brothers as they climb out of the car, and the smile diminishes when the Vestal Amata emerges after them.

We've got three churches in town, the madam says and folds her arms across her chest. They're not in the best condition, but they're still full of relics. Families like to stay there sometimes when they pass through.

In the windows of the gabled house behind her, there appear faces of girls all lipstick and powder. Their eyes dash back and forth, curious about the newcomers.

No, ma'am, Abraham says and limps forward on his wounded leg. I reckon this is the place for us, Vestal or no Vestal.

The smile reappears on the madam's face.

Then come on in, she says. Homestyle comfort right here in little Dolores.

The town is grey and low, spread out in the small valley between the foothills of a mountain range to the north-east. Like most survivor towns, the outlying structures are run-down or fully collapsed, and all the residents have huddled into a few maintained buildings in the centre of town. Across the street from the Rio Grande Southern is a long ranch-style building like a train depot, with a raised porch that circles it entirely. At one end is a sign for what probably used to be a barbecue restaurant. The words Flying Pig are painted across it, and it looks like someone in town has restored the sign to its original colourful state. Except, dangling from the overhang of the place, there's a skeleton of a swine to which some scallywag has wired white wooden wings. And such is the playfulness of the town called Dolores – muddied with grim horror.

The sky overhead is slate grey and shallow with ugly clouds. Likewise, the street is pocked with dirty puddles of icy snow, the painted median lines long weathered away, the verge of the tarmac crumbled with use and age. It is a place to make you feel crushed, squeezed to suffocation between a low sky and a flat earth, as though life here continues narrowly, in a thin margin between earth and atmosphere. The residents stoop in towns such as this for fear of striking their heads on fallen skies.

The three travellers are escorted into the Rio Grande Southern by the madam. Abraham stays in the lobby of the place with the Vestal Amata and a small host of women wearing all variety of nightclothes, while Moses follows the madam into a back room to make arrangements.

Watch her, Moses says to his brother and points to the Vestal.

Aye aye, brother, Abraham says and smiles at the roomful of women.

In the madam's office, the woman talks terms.

It's a luxury establishment we've got here, she says. There's a price for bedding down here.

What's the price?

What've you got?

We've got pills, uppers mostly. Some electronics it looks like you could use. Some ammunition if you got the right kind of guns.

It sounds like you might be able to afford us. What is it you want?

Rooms for the night. Three near each other. Board. A girl for my brother.

What about a girl for you? Or are you with the red-head?

Ain't nobody with her like that. A girl for me too, I reckon.

So the redhead's left out of it, is she?

She don't need any of that business. She's a Vestal.

A what?

A holy type.

That girl out there? That redhead? Honey, I think you might have misread a few things. But your business is your business. Let's go out and see what you have in that car of yours – and maybe we can seal this deal.

*

Abraham has taken to wearing the harlequin Albert Wilson Jacks's gift to him around his neck on a leather shoelace. He plays with the black plastic thing when he is bored, picking at its exposed metal end. When Moses is done making arrangements with the madam, he returns to his brother, who points to one of the older women in the lobby.

That whore there knows what this thing is, he says.

She says to me, Hey, I know what that thing is. It's a yewess bee drive. And I says, A what kind of bee? And she says, A *yewess* bee. She says it plugs into a computer.

Do they have one here? Moses asks.

Huh-uh. She says they don't have much call for computers round here.

Which woman?

Abraham points her out. She's dressed more elegantly than the others – wearing a classy cocktail dress and sitting properly with one knee crossed over the other.

Okay, Moses says. I arranged things for the night. Your pick of the girls. But I'm warning you – go easy. This ain't a town to get jammed up in.

You got it, brother. Easy's my middle name.

So Abraham picks a girl – the one who looks youngest and most frightened. He pulls her along up the winding staircase, taking her by the upper arm just under her shoulder as though he is punishing a child for some misdeed.

Then the Vestal Amata is standing before Moses, speaking low.

You ain't takin one of these girls, she says to him.

You got you your own room – right next to mine. Ain't nothing going to happen to you.

That's fine, but you ain't taking one of these girls. If you do, I'll run off – like I did before.

Where'll you run to? Cold out there. Colorado's not got such good walkin weather.

I don't care. I swear to God I'll run off. I'll hitch a ride on out of here.

He looks at her, trying to figure the girl's brain. It's a muddled thing, that head of hers. She's like an optical illusion, different each time you look at her.

What do you care about it anyway? I got the feeling you ain't so pristine about the business of the world.

She slaps him. But ferocious as she is, she's also a small thing, so her wee palm does little damage. She slaps him again.

This time he picks her up and tosses her over her shoulder.

I figured you might try somethin like this, he says. I got it arranged.

She kicks and strikes at his back, but he carries her up the stairs and to the room designated as hers, where he tosses her on the quilted four-poster bed. The window of this room is boarded up, and there's a lock on the door.

Get some sleep, he says to her. And let's keep our business in neat and tidy corners, what do you say? I'm carryin you from one place to the other, that's all. I may port saints, but I ain't one. Understand?

Then the expression on her face changes. The anger melts to sadness before his eyes.

Just because I ain't a true Vestal don't mean I ain't of spiritual bent, she says. You mistake me, Moses Todd. I know right and wrong. I can tell the difference – in myself and in others.

How do you know for sure? he says. How do any of us? I reckon I'll take my own counsel on such matters.

He doesn't wait for a response but rather shuts the door and locks it up tight so she can't get out.

Still, he can't get the Vestal out of his head, and he can't get comfortable with his woman once she's taken him to her room.

It's the older woman, the one who knew about the yewess bee.

Maybe you just want to sleep for a while, she says. Don't worry about it – we've got all night.

He is silent, lying on the bed and staring at the ceiling.

We don't get real men around here much, the woman says, winding herself around the poster at the foot of the bed like a snake.

You can quit that talk, he says. I ain't a man in need of being built tall.

As you wish, she says and sits down in the chair in the corner near the foot of the bed. My apologies. You're not like your brother. What would you like to talk about?

You had a name for the thing around my brother's neck. A yewess bee. A computer gadget.

That's right. You should have the same name for it. You look to be about my age.

I never was much of a computer person – neither before nor after. What does it do?

She shrugs.

It could do lots of things, she says. It stores data. Who knows what the data does. Probably nothing.

How come you know so much? What were you before?

I was a secretary for a real estate attorney. I was just getting started.

And now you're here doin this.

Moses shakes his head, commiserating.

The woman recoils a bit in her expression, as if bitten. She moves to the window of the room and puts her back against it, folds her arms over her front.

You think I regret it? she says. Living didn't used to amount to much. Now it counts. I used to be a secretary for a real estate attorney. Now I'm a survivor of the apocalypse and a whore. I endure where others don't. It matters. Just breathing means something now. Have you got a problem with whores?

Moses cringes, chastened. He looks down at his dirty, brutish hands.

Not as a general rule, he says.

Then the woman softens a bit. She comes and sits on the edge of the bed, where Moses lies on his back looking at the ceiling.

You and that redhead, she says. You two are together somehow?

Me and the Vestal? Huh-uh. She's just my charge is all.

You're a hired gun?

Somethin like that.

So what are you being paid?

Moses goes silent. He gazes at the ceiling. He ponders when was the last time he laid beneath a roof and called it home. The world, for him, just keeps going on and on and on, long after he thought it ever would.

Come on, he says and reaches for the woman. Lay here and just let me get some shut-eye for a bit. Then we'll get down to business.

*

When he wakes in the morning, there is a tumult downstairs. He rushes down thinking that his brother has got into trouble again – but this time it's not the riot of threat but rather the riot of laughter.

In the sitting room, on a burgundy couch, he finds the Vestal Amata making merry with a passel of men. Townsmen – a number of the faces Moses recognizes as those of the men who were holding their rifles at the ready when they rolled into town. The redhead herself is lying across two of their laps, her bare feet resting on the arm of the couch, her toes wiggling playfully.

Here he is, she says of Moses to the men. My Rock of Gibraltar. Come on in, Gibraltar. The boys and I have had quite a night.

A couple of the other girls sit in the room also, but Moses sees that they are distinctly unhappy with this redheaded interloper.

Brucie there gave my feet a nice hot salt bath, says the Vestal and points to a tough-looking man who nonetheless flushes when she says his name. Men are lovely, she continues. You try to pay them back in kindness, but they just give so much it's difficult to keep up.

She wiggles her toes again, and Moses wants to chop them off and put them in a jar like bloody fireflies.

He goes over to the Vestal, takes her by the arm and lifts her from the laps of the men.

Hey, there, mister, says one of the men, a note of warning in his voice. They have already become possessive of her.

Moses gets ready for a fight, but the Vestal defuses it.

It's okay, boys, she says. He is my saviour, after all.

I'll save you, one man says.

Yeah, me too, says another.

The men laugh, and the Vestal laughs with them.

You know the rule, boys, she says. Only one saviour per girl. Let me talk to my Gibraltar in private for just a little sec.

He takes her into a small parlour down the hall and shuts the door behind them.

What the hell was that? he says.

It's the boys, she says and smiles slyly. Her eyelids are heavy, and she steadies herself against him.

You been drinking, he says.

Only all night.

You were locked in the room.

I pinky promised not to bolt. They gave me my freedom. Said they would watch me. It cost me a groaning or two, but they ain't a bad bunch.

He looks down at her, horrified. Her toes are still wriggling against the plush rug, and it makes him feel sick.

What's the matter? she says. You need a little touch, too? I figgered you got enough last night, but p'raps that matronly lady didn't quite satisfy.

She puts her hand between his legs, and he swats it away disgusted.

But – but, he stutters, the things you said last night . . .

She laughs high and clear, slapping her palms against his chest as though he were a drum, an instrument in her own perverse and ritualistic dance.

Oh hush, she says. You knew we were just playin, ain't you? Come on, ol Mosey – this girl was *raised* in establishments of ill repute. I cut my eye teeth on a big-boss cherry picker when I wasn't hardly twelve years of age. The celebrations of the flesh ain't nothing new to me. You want to be a bad boy? Well, then I can sure as anything be a bad girl.

He pushes her away from him.

You're a liar, he says. You ain't honest.

She stands for a moment looking surprised, but then she wobbles and leans against an oak desk – and a mild smile of resignation grows on her face.

Honey, she says, honest ain't the half of what I'm not.

He leaves her there and fetches his brother from upstairs. Abraham is sleepy-looking and irritated.

How come it's so early? he says.

We're gettin out of here, Moses says. She's a whore.

Who's a whore?

Come on. We're taking her to Colorado Springs and we're gettin shut of her.

For a moment, in the sitting room, it looks like there will be a fight when the men discover Moses and his

brother want to take the Vestal away, but the girl mol-
lifies the men with sickening sweetnesses and they
relent.

Out in front, Moses is stopped by the woman who
shared his bed the night before.

Go easy on her, she says.

What's it your business? he says.

It isn't. I'm just telling you. Womanhood's a tricky
thing. You're always walking a tightrope between what
men want and what they think they want. It's a long
fall either way.

The trials of bitchery ain't nothing to me, he says.
I choose not to excel. I turn my back on em.

And so he does. And on the woman herself. And
he does not speak again until he and his brother and
the Vestal Amata are well gone out of the small town
of Dolores, the frozen highway stretched out before and
behind them like a bad thought you can't escape.

*

Into the mountains they drive, and there are very few
dead here. They are buried beneath the snow – dead
permanent or frozen in grotesque animation, it makes
no difference, for they are no threat. The evergreens are
dense here, and the snow is old fall, collected deep. The
road is somewhere beneath them, they know because
they observe the cut through the trees – but they
cannot see the tarmac until it is revealed behind them
in parallel tracks from the tyres. Should they get stuck,
should they slip off into a ditch, they are aware that

they will likely die – too deep into the wilderness are they now to walk their way out.

So Moses drives slowly. Abraham sits beside him in the passenger seat and the Vestal sleeps deeply, curled into a ball across the back seat.

You gonna tell me why we had to get out of that town so quick? Abraham asks. I didn't do nothing untoward. I was lookin forward to sleeping in.

It wasn't you, Moses replies. It was her.

He turns to look at her. She is far gone into sleep after her night of carousing.

The girl's a whore, he goes on.

Who? The Vestal?

She's a whore's why she took to that place like it was her foster home. There ain't a drop of holiness in her. She's had the purity all sold out of her.

But a whore? Like a professional?

She good as told me it. She ain't to be trusted.

Abraham cranes his neck to look at the girl sleeping in the back seat.

An honest to God whore, huh? he says. If I'd knowed that before . . . You reckon I could bang her now, Mose? It being her vocation and all?

Moses says nothing in response. The world is a grim and empty place. The appetites of the dead – Moses knows they ain't nothing to the icy hearts of living men. All gone to naught, like a frozen hand laid over some Eden, all the blossoms of the true and holy shrivelled to sumpy weed and iced over to knotted hard and fragile things. And maybe what happened was that all the pure and good got raptured up while what remains is a populace gone all ugly and cankered at the seams. His own blood, too. His brother not excepted, nor himself neither. For the pursuit of good is a constant labour, and he ain't always got the strength in his heart.

*

The sun is directly overhead when the car breaks down. They are shaken by an enormous pothole hidden by the snow, and then the car skews a little. Something in the undercarriage knocks loud, and they are stopped dead.

The brothers climb out and Abraham looks under the car.

The axle's broke, he says. We're not goin anywhere.

Moses looks up and down the road, but there's nothing to see.

It's a goddamn trial is what it is, he says. How do you feel about freezin to death, brother?

Well, Abraham says, it sure ain't the way I thought I would go. But it seems clean at least.

Clean? You got some mind on you, Abe.

His brother takes this as a compliment and beams wide.

Then the rear door of the car opens and the redhead climbs out, rubbing the sleep out of her eyes and yawning.

How come we're stopped? she asks.

The axle's broke, Abraham tells her and smiles. We're dyin clean.

She casts a look of confusion at Moses, but he does not meet her gaze.

Come on, he says to both of them. We might as well go forward cause we know there ain't anything behind. Don't take nothing you don't need.

So they bundle themselves up and walk forward through the deep snow, raising their faces to the noon-time sun.

And maybe there are a handful of blessings left in the world after all, because it is only a quarter of an hour before they find a cut through the trees to their left.

What is it? says the Vestal.

Looks like it could be a path, Abraham says. Mose?

Could be, Moses says. Could be there's something at the end of it. Could be it's nothin at all. You want to chance it?

Might as well, Abraham says. After all, we can *see* there ain't nothing for miles in the direction we're headed.

So they follow the cut through the trees, climbing up an incline to a plateau where they find a clearing in the woods. In the middle of the clearing is a small cabin with a collapsed chimney and a sagging porch.

Hallelujah, Abraham says. Looks like we found ourselves a place to not freeze to death.

Inside, the cabin looks like it was abandoned many years before. Some of the floorboards are rotted through, but nothing is out of place. It isn't until an hour later, after they have hauled their things up from the car and while Abraham is on the roof clearing the bricks out of the collapsed chimney and Moses is securing the porch, that the Vestal Amata finds the dead man.

There's a pond behind the cabin, its surface frozen over. Under the fallen snow, it's hard to tell how large the pond is, but the trees around it are cleared to the size of a baseball diamond.

I didn't even know it was there until I slipped on it, the Vestal says.

They can see the place where the Vestal slipped, the snow has been dusted away from the surface of the ice, leaving a clear patch.

Look, she says and points. Slug under glass.

They gather around the cleared patch and look down. The ice is clear, and caught under it, like some kind of horrible fish in an aquarium, is the face of a dead man gazing up at them. His body has gone soft and bloated from being underwater for so long, his eyes milky, his flesh gone pale, nibbled at by fishes, his skin peeled off and floating around him like a nest of seaweed. They could have thought him just straight dead if it weren't for the fact that his eyes are blinking up at them sluggishly. As they watch, the dead man raises a hand to them, his movements slow, made almost ghostly by the freezing water in which he is entombed. He places his palm against the undersurface of the ice.

Moses knows it to be a grasp of hunger, but because the dead man doesn't seem to be able to bend his stiffened fingers, the outspread palm looks like a gesture of greeting or welcome. The eyes continue to blink, slowly.

It is pathetic and awful, the slug trapped underwater and undrownable – like a man staring up at them from the very mouth of the void, waving his goodbyes as he descends, floating down peaceful into the great black.

There is a darkness to nature – the unhurried ways of birth and death.

Jesus, Abraham says. If that ain't a sight. I'm gonna be seeing that for weeks now every time I close my eyes.

It's sad, says the Vestal Amata. He's trapped.

I wish I hadn't of seen it at all, Abraham says. I don't need my brain haunted like that.

What do we do? asks the Vestal.

Nothing *to* do, Abraham says. He ain't gonna hurt anybody. He might thaw out come spring, but we'll be long gone or long dead by then. Come on, let's get back.

Abraham turns and head back to the cabin.

Mose? asks Amata.

Moses has been gazing at the man beneath the ice. He wonders how much the dead man can see – how well those eyes still work. What must be the world to him? Shadows of light and fog, fish nibbling at your skin, your eardrums rotted to blissed silence.

It's like Abraham says, Moses replies. Ain't nothing to do.

He rises and walks back to the cabin, and the Vestal follows soon after.

Except much later that night, after the sun has set

and they have gathered dry wood and started a fire in the fireplace, after they have settled on accommodations – Moses and his brother on the double bed, the Vestal on the couch – after Abraham's snoring harmonizes with the crackling of the embers in the fireplace, the sap of the tree branches popping and hissing, the firelight casting dramatic shadows on the ceiling, after everything has settled to haunted inaction, then Moses finds he cannot sleep.

He rises in the dark, puts on his boots and overcoat and steals out quietly into the night.

Twenty minutes later, he is still there at the pond, kneeling prayer-like over the ice, when the Vestal Amata finds him.

Don't be startled, she says and comes up from behind him. It's just me.

I know, he says.

Well, I didn't want you shootin me for a slug or anything.

He does not respond, and she stands over him where he kneels. He sees her pull her coat tighter around her.

It's too cold for you out here, he says. Get on back inside.

I been colder, she says.

When? he asks.

What?

When've you been colder? Tell me a story.

She must detect a hostile challenge in his voice, because she doesn't respond. Instead, she kneels down in the snow beside him and looks at the face, barely visible in the moonlight, staring up at them from beneath the ice.

For a while the two say nothing. There are hoot owls in the trees, and they make a lonely sound.

Finally, Moses speaks, but he does not look at her – nor does she look at him. Instead, they both gaze down at the bloated, cloudy face beneath the water, as though a dead man were the only kind of true hearer of tales.

You ain't holy, he says.

No, she replies quiet. I ain't.

Are you a whore?

I've been a whore, she says without flinching. I've been lots of things. For a while I just wandered. When you ain't got a destination, you find yourself going down all kinds of different roads.

How come you talk like you do? Different ways.

She shrugs.

I picked it up. I been high and I been low. You learn things when you travel around a lot.

Me, I travelled around a lot more than you, and I ain't learned any mannered speech.

She shrugs again.

I'm a people pleaser, she says. I like to fit in. It's different when you're a woman and you ain't got a gun. Sometimes your only weapon is a ticklish subterfuge. You, now you're like a grizzly walking on two feet – I guess you never had to subtle your way through anything.

I guess not. Subtlety ain't my strong point.

I recognized that.

She laughs, and Moses chuckles along with her. Then they sit in silence for a while longer. The Vestal leans back on her hands and looks up at the night-time stars. Ever since the world has gone awry there are many more of them, and they are brighter – like the shimmering dust left behind after some levelling destruction.

Then Moses begins to talk again.

So, he says slowly, if you ain't a stranger to whore-dom—

Among other things, she reminds him.

Right.

I mean, I never had any whore business cards made up.

Understood, he concedes. Among other things. If you ain't a stranger to it, how come you were so intent on keepin me from the girls back there?

She smiles up at the stars.

It's pretty out here, she says. You do find it some-times, don't you – even in a world of death?

That ain't an answer.

The good thing about being a tricksy bitch, she says, is that you don't have to tell all your secrets.

True enough, Moses nods. Everyone's entitled to their secrets, tricksy bitch or otherwise.

She seems content not to answer for a few minutes, but the question still lingers in the air between them. After a while, she sits forward and brushes the icy dirt from her palms.

If you want to know the truth, she says, it wasn't any-thing in particular. It just seemed wrong. I don't mean *wrong* wrong, not wrong for the world at large. Just wrong for you. Does that make sense?

He nods slowly.

I reckon it does. Your life ain't a target for the world to shoot at. The world is a target for your life to shoot at.

She looks at him and smiles.

Somethin like that, she says.

Again they gaze into the face of the dead man beneath the ice. His clouded eyes blink peacefully.

So then how come? Moses says. How come the dead don't want you?

The Vestal shakes her head.

I don't know, she says. Honest to God. All I know is it ain't my pure soul shining so bright it blinds em.

Moses narrows his eyes at this mystery. They are quiet. The Vestal Amata leans her head on his shoulder, and they sit for a while without saying anything. He can feel her small body shivering.

Go on back to the cabin, he says. Get warm.

Okay, she says. You coming?

In a little while. I ain't quite done stargazing yet.

So she returns to the cabin, and he remains out there in the frozen wild, his only real companion the trapped and pathetic dead.

*

They stay the next five days in the shelter of the cabin in the woods. They scrawl a sign on a wooden plank and nail it to a tree down by the main road. It says:

SURVIVORS IN NEED OF RIDE
THIS WAY

And it has an arrow pointing up the path. It is the Vestal's idea, but Moses knows that bandits frequently use such signs to trap the unwary and that no experienced traveller would ever follow one. Still, the days are long, and it is something.

Moses hunts squirrels for food, and Abraham cooks them in the fireplace, boiling snow for water. They do not speak of what is to come, because it feels as though time has stopped dead, as though they have stumbled into some grand hiatus, a still centre around which the rest of the world rotates.

Abraham tends to the wound in his thigh. He limps around, teeth grit, and sweats at night despite the cold.

Once, while he sits on the floor by the firelight, pouring water over the wound to clean it, the Vestal looks down at him.

That leg of yours is in bad shape, she says. It stinks.

How do you know that's my leg and not just me? Abraham replies. I ain't exactly known for my ambrosial odours.

I know the difference between regular man stink and the stink of flesh rot. You don't get that taken care of you're gonna lose that leg. And out here, you lose that leg and the rest of you won't be far behind.

It ain't nothing, he says. Then he leers up at her and says, It ain't nothing a quick mouth job couldn't fix.

She does not flinch nor even give any indication of noticing his lewd suggestion.

I'm serious now, she says. Infection like that spreads.

He waves her away with his hand.

It ain't nothing, he repeats. I'll sweat it out.

Then he goes back to tending to the wound. But he can't let the girl alone, and that very night Moses hears him hobbling across the creaky floor of the cabin not long after they have settled in for sleep. Perhaps he believes that Moses is asleep, or perhaps he does not care – but he leans down over where the Vestal lies on the couch.

Hey, he says to her in a soft voice. How bout a little touch? Just a quick poke like – what do you say?

Shoo, Abraham, she says. Get back to bed.

Come on, he says. You had worse than me, I know it. Me, I'm like a bunny rabbit – quicky dicky. Sweet and simple.

I don't let stinky dying men poke me, she says. Go to bed.

All the more reason, he says. A dying man's last wish – would you begrudge him it?

Shoo, Abraham. Go shish-kebab a squirrel. This pussy just ain't got your name on it.

Moses sees her turning her back on him, burrowing herself into the couch.

Abraham stands appalled for a moment, balancing on his one good leg.

Well, I'll be goddamned if it ain't the *only* name not

on it, he says to her, his voice hissing with vitriol. You got the whole phone book down your pants, girl.

Pretending to sleep, Moses waits to see if his brother will take more action. He is a man who does not react well to rejection of the womanly sort. But Abraham is too aware of his brother's presence in the room, so he turns and stumbles with great noise back to the bed he shares with Moses. Moses can hear him cursing a litany in a whisper under his breath.

Goddamn high-falutin whores, he says. What's everybody keepin themselves so pure for anyway? Armageddon everywhere you look, and everybody's still so uppity about a little bump. Like a goddamn piss in the woods. Who cares? You do it and then you go back to the business of not bein dead. Instead we got ourselves a world of princes and princesses and dukes and dukettes – and everybody's wearin white robes and readin bibles and puttin flowers in each other's hair. Just once I'd like to meet somebody without such a goddamn fine-tuned moral compass.

When he gets into the bed beside his brother, Abraham tugs the bristly blanket off Moses and curls up in a sweating ball of curses.

Moses waits. He does not sleep much. The embers in the fireplace pop and glow.

*

Five days they stay in the cabin. Five days in the woods where, at night, they can hear the flakes of snow tapping light on the windowpanes, they can hear the branches of the trees cracking under the weight of the fall. If it snows at night, in the morning Moses clears again the ice from behind which the dead man gazes. Moses hunts, the Vestal cooks, Abraham stumbles around the clearing and tends to his wound.

What is it if it ain't a miniature family we've gone and built here? Abraham says.

Five days, Moses thinks. And goddamned if it doesn't feel, in fact, like they have built something. A something out of nothing. Like a building on an empty lot. A thing that wasn't there before but now stands undeniable and true.

Nights, when he can't sleep, Moses goes and sits by the pond and looks up at the sky along with the dead man. Sometimes the Vestal Amata joins him, and sometimes she doesn't. They talk, and she picks at the ends of her long red hair. She tells him about herself. She was born in Oklahoma City, she was raised by her mother. Her father she doesn't have much memory of. He went his own way when things went bad. She was five years old, and for a long time it was her and her mother, finding places to hide from the hordes of the dead. Then her mother died when she was nine. Not eaten. She just got sick and kind of faded away. Some stories end that way, the girl explains. After her mother died, she was taken in by a whole lot of different people. Some were okay and others weren't. Now she's twenty-five – which is exactly the same age as Abraham.

For brothers, she says, you two got some age between you.

Fifteen years, Moses confirms.

That's a big difference, she says. And it ain't the only thing different between you.

Moses shrugs.

We got different mothers, he says.

I'd listen to a story, if you'd recount it.

It ain't much of a story, but I don't feel like tellin it at the moment. Maybe a different night under different stars. These ones are too hopeful.

Okay, she says.

He can feel her gaze on him. She does not look away for a long time. He sits up and leans over the ice of the pond.

Everybody's lookin for their own personal entrance to heaven, Moses says. Mine looks different from my brother's – and yours different from both.

Moses reaches out a finger and taps on the ice over the dead man's face.

Him too, he says. Look at him there, nose pressed up against the window of heaven.

The Vestal Amata leans forward to look. She brushes her palm gently across the surface of the ice. Then she looks up into the night sky as if to see what heaven he might be trying to get into.

Everyone's always tryin to find an entrance to the kingdom of heaven, she says. Me, I ain't so interested in entrances. All I want's a kingdom of exits.

Moses wonders what she means, and then he thinks he understands. He too has looked this way upon the world at times. He eyes her, the curve of her neck craned upwards, the moonlight catching it pale as the snow, the auburn of her hair like a tangle of nightwood. And then a smile cracks the cool reflection of her face, and she laughs high and tinkling like a Christmas chime. Suddenly he is suspicious of the sincerity of her words – as though she is accustomed to being the awed audience of her own performances. He wonders how much, in fact, she believes her own stories.

But she smiles brightly. So, so bright.

She looks down at the dead man in the ice again.

How long do you think he's been down there? she asks.

Too long, Moses says and rises to his feet.

Where are you going?

I'll be back.

He goes to the broken-down porch of the cabin and returns with a rusted red fireman's pick-axe.

Watch out, he says to the Vestal.

Then he raises the axe over his head and brings the blade down on the ice to the left of the dead man. A crack extends through the surface of the pond, and water splashes out. Then he hefts the axe twice more – once on the other side of the dead man and once beyond where the head is. Then he sets the axe down and slides the loosened sheet of ice away leaving a rectangular patch of water where the dead man is.

Moses kneels in the water at the edge of the pond, before the floating slug. The ripples in the water diminish until the surface is flat and unmoving. Then the dead man begins to rise.

But he has been underwater for too long. The face, as it rises out of the water, melts away, the loosened flesh slipping off bone, the mush of his features splashing into the water, scalp and ear floating mildly on the surface like lily pads. The jaw seems to open, too, but it does so by gravity rather than hunger, because the muscles are rotted away as well. The man cannot hold himself above water, and as soon as his shoulders clear the surface he falls back again. Again he rises, and again he falls back.

Moses doesn't know what he expected to happen. Perhaps he thought the man would rise like the body of a saint, held aloft on columns of light, lifted to cloudy heaven. Maybe he thought the man would emerge dripping, cleansed, baptized, and steal away into the wilderness to encounter fully his final communion with the earth.

What Moses had wanted was to free the man. But this horror does not look anything like freedom.

He bows his head and sighs as the slug rises again and falls back, the wrinkled flesh of his fingers sloughing off as he reaches for purchase at the edges of the ice.

Then Moses stands and picks up the axe again. He turns it over and uses one hand only to bring the pick end down and bury it in the dead man's skull.

The pick slips out as easily as it went in, and then the body sinks again for the last time.

Moses looks to the sky again, but nothing has changed. The stars are the same ones he saw before. They are the same hoot owls that once again commence their haunted calls. He is still thigh deep in the pond, but he cannot feel the cold.

He turns to the Vestal Amata who has watched the whole thing in silence. He starts to say something but then trails off:

Well, at least . . .

At least what? the girl asks.

But diminished so to smallness is the world that the least of anything is difficult to determine.

*

That is their fifth night at the cabin. Moses does not know how he will endure a sixth – for slowing down means growing blind to promise, and a cessation is the ignoblest kind of death. So what will a sixth day look like? What sallow universe will be born?

But he does not have to discover it, because before dawn on the next day the visitors arrive.

Seven

It is the Vestal who wakes Moses when the light is still grey and misty. It is no longer snowing, and instead of the tap-tap-tap of the flakes on the windowpanes, there is only a muffled silence that sanctuarizes their small and fractured home.

The Vestal says nothing. She simply puts a hand against Moses' cheek, and he wakes. He opens his eyes to see her holding a finger to her lips, hushing him. She points to a window and bids him to wait and listen.

He remains still, and then he can hear it. The stuttering groan of snow beneath clumsy boots. It is difficult to sneak up on someone in the snow. The ground itself cries out your presence.

Did you see them? Moses whispers.

The Vestal nods.

Three of them, she whispers. Two men. One woman with a bow. Fletcher's people.

Moses wakes his brother, and they creep to the windows, peeking out from behind the ratty curtains they kept closed in case of just such an intrusion.

The men'll come through the door – both at once, Abraham says. The woman with the bow, she'll stay back, watch for runners.

Right, Moses says and nods.

What do we do? the Vestal asks.

Moses turns to her. They are all three crouched to the floor.

You want to go back with him? Moses asks her.

No, she says and shakes her head. Why would I—

You're goin with him or you're comin with us. My brother and I, we put our necks out there to get swine-cut again, you're comin quiet. No more sneakin off.

She looks at him straight, her eyes narrowed, as if she would consider this. As if her word of honour were a puzzle box she is trying to open behind her back.

Decide, Moses says.

Fine, she says quickly. Fine. Agreed.

Moses then turns to his brother.

The two that come in, he says. You and me'll take em. No noise. Let the Vestal be the bait.

*

When the door opens, there is first one man – wrapped up in leather and carrying an Uzi swaying in an arc before him, as though he would pepper the room with rounds if given a reason. But as soon as he sees the small figure on the bed, he lunges and holds the Vestal down with brutal and gleeful force. He swings the automatic weapon around to his side on a long leather strap.

Found you, ain't we? he says. Brucie, get in here!

Then the other man, a twin of the first, comes into the room, smiling and carrying two pistols.

Where's your boyfriends at? says the one named Brucie. He chortles. They use you up and leave you behind? I guess that's what you get when—

But that's when he spots Moses, emerging from behind the door like a bearded leviathan, a monstrous bladed weapon raised above his head.

Brucie opens his mouth to say something, but before he can utter a sound or raise his hands in defence, the weapon comes down and shatters his skull, exploding his head and sending thick spumes of bone, blood, gristle and brain in a multifoliate bloom across the floor and walls.

The other, splashed with the wastage of what used to slosh around in his compatriot's brainpan, shuffles back quickly on the bed, reaching for the Uzi – but Abraham rises from a pile of dusty blankets behind him, reaches around the man's neck and buries a knife in his throat up by the ear. An arterial surge of blood erupts from the wound, but the man still struggles – so Abraham draws the knife deep and true around the underside of his jaw-line. The man's head falls backwards against Abraham, cut off near to entirety, his neck now opening up in a huge thickly pumping cicatrix. Abraham lets the body drop to the floor and then drives his blade through the man's eye socket to prevent him rising again.

It is done. The three wipe their eyes clean of blood. The Vestal picks a bit of gristle off her cheek. She does not flinch. Moses waits for her to flinch, but she does not flinch. A hard woman, that one. A woman raised in the midst of gore, chaos.

What about the other one? the Vestal asks. The woman outside.

Moses takes a sighted rifle from the corner and hands it to his brother.

Abraham's got the eye, he says.

Abraham takes the rifle and goes to the window, putting the barrel between the curtains right up to the glass pane.

You got one shot, Moses says to his brother, or she'll bring the whole cavalry up here. Can you do it?

I reckon I've done plenty of headshots from this dis-tance.

Here, Moses says. He takes a pillow from the bed and wraps it around the muzzle of the gun to hush the report.

Can you still sight it? he asks.

Sho, his brother answers.

One shot, Moses says.

One shot, Abraham says.

They wait while Abraham sights it. Moses looks out the window through a narrow gap in the curtains. He can see the woman's figure there in the snow, holding the bow with an arrow nocked loose in it, looking towards the cabin and shifting nervously. Every few moments she lets her gaze go back down the hills behind her towards the main road where the rest of her company sits in wait. Moses watches her, and her breath comes in clouds from between her lips.

Hold up, Moses says to his brother.

What now? says Abraham.

Moses turns to the Vestal.

You know that woman? he asks.

The Vestal nods.

She's a sport archer. Can land an arrow between a slug's eyes at a hundred yards.

She would kill us?

The Vestal nods.

Or have us killed, she says. She ain't a bad person. But she's a soldier, and she's got loyalties like the rest of us. Hers are to Fletcher. He protects her.

Moses sighs and nods.

Okay? Abraham asks.

Okay, Moses says.

Once again he looks through the window. Abraham takes a number of seconds to steady himself. Then there's a muffled report, a quick crack at the window-pane, and outside in the snow Moses sees the figure of the woman drop the bow and slump down quietly in the serene drifts.

They wait for a few minutes, listening. But there is no rush of aid coming up through the trees – no panicked response. The people below have not heard, and silence catches in the branches of the trees like some vast spider's web.

*

Moses leaves the other two to wash the gore from their faces with melted snow. He goes a long way around through the trees to where he can see the main road in the distance, the extended line of parked vehicles that is Fletcher's caravan. Then he returns to the cabin.

We're stuck, Abraham says. Ain't we? We ain't trekking through the woods, and we ain't got a car.

They've got cars, Moses says. There's one at the back, away from the others. One man at the wheel, sleeping. We go through the woods, come up from behind. Quick, before anyone knows.

They'll see, says Abraham. They'll give chase.

Let em, Moses says. They track good, but they're slow. We'll outrun them.

Abraham nods. He massages his stiffening leg with snow.

But he can't hardly walk, the Vestal says and points to Abraham. How's he going to tromp through the woods and make a dash for a car?

I ain't, says Abraham, looking at his brother. I'm stayin here.

What? says the Vestal. They'll kill you.

Naw. They'll be too busy huntin you two. I'll go up

165

in the trees a ways and hide out a couple hours till they're well gone. Moses'll drop you where you're going. Then he'll come back here for me. Ain't that right, brother?

Moses says nothing for a moment. His eyes meet Abraham's, and something passes between them.

Can you conjure a better plan? he asks Abraham finally.

I surely can't, says Abraham, grinning a little.

It'll be a few days, Moses says. Can you last it?

I can last it. You for certain you can find this place again to come get me?

Moses shrugs.

If I don't, he says, there's someone in the pond out back could use some company.

Moses smiles and chuckles a little, and Abraham laughs with him.

You ain't much of a brother, Abraham says. Are you?

Ain't neither of us anything to make a daddy proud.

Abraham squints up at the sky, as if in remembrance of something profound.

It don't matter, he says. Our pap is long gone. Likely he was the first slug that ever was. The one that started this whole thing. Just one stubborn prick refusin to stay dead. Don't that have a ring of truth to it?

Moses smiles and nods down at his feet.

It does, he says. It surely does.

For a while again they are quiet, kind of kicking their feet in the snow and looking everywhere in the world except at each other.

Hey, Moses says at last. Do me a favour.

What's that? says Abraham.

They won't come for you. But if they do – if they do come for you, then kill em good, okay?

You got it, Abraham says, a smile spreading across his face like that of a child who has garnered the approval of a difficult parent. I'll kill em real good. I'll make tobacco pipes out of their bones and be smoking em when you get back.

*

The man at the wheel of the small car is still sleeping when Moses returns to it with the Vestal Amata. The caravan sits idle along the road. Towards the front of the line, many of Fletcher's people have got out of the vehicles and are tromping playfully through the snow. One woman with a bandana around her head is making a snowman and decorating it with the eyeballs and nose and scalp cut from a slug. Fletcher himself is there, too, standing atop the truck at the very front of the line, his wide sombrero perched on his head and a bottle of wine in his hand. He drinks and laughs at the antics below him and then drinks again. Every now and then he glances up towards the cabin. He wonders, perhaps, why it is taking his three soldiers so long to return. But he is reluctant, no doubt, to go up there himself after he was taken hostage last time.

Moses and the Vestal climb down through the trees to the road twenty yards behind the end of the caravan. They creep up behind the small car with the sleeping man. Moses is about to make his attack when the Vestal stops him.

Let me do it, she whispers. We don't want to raise the alarm just yet, and I'm willin to bet my touch is just a wee bit more delicate than yours.

Moses nods.

Try not to kill him, Moses says, if you don't have to.

She shakes her head and smiles at him.

You and your notions, she says. It's like you're livin in a different time. And not even the one we lost but a different one altogether.

He's sleeping is all I'm sayin.

I hear you. Give me your belt.

He gives it to her, and she tears a strip of fabric from the hem of her skirt.

Moses watches her as she creeps up behind the car on the driver's side until she's at the window, which is rolled down. She reaches in and touches the side of the sleeping man's face, caressing his cheek lightly with her fingers. In her other hand, Moses can see she has the belt and the wad of fabric.

The man wakes suddenly to see the redhead's smiling face hovering before him.

It's you, he says.

It's me, she says and kisses him.

He must wonder if he is still asleep, or if he has fallen into death and heaven by the back route of somnolence. He is old, his hair thin, grey and wispy. This man is no fighter. He closes his eyes again and relents to her kiss, which is deep and long and, Moses notices with disdain, undeniably professional. It is longer than it needs to be. The man is subdued – he is acquiescent, and still she continues to kiss him, one hand gripping the back of his head as though it is still possible to draw him closer, as though she would consume him, as though her appetites are the same as those of the dead.

Moses sees the other hand reach up with the wad of fabric.

She stops kissing him suddenly.

I always liked you, she says to him. You were always nice to me.

He smiles a little.

Then she takes the fabric and jams it into his mouth.

An expression of tragic betrayal comes into his eyes – and so surprised is he that he doesn't even struggle against her for a moment – not until after she has already got Moses' looped belt around his neck like a leash.

Then she opens the car door and pulls him out by the end of the belt. He reaches for the fabric in his mouth so that he can cry out, but Moses is there, taking his hands and holding them still.

In such a manner, they drag the man through the snow and into the trees by the side of the road and tie him to one of the trunks using the belt and strips of torn fabric. He does not struggle much, for he is set upon by the woman he once knew, who kissed him even, and a man he does not know but who is a Paul Bunyan of a man who looks like he would brook no resistance. Besides, the Vestal Amata keeps reassuring him they aren't going to kill him.

See, she says and points. The road's right there. They'll see you from it. They won't leave without you.

He's the doctor Fletcher keeps with him, the Vestal says to Moses as they make their way back to the car. Peabody's his name. He cured me of the clap once. He's an okay guy.

Hush up, Moses says. Let's just get ourselves out of here.

Moses climbs into the driver's seat, and the Vestal gets in the other side.

You ready? Moses says.

I'm ready.

Moses glances once more into the woods at the man called Peabody who at some time in the past cured the Vestal of her gonorrhoea and is now tied to a tree with mild staring eyes. Then he starts the engine, puts the car in gear and accelerates as quickly as he can without letting the tyres spin on the ice.

At first the others don't seem to notice – then, as they pass the first few vehicles of the caravan, some of Fletcher's men begin calling out. By the time they reach the front of the caravan, guns are unsheathed and aim is being taken – and Moses can see Fletcher himself in the rearview mirror – standing there atop the truck, throwing in fury the half-empty bottle of wine so that it spins end over end through the air and spills its contents onto the snow, staining the earth with a burgundy that looks like day-old blood.

Some potshots are fired, one of them thunking into the plastic of the bumper – but they are too far gone for an effective hit.

Now what? says the Vestal.

Now we outrun em, Moses says. They're slow, but we've got a tail we got to stay ahead of. Besides, Abe's waitin on me. Let's get this business finished for once and all.

*

They drive five hours straight, though the roads are icy and slow going. They pass places with names such as Mountain Village, Sawpit and Loghill. The road begins to decline, and they find themselves coasting down out of the mountains where the snow diminishes and finally disappears altogether. In a city called Montrose, they veer off onto a highway going east. It is good driving for a while, and Moses sees no sign of the caravan behind them.

Maybe they gave up, says the Vestal. I can't be worth all this.

Maybe they gave up, but I do doubt it. The more I take you away, the more of a holy grail you get to be to Fletcher. There's not much can come between a man and his grail – particularly not reason.

A what?

Grail. It's a cup.

A cup?

Not a cup. A goblet I guess. The one Jesus drank out of.

Jesus drank out of a cup?

That surprises you?

I don't know. I guess I always pictured him drinking out of his hands like you do at a river or something.

Well, he drank out of a cup at least once. And there for a while everyone was lookin for it.

When? When were they looking for it?

I don't know. The time of the knights.

Did they find it?

He considers this.

You know something, I don't remember that part. Maybe they did and maybe they didn't. Anyway, it was the looking for it that counted.

You know a lot.

He looks at her to see if she is making fun of him, but she doesn't seem to be.

I don't really, he says. It was just different when I was growing up. You had time to learn a lot of things that didn't matter much.

For a while they find themselves driving parallel to a large, elongated reservoir. There are no signs of life on either of its shores – just pale-brown hills under the rutted sky. They come to a place where the road turns and crosses a two-lane bridge over the reservoir to the north shore, but there is a pile of burned-out cars blocking the route.

Is that where we need to go? asks the Vestal.

Yup.

Can we go around another way?

We maybe could. But it'd be a long way out of our way, and I don't like the risk of it.

Can we move the cars?

He looks at her.

Then what? she says.

We walk across. I reckon we can find another car on the other side. Plus it'll slow Fletcher down considerable. Those that move in bulk don't do so good with obstacles.

So they take their things and put them in duffel bags. Then they say goodbye to the car and run it down the slope into the reservoir to confound Fletcher's trackers for a little while at least. They watch the car sink, as though it were a symbol of something important.

Then Moses climbs up on the parapet of the bridge and helps the Vestal up behind him. They walk on the parapet until they are beyond the pile of cars, then they hop down onto the concrete and follow the broken and faded centreline in, she on one side and he on the other.

Halfway across, they find three dried-up corpses that begin to rise when they hear footsteps. As the slugs pull themselves up, Moses can see their brittle white bones cracking from misuse under their loose skin. There is a clicking coming from their throats, as though their tongues and gullets had shrivelled up and speech were now a thing of bone and grit.

Stay back, Moses says to the Vestal Amata as he drops the duffel and pulls from it a pistol.

Sure, I'll stay back.

The Vestal walks casually to the side of the bridge and hoists herself up to sit dangle-footed on the parapet. Moses has forgotten, for a moment, that the slugs pose no threat to her, but he is reminded by the complete lack of alarm in her expression – as though she were taking her seat for a weakly acted matinee performance.

As the three slugs drag their feet in his direction, he takes aim and fires. The first shot goes wide. The second is too low, hitting one of the slugs in the chest, and the third blasts off an ear. On the fourth shot, the slug on the right drops back down to the ground. The other two continue forwards. Moses takes aim again.

I see you ain't a sharpshooter, says the Vestal from her seat. She breaks in half a twig she's been carrying and uses it to clean her teeth while she watches.

It takes him five shots to bring down the second one.

You're burnin through our ammo, says the Vestal. Well, at least it'll make a lighter load for us to tote.

When he fires the pistol at the third and hears the click, he is reminded that he needs to reload. He reaches down to do so, but the slug is only a few paces away now – slow in movement but undeviating in purpose, more machine than animal, its rusty, ossified mechanics grinding away with click and bristle, enslaved to its single appetite.

Before Moses realizes, the dead man's hands are on him, his sandy, brittle fingers pawing at Moses' jacket. Moses drops the gun – it's too late now to load it.

Instead, he takes the creature by the neck with both hands to keep the deadly snapping jaw away from him. The dead man has little strength left in his body, so Moses can hold him, like a snake wrangler, out of danger, but there is little else he can do without releasing the slug.

He is still undecided about his next move when the slug's face explodes before him, splashing his own face with moist, papery gore. He can also hear the bullet whistle by his ear, and when he drops the dead man to the ground he can see the Vestal standing behind him, her pistol still aimed at where the slug's head was a moment before.

Goddamnit, he says to her. You could of killed me.

She looks at the pistol as though confused by its purpose.

I didn't think it would go all the way through him, she says. Did I get you?

He grabs the gun away from her, his heart trilling in anger.

Naw, you didn't *get* me. Though it ain't for want of tryin. You're a goddamn menace.

Well, pardon me for tryin to come to your rescue. It seemed like you were in some peril – I ain't ever seen so many bullets flyin wild.

Moses stuffs the guns back in the duffel and swings it over his shoulder. He does not want to look at her. She is a reckless thing, a shameful thing.

You know something? he says. I got a theory on you, and it's a goddamn miserable one.

A theory! I bet nobody ever mistook you for a philosopher.

I got a theory that maybe you wore out your soul whorin and deceivin. Maybe some part of you's already dead – which is why they don't take you.

The moment is stricken by silence. A breeze blows cold and harsh across the bridge. Moses moves his feet against the sandy tarmac but makes no show to walk away. It would seem that there are no directions leading away from this moment.

Jesus, says the Vestal quietly. That's an awful theory.

I told you it was, says Moses almost in a whisper.

Is that really what you think?

He shifts his feet against the tarmac again. He would walk away from everything in the world if he could. A wandering man.

Hey, look, he says, straining a note of apology. I'm shook up. You did me a service here. I ain't the shooter of the family.

They walk on in silence to the opposite side of the bridge where Moses climbs down to the water's edge and washes the blood out of his hair and beard.

The Vestal sits by him, soaking her feet in the cool water.

So you never really learned how to shoot, huh? she asks.

He holds up his right hand, palm downward, to show her. It is a thick, calloused paw, and it trembles as if in withdrawal from punching.

I ain't so steady, he says. I guess I'm more of a cudgel man.

I would say so.

*

They walk, and they examine the cars abandoned on the road. It is more difficult than Moses had thought to find an operational vehicle. The tyres are blown out from the heat, the gas burned out of the tanks, the engines rusted still. The weather in this area is harsh. It is easier in the south, where he is from.

They walk all day and find no vehicle. They stay on the road that follows the reservoir's north bank, and in a few hours they are beyond its tip where the barren dirt plains give way to patches of pasture and farmland. Up ahead in the distance, Moses points to some buildings – but the sun is lowering on the horizon.

It's a town, he says. Gunnison. We've been seein the signs. We can probably find a car there, but it ain't advisable to approach a strange town after dark. You like to have your eyes open for whatever's comin your way.

So they find an abandoned farmhouse where they can stay the night. They gather wood and start a fire in the fireplace, and there are some cans of chili left behind in the cupboards, so they heat those and put them into ceramic bowls and eat with spoons. They sit next to each other on the couch and watch the fire and wait for their eyes to become heavy with sleep.

This is nice, says the Vestal Amata, ain't it? It's like

we've set up housekeeping. Like we're a newly-wed prairie couple or something.

Moses grunts non-committally.

They are quiet. They wait. Then the Vestal speaks again.

You worried about your brother?

He'll last it, Moses says. He's hard like a tree root.

He is at that. You two are very different. He ain't the most decent man in the world. I guess you know that. But you protect him.

I'm his brother, Moses says. I ain't much of anything in this world – but one thing I am is Abraham Todd's brother. For good or poor.

For a while Moses says nothing else, and it seems as though the conversation will end there. Then he breathes in deep, still gazing into the fire, and speaks again.

He could of turned out different given different circumstances. I guess we all could have. But I'm talking about before. Before the slugs even.

You must of seen him grow up, says the Vestal.

I did and I didn't.

You got a lot of years between you.

We sure enough do, Moses confirms and stares deeply into the fire as though his entire history were contained in the flames. We got different mothers. My father, I didn't know him. He left before I was born. I got raised up by my mother. I knew *of* him, though, my pa. You heard about him all around the county. There wasn't any honour or nobility to him. He was just your run-of-the-mill degenerate. He never had much to say to me, nor I to him. When I was fifteen a young girl died givin birth to a baby boy she claimed was his. She was fourteen years of age, that girl. Her boy was Abraham.

He pauses, and for a while nothing is said. There is a pop in the fireplace, and an ember leaps out and comes to rest on the floor before them. It glows, the little burning punk, and then smokes itself out.

Your father raised him? the Vestal asks.

Naw, Moses says. He never admitted Abraham was his. Wouldn't submit to a test. Abraham had it hard. He was raised by the state. Foster homes and institutions. There wasn't nothing I could do – I was just a teenager. But I listened around about him. I always knew where he was. He had it hard, Abe did. Just a little scrawny twig of a boy, and nobody on his side.

He pauses again and looks out the window into the distant dark, and he wonders if maybe the boy is still out there somewhere in the reachable past.

When everything went sour, he goes on, my ma got taken early. I was twenty years of age by then, wanderin here and there. I wasn't there to protect her. By the time I got back to my hometown, she was already gone. There weren't much left at all, just a bunch of people all panicking themselves to death in the hospital. I found Abe there, took him with me. No one stopped me. No one was stoppin anybody at that time.

Moses breathes deep.

Anyhow, he says, whatever took him, whatever

malignancy's got him in its teeth, he was already took when I collected him at five years old.

The fire snaps again and fizzes. It is guttering down now, glowing red like a beating heart that refuses to stop.

Say, he says and turns to her where she sits next to him on the couch. Back there. The thing I said about you – your soul.

Forget it, she says. She leans her head on the back of the couch and gazes at him. Her eyes sparkle like embers popped from the fire.

Mose, she goes on. Did you ever have a woman? You know, a real woman of your own? A wife?

He opens his mouth to respond and then closes it again, as though something is short-circuiting in him. He opens his mouth again, and this time the words come out.

A wife, he says. Yeah, a wife. And a kid, too. A daughter. I was supposed to meet em in Jacksonville. The caravan they were in, it never showed. Could be they're still out there, but I reckon not.

He feels something in his throat, his chest. He coughs and bites down hard as though to keep something from erupting inside him.

I would of took care of them, he says, raising his finger and pointing it hard at the Vestal, angry even. I would of killed anything – anything to come near them with malign intent. I would of – I would of been a good – I swear I would of killed—

His words stumble over each other, and he has no

control of them any more. They are spilling out of him, and he is embarrassed. But then the Vestal stops him, perhaps in an act of glorious pity – rises suddenly and climbs onto his lap and closes his mouth with her own so that the words stop coming. Because it is the words that are most treacherous, the words that spread like ripe contagion, the utterance that makes things true – calamitously and inexorably true.

Wait, he says, because the words keep coming – out of spite they keep coming.

Wait for what? she asks.

Just a thing I got to know, he says. How come you ran away? There's somethin in you. You could help people. How come you don't want to go to that citadel?

She shrugs and shifts on top of him, her loins pushing down on his lap.

I don't know, she says. Everybody's lookin for answers. I don't want to be anybody's answer.

She moves to kiss him again, but he pushes her away a second time.

And this? he says. Ain't this an answer?

You big dope, she says and takes his face in her hands. This ain't even a question.

Then she kisses him again, stops the words dead. Dams up the unceasing stream of language. Moses takes her little body in his hands, such a small powerful thing.

And the Vestal, her red hair falling around his shoulders – she stops the words, stops his mouth, both their bodies caught in a sudden seizure, gripped to blissful stillness, swaddled and safe in the cool, hard limits of human contact. He sees again the pendant she wears between her pale breasts, the small wooden cross – and it is a sign for him of something true, some honest faith in this wild thing of a woman. They are together, and what they create in their union is not a new something but rather a whole and complete nothing, a void that sits quiet and calm on his heart, that makes his breathing shallow and at peace, that gives erasure to many scripts of tragedy that have palimpsested themselves over the vellum of his greying mind.

To stop. To cease, just for a moment. To turn your back on the world, to close your eyes – to see the nothing that is *not* rather than the nothing that *is* everywhere around you. To just be quiet in your mind for a little minute.

There are paradises even yet on the abandoned plains of the earth – and they are not filled with fecund flowering Edens but rather just with sweet unerring silences.

The Vestal's flesh is white as a lily, but she is unbreakable – even for hands as worn and brute as his. He is safe in his inability to hurt her. She is empty, and beautiful as one of those ancient urns that tell stories – and she is unblemishable.

*

That's right, Moses says to the caravaners. I had a wife once. You heard it true enough. You'll ask how come I ain't mentioned it yet – so cardinal it is to the understanding of who I was, who I am still.

It is full dark now, the fire down to mere embers. It is no longer possible to tell who is listening and who has been taken by sleep. No other person has said anything for a great while. They are caught in the sickly dark hours between late night and dawn. The great one-eyed man continues to speak without recourse to the number who either hear or don't hear him – as though his story were a fated thing, a toy machine that, once wound, must keep spinning wild on its metal wheels until it finds its own still end.

You'll say, maybe, that I've misled, Moses goes on. If so, I apologize. To you. To her. It ain't nothing, an apology. Just a notion, like any other. You can utter it like an incantation, but if it brings somethin to bear you've got more out of it than I ever have. I'm sorry. I declare it with every step I take on this earth. I'm sorry. I'm sorry. I had a wife once. And a kid, too, a daughter. It was a long time ago – half a life ago. My wife, well she was a beauty too, don't doubt it – but in a different way. She wasn't fancy – not spectacular with herself or nothin like that. She was just pretty in a plain way. And nice. She was pretty and nice. You miss things like that now – you, me, the whole world. She – my wife – she wore her hair tied up in a ribbon. It was a pink ribbon, if you want to know. Simple, pink. It was nice.

The silence draws itself out, a breath held in anticipation of falling.

The truth is, he goes on, I don't like to think about it. You try to let dead things lie – try to look things in the face for the present fact of what they are. You try.

He pauses again.

And for the redhead, too, he continues. The Vestal. I had no business messing with her. But you ain't always able to see. Sometimes you bumble around in the dark. Sometimes you reach out and there's someone there, and you grab them. It may be instinct, but it ain't pure – it don't bear on goodness. I'm sorry, I'm sorry.

He shakes his head, gazes into the dying embers.

She smelled salty, he says. Like oceans.

*

But she is practised in the ways of witchery – a transmogrifant who in the light of morning wears a face different from the one you see by the moon and stars. She is so many things. She is an impossibility with an unperturbed face.

She is not beside Moses when he wakes in the morning. He goes hunting for her and finds her in the kitchen, sitting at the linoleum table and cackling like a hag. She has found a pair of kitchen shears and she is in the process of cutting off her long locks of red hair. They fall to the ground around her as though she were an autumn tree shedding its riotous leaves. And her laugh – it is not hysterical but cruel, diabolical rather than panicky.

Now you're soul-split too, she says and points the shears at him. If I'm broke, then so are you. If I'm dead and empty, then so are you. Whatever hell I've got boiling inside me, you loved it – and that makes it part of you too.

She laughs again.

Who do you think you are? she continues. Your soul

ain't better than mine. You ain't lookin at me from some high tower. You're down here in the muck with the rest of us. You want order? You can play at order and righteousness all you want, but the world ain't got any obligation to conform to your notions.

He looks at the nest of red in which she sits.

Your hair, is all he can utter.

Time for a new look, she says. Sometimes you got to wear your ugliness on the outside of you. The amber tresses ain't me any more. Haven't you heard? I'm the walkin dead – just a slug that's been trained to talk and fuck.

He turns and walks out of the kitchen. He goes outside and sits with his duffel on the front porch. He finds a cigar he's been saving and smokes it while he waits.

There is not a person in sight, living or dead. Sometimes it can be this way – just quiet and still. The sound of a breeze through the high grasses, the creak of an unoiled barn door, the sandy brush of dust blown across an abandoned macadam road. Sometimes there is nothing for miles and miles around to remind you of the way things used to be. The world is so big – the amount of empty space is deafening. Who could of learned to live on this vast and poisonous air? What kind of man?

To end up in this place. Moses has gone wrong somewhere. The woman in the house behind him – she shouldn't of been his burden. He's the wrong man to bear such a trial. It ain't that he's a good man – not by any measurement – but he's got to believe there are laws. He's got to believe there are things you're supposed

to do and things you ain't – or else what's it all for anyway? There are everywhere you look forks in the road.
If there weren't some purpose to choosing one or the
other, then – then what? Then he and the world would
be paralysed with quandariness.

So maybe that's what's happened after all. The
whole world at a crossroads – and no reason to go
either one way or the other.

Finally, she emerges from the house. Her hair is
chopped short and ragged. Uneven patches stick out
every which way, and she looks more like a child than
ever. A ferocious and feral child – all spit and hiss and
gnashing teeth.

You ready? he asks, looking away from her.

I'm ready.

Okay then, he says and rises. Let's get it done with.

*

In the next town, Gunnison, an hour's walk away, they
find a car lot and search until they locate a vehicle that
still runs. They do not speak. Moses glances down the
road behind them and wonders what he would do if
Fletcher caught up to them right now and wanted to
take the redhead away. He imagines handing her over
with an old-timey bow and flourish. He imagines it,
and it gives him pleasure – and he checks himself for
he does not want to become someone who lives exclu-
sively in the mind.

They drive east. The roads rise in twists and turns
over another mountain range. They see snow on the

ground again. Moses thinks of his brother waiting for him to return, his leg festering.

Again they pass out of the mountains, and again through wide plains of farmland all gone fallow. They stop and look at the maps Moses carries in his satchel. They continue.

In a place called Penrose they turn onto a new road and follow it north. There is nothing for miles. A big blank, the whole world unravelled – gone back to immensities of stone and sky.

But half a day after they find the car, they arrive at Colorado Springs. It is thick with the slow dead. The city holds warmth enough to keep the dead animated, but they move with painful slowness across the icy streets. The faces of the slugs here all wear the same blue pallor, and frost settles glistening in their hair and eyelashes. They reach out their arms at the car passing through, but there is nothing to be done. In some cases, their clothes have frozen into the ice on the ground, and the slugs are leashed there, trying fruitlessly to rise. They will not be able to do so until the spring thaw. Until then, they close their eyes against the snow that falls peacefully on their upturned faces.

The place they are looking for is north of the town itself, so they drive through. They turn up another road, and the Vestal Amata points to the road.

Look, she says. Tyre tracks. Cars have been through here. A lot of them it looks like.

Moses nods.

It's a good place to hole up, he says. The dead ain't much of a threat – at least half of the year.

They begin to see skeletons of old fighter jets parked on concrete platforms, landing strips and radio towers every which way.

Where is this citadel we're going to? asks the Vestal.

It's military. The friar said it was part of the Air Force Academy.

The Vestal shakes her head.

Goddamn army men, she says. They're the worst for surviving ugly.

What's that mean?

It means I don't trust em.

Maybe it ain't for you to trust them – but for them to trust you.

God and the army – two things that ain't ever worked so well for me.

What about that pendant you wear on your neck?

What about it? she says, placing a palm against her chest. It was a gift, that's all. The symbol of it's neither here nor there.

They round a bend and come to a large gate in a fence that runs out of sight in either direction over the snowy foothills.

Moses stops the car before the gate, and two soldiers emerge from a guardhouse. One stands at a watchful distance while the other comes to the window of the car.

Are you hurt? asks the soldier.

Not to speak of, says Moses.

Are you seeking shelter?

Huh-uh, Moses says and shakes his head. We got business. I was sent by a friar in Tucson. He said to bring her to the cathedral here. She's a vestal canoness.

A what?

I don't know what it means either. I was just told to bring her, so here she is. You'll like her, she does tricks.

The soldier leans down to look at the Vestal Amata, who glares at him. Then he stands and goes to the guardhouse while the other soldier stands watch.

I ain't a pet to do tricks, she says in a low voice to Moses as they wait.

Ain't you?

Look, Mose, she says and turns to him. I don't like it here.

Her voice has a quiver of nervousness to it, but he doesn't know how far he should believe her.

It ain't exactly my vision of home either, he says.

We don't have to do this, you know. We could turn around right here.

Moses tightens his hands on the steering wheel. He looks grimly forward through the grey clouds that have settled over the landscape.

You got to finish things in life, he says finally. It's important.

The gate before them rolls open and the soldier returns to the car window.

You can proceed inside, he says and points not with a finger but with his full open hand. Take your second right and then your first left after that. The chapel's ahead. You'll see it. Pastor Whitfield will be waiting for you.

Moses pulls the car slowly through the gates, and the Vestal Amata begins a quiet and breathless plea.

Moses, Moses, she says. I ain't dirty, Moses. Really, I'm not. I ain't a holy woman either. I ain't clean nor dirty either one. Moses, I'm just me. I don't want to be anybody's solution. I don't want to be anybody at all. Moses. Moses, please. I know I've been a burden on you.

She is frightened. He has not seen her as a frightened girl before, and he has seen her as many things.

We're just findin out is all, he says and looks straight ahead. You could be of help to people. We're just findin out why it is you're different.

I don't want to know, she says in a voice that's almost a whisper. I don't want to know. I don't. I really don't.

The snow has started to come down now, drab grey and inhospitable. It whips around in flurries and gusts. It fills in all niche and nuance of the world. It blocks out the sky.

Eight

The citadel is a thing to behold.

They get out of the car and block their faces from the windblown snow. They can see figures, living men and women, walking to and fro unhurriedly across a court-yard. These are people who have grown accustomed to safety. They have lived behind these barriers for who knows how long – and they no longer have the wil-derness inside them. The courtyard is a wide square expanse around which the low buildings of the com-pound are situated. It might be grass under the ice, or concrete, or something else entirely – but right now it is simply a plain of colourless drifting snow. So too the distant foothills – so too the sky. The features of the world grow indistinct inside this spitting cloud. It is a place that loses its absolutes – a lightless murk neither of earth nor air, a suffocating desolation where people roam like ghosts grown used to the purgatory they inhabit.

One man wrapped up in a parka walks by them. Moses stops him.

The citadel, he says to the man. Where is it?

The chapel? says the man. He points across the courtyard and continues on his way.

Then, in the distance, they see the spires of the structure. There are seventeen of them lined up in a row, grey spears standing ten storeys tall against the grey sky. It is unlike anything Moses has ever seen before. Dangerous is what it looks like, a structure of sharp steel edges and spikes – looking so like a weapon that Moses imagines it swung by one vicious giant against the jugular of another. Or a row of monstrous teeth, calcified to pale white – the petrified jaw bone of some ancient dragon.

Jesus, Moses says. That don't look like any cathedral I've ever been in.

Moses, please, says the Vestal Amata and takes his arm at the shoulder. The snow is collected on her choppy red hair – as though the winter itself would make her disappear.

Come on, he says. I been around a long time, and if there's one thing I learned it's that the things that look most dangerous usually ain't. It's the ridiculous-lookin things you got to watch out for.

So they cross the courtyard, holding their arms before their faces to block the wind and snow. They are not dressed for this weather, and Moses can feel his beard icing up.

They go around the side of the chapel. A ramp leads up to the glowing doors like the protruded tongue of a sleeping beast, and they climb it. They enter through the wide double doors and find themselves in a huge hall lined with pews – the buttresses of the seventeen spires creating a row of triangular ribs inside that gives you the impression of having fallen into the belly of a beast. But there is an odd violet glow in the place, a perverse warmth that does not seem to jibe with the bitter grey outside.

Then an old man approaches them. He wears a suit and tie and moves with surprising alacrity from some alcove in the side of the place across a line of pews and up the aisle towards them. It is the Pastor Whitfield, and he introduces himself with a smile.

You are seeking sanctuary, maybe? the old man asks. We welcome all.

That's nice, Pastor, says Moses. But I'm just carryin her for a friend. A monk who goes by Ignatius.

The old man smiles widely and claps his hands together.

Ignatius! he says. A dear old friend of mine. I'm so pleased to hear he is still with us. Are you part of his congregation?

Us? Moses says. No. Well, I ain't at least. He told me to bring you her. She's a Vestal.

The old man looks at the girl with the cropped hair and smiles benignantly.

A Vestal, he says. I'm not sure I understand. She's . . .

She's special, Moses says.

We're all of us special in one way or another. I'm sure this young woman—

Special as in the slugs don't want her, Moses blurts out. The man's kindness makes him nervous – along with the purple glow of the place, the sense of peace, the downright civilized tone of it all. He is unused to the niceties that come along with comfort and safety.

They don't— the old man begins, but stutters. They don't—

That's right, Moses confirms. They don't want her. It could be she's an angel or somethin. At least that's what the friar speculated.

You mean, the pastor says, she's immune?

Immune? Moses says and looks to the Vestal. I don't know if you'd call it immune. If she died would she not come back? Beats me. But they're not interested in makin her a meal. I reckon we could give you a demonstration if you got any slugs around. I don't know if it means anything.

If what you say is true, sir, says the pastor, then this young lady means a great deal indeed. But maybe more to science than to the Church. Please follow me. I would like to introduce you to some of my friends.

Moses doesn't like being called sir. He can't remember the last time it was done. It fits him ill. He longs suddenly for the barren wilderness, the brokedown country roads, the collapsing structures, the wandering dead. It is there, in that place of ragged leftovers, that he knows how to behave.

But the old man seems kindly, and he offers them coffee, which Moses hasn't had the delight of in a long time, and he loans them coats to wear as they cross the wide expanse of the snowy courtyard again. And so he follows the man, and the Vestal, still skittish, follows Moses. And when they are inside the buildings of the compound it is almost possible to forget that the world ever became the wilderness it did.

*

It is a community. A whole functional community, clean and calm behind guarded electrical fences and concrete walls. There are soldiers, yes, marching with neat precision, but there are others, too. Civilians to be observed in the glowing windows of bunkhouses, even children. Technicians tinkering with machines, sitting in front of computer monitors. And scientists and doctors walking busily to and fro in white lab coats.

Moses wonders if this is the order he has been craving – if this is what order looks like. It has been so long. So long. He keeps a hand near a pistol on his belt in case of a trap. He looks warily around corners before he turns them so that he won't be taken by surprise. The Vestal, too, seems to wither under the fluorescent lamps lining the ceilings of the compound. She cowers against Moses' chest.

Strange, he thinks. The girl has been through so

much. She has been beaten and lost and whored and imprisoned and broken and put back together – but she has never been simply safe. It must taste sour to her. Unnatural.

Yes, Moses thinks, that is what the girl must feel.

They are led by the pastor to a research wing of the compound and introduced to men and women who are cordial and businesslike. They smile politely and disbelievingly when Moses tells them about the Vestal. But then the Vestal does give a demonstration, three soldiers standing by ready to shoot the female slug in the head when she goes for the girl. But she doesn't. The Vestal walks right up to the slug and stands before her. In the bright lights of the lab, everyone watches as the two lock curious, pitying and befuddled eyes. A long string of drool falls from the lip of the dead woman but she makes no move to wipe it away. Then Moses sees the Vestal's lips move, as though she were speaking to the slug – just briefly, a phrase. But he is standing behind glass with the scientists and cannot hear what she says. Later he asks one of the soldiers who was in the room with the Vestal.

What did she say? Moses asks. To the slug, I mean.

The soldier shrugs, still stunned by the demonstration.

She said it soft, the soldier says. I couldn't really hear it. But it sounded like, Where are you?

After the demonstration, the scientists sit the Vestal down and proceed to ask her a series of questions, many of which have to do with the things she has eaten or the drugs she has taken or the places she has been.

While the interview is taking place, the Vestal keeps glancing over at Moses, who nods seriously. It is a reassuring nod, but also one that says she is obliged to continue.

After a while, Pastor Whitfield himself approaches the desk where the scientists are talking with the Vestal, and he suggests that they give the girl a break.

She's travelled a long way to be here, he says to the others. Let's give her some supper and some time to herself. Can we resume at another time?

The scientists agree and begin to discuss their notes among themselves. Whitfield takes Moses and the Vestal to a dining hall, where they eat hungrily. Around them, at other tables, are civilians who do not even notice the newcomers. This place, it must host many travellers. Children run around the tables, screaming happily, their cries echoing from the raftered ceiling. It is nice, this place, and yet Moses winces as though prickled by the sounds of joy.

How do you enjoy our food, my dear? Whitfield asks the Vestal.

It's lovely, thank you, says the Vestal in her most formal and subservient voice.

Then she excuses herself to the restroom.

Pastor, Moses asks when she has gone. You're a man of God.

I am.

A true man of God?

The pastor smiles gently.

I am a man of a true God, he says. We all endeavour to be true men, but our successes on that front aren't to be measured here in this place.

Moses considers this and finds it a fair response.

And this place, he says to the old man. It's safe?

As safe as any I've—

For her, I mean.

I see. You wish to be reassured that we will not hurt her. Because the girl has been hurt enough, yes? For someone who identifies himself simply as her delivery man, you are generous to be concerned about her. I assure you, Mr Todd, we are not in the business of hurting people. We are a sanctuary here. There are still some of those left, you will be happy to hear.

Moses nods.

One more thing, he says.

Whitfield opens his hands palms up as if to offer himself for service.

When I told you about her, Moses says, you took her straight to the doctors.

The pastor nods.

Is that cause—

Moses starts to ask his question but stops short and looks around as though someone were spying on them. He shifts and leans in closer to the pastor and continues.

Is that cause you don't believe she's holy? Cause you believe it's just a thing with her body rather than her soul?

The pastor smiles, folds his hands and leans forward

as if he would meet Moses in conspiracy over the table-top.

I'm a man of God, says Whitfield. You said so yourself. It's my business to believe that God has a hand in everything. It's an article of my faith that things are the way they are because they are supposed to be that way. Is the girl divine? Absolutely. And so are we all.

But—

But the two things are not mutually exclusive, the pastor continues. Her body may have some divinity it can share with the rest of us. The soul, the body . . .

Whitfield waves a hand as if to dismiss them.

. . . Our desire to distil one from the other is a child's game. For good or bad, you are your appetites as well as your expiations. You are just as much what you *would* eat as what you *do* eat. Look around you. The dead risen. The body has its harmony, too. Where is the soul?

Whitfield knocks against his own sternum.

Right here, he says. In our playful and meagre guts.

The pastor sits back, and so does Moses, considering what Whitfield has said. After a few moments of silence, Moses speaks.

Faith sure has changed, he says and shakes his head.

Not much, Whitfield says and smiles. It's just got a little bigger. Things tend to do that when you open your eyes to them.

*

We have rooms for you, says Pastor Whitfield after they have eaten. He shows them into what looks like a dormitory wing of the compound, but there don't seem to be civilians living there. Moses wonders if they will try to keep them locked up, but the rooms they are shown are snug and clean and have unbarred windows opening onto the courtyard.

We can make you both very comfortable, he goes on. We didn't know whether you were . . . together, so we've found two adjoining rooms. Use them as you see fit.

The Vestal looks up at Moses. He sees her white face out of the corner of his eye, but he does not return her gaze.

Actually, Pastor, Moses says, I can't stay. It's my brother. I left him in a bad state – told him I would come back. He needs help. He got shot, and the wound's got infected. When he's took care of I'll come back. Abraham and me – both of us will.

Whitfield says he understands and goes to gather some antibiotics from the medical wing.

Do you trust em? asks the Vestal when Whitfield is gone.

She sits on the edge of one of the beds, her arms crossed over her chest.

They seem all right, Moses says.

They're too nice.

Some people are just nice, I reckon.

I don't want to be an experiment.

You ain't an experiment. Everybody just wants to know why you're different. They figure that out, maybe they can put things back to the way they were.

I don't care about things going back to the way they were.

Moses opens his mouth to demur then realizes something.

I don't really care much about it either, he admits. Some worlds you're just made for, and I'm made for that one out there. But it ain't everybody so adaptable. You might do somethin for those people.

She keeps her arms crossed and looks out the window, the snow falling in hard streaks against the darkening sky.

I don't want to stay, she says stubbornly.

I'll be back, he says. Two days. Then we'll figure things out.

Let me go with you, she says. We'll fetch Abraham and then we'll all come back, all three of us.

They ain't going to hurt you, Moses says. The sooner they get their research done, the sooner all of us can leave.

Your job's done, she says. You can leave now. Ain't no obligation bringin you back.

There is a challenge in her voice. She wants to be corrected. She wants a promise from him. Moses wonders if this is a woman he can make promises to. He wonders how much of her is a lie. Even now. The fear in her eyes – it could be just another performance.

I'm comin back, Moses assures her. I ain't entirely done with this place. Abraham's gonna want to see it with his own eyes. And maybe we can recuperate here for a bit. Besides, you're my beheld responsibility. Even though you've been workin contrary to it, it's my thought to keep you safe till the full stop of this journey. Maybe this is it, but anyway I got to make sure I ain't delivered you into hazard.

Fine, she says.

But she won't look at him.

He goes to the door of the room and turns around once more before going out.

I'm comin back, he says. Two days. You'll be okay.

Then she does turn to him, the full blaze of her eyes whipping sharp at his.

See, she says. Whatever I am, so are you – but worse, cause you can't admit to it. You ain't no gentleman, Moses Todd.

He looks at her a moment longer. Some part of him desires to take that crazily cut redhaired head and hold it against his chest as he would a small, shivering animal. Yet another part of him, a confused and muddy and thickly despairing part of him, would like to wrap his hands around the girl's neck and squeeze until she is quiet, until her witchy words no longer have the power to sink him so low.

No, he says. I guess I ain't so much of a gentleman. Guess I never have been much of one.

He waits a moment longer, but she has nothing more to say. She turns again and looks out at the pelting snow. Their voices have been muffled and wrong in this building of plaster and concrete.

I'm comin back, he says one last time.

Then he turns and goes.

*

Whitfield brings him a bottle of pills.

Biaxin, he says. It's an antibiotic – a powerful one. The doctors tell me it should keep your brother's infection from spreading. But you'll bring him back here? We have the facilities he needs.

Moses agrees and stuffs the pills into the pocket of his jacket.

I thank you, Pastor, says Moses. I'm in your debt.

Whitfield clears Moses' debt with a wave of his hand.

The world we're living in now, Whitfield says, nobody owes anybody anything except kindness.

You've been more than generous to us. I ain't so accustomed to it. I don't expect I know how to act around it.

The pastor smiles.

I've seen rougher than you, he says. This country hardens people.

*

Back on the road, travelling the inverse of his former journey, the world looks reversed. There have not been many times in his life that Moses has retraced his steps. He is defined by forwardness – a true frontiersman, foraging the wilderness, chopping through the untamed tangles, burning to ash the road behind him. And there is ever more. There are an infinite number of roads – an embarrassing possibility of directions to travel. You can keep moving your whole life and never cross the same intersection.

Not wishing to meet them face to face, he looks for signs of Fletcher and his caravan. But he finds no trace of their immense footprint. Perhaps they have lost the trail – or perhaps they have gone a different way.

Back at the citadel, they filled his tank with gasoline, so he drives straight through without stopping. He knows, having just come from them, which roads are good and which are bad – and he takes detours where necessary. Still, travel is slow. He remembers, in his youth, when miles and minutes were commensurate. On the freeways of the nation, you could measure the one against the other with modest accuracy. But now, with the crumbled tarmac, the piles of abandoned cars, the collapsed overpasses, everything moves more slowly. The traffic of the dead and gone – there is no more dense population anywhere.

The sun goes down, and he makes his way in the dark. Normally he would stop rather than risk damage to the car by driving at night. But his brother is waiting for him, his leg rotting away by the hour. He can see it, the rot, spreading through Abraham's body. A creeping rot gripping his heart and lungs, greening his brain with sour fungus. His brother, a creature of rot and decay. And so he is – and so he ever was.

He drives, and the muffled silence of the car is powerful. He has not, in his life, been much alone with his thoughts. It has been him and his brother. But now, by himself in the car, his large body balking against the small seat, driving this desolate road under a sky full black like drowning – now he perceives entire the eminence of the unbreathing lacuna in which the world has found itself.

He thinks about his wife, his daughter – and he does not wish to. He steps on the accelerator, trying to outpace his own memories. He will run from them where they cannot follow. He swerves between the mountains of wreckage on the road, faster and faster, clipping abandoned vehicles, shearing off the rearview mirror on the passenger side. Still, the thoughts follow him. And they come with other thoughts: his brother, that blasted-out shell of a man, all yellow teeth and grotesque appetite – and the Vestal, too, that pale luminous face like a moon behind clouds, her red hair spilling in chopped locks around her, a madwoman gone tricksy in the manners of the earth, the gorgeous get of a blighted world, so perfect in her lying everything, so—

And would she be . . . would she stay? . . . So pliant as the road takes her – so false and calamitous—

Suddenly there's a figure in the road, ambling towards the centre line, and Moses turns the speeding vehicle but strikes it anyway. The slug's body fractures and spins madly, its legs propellering up into the air, a macabre carnival act, the head swinging down and forward to crash with a wet thunk into the windshield right in front of Moses' face, a grim explosion of wasted meat, a spiderweb shattering of glass.

Moses jams the brakes, the car skids on the icy surface of the road, flings the slug off, spins around two full times before coming to a rest in the dead centre of the road.

And he's breathing fast and heavy now, leaning forward and resting his forehead on the wheel.

The impossible raucous silence of everything. Nothing sounds more like annihilation than deafening quiet.

He throws open the car door and looks back on the icy road where the body lies. There is no need to put the slug down – his head is split wide from the impact. He looks down the road, the pool of light cast by the car's one unbusted headlamp.

Lord, Moses whispers. Lord, lord, lord.

As a prayer it isn't much, but it is as good as any on this lightless plain.

*

The car still runs. He gathers a handful of snow from the ground and uses it to wipe the gore off the windshield. Then he continues. He drives through the night, more slowly now, the calamity in his head dampened again by his own iterant voice filling the small space of the car, his voice repeating over and over something he learned as a child in school:

Four score and seven years ago our fathers brought forth upon this continent a new nation conceived in liberty and dedicated to the proposition that all men are created equal . . .

He speaks it in its brief entirety as he learned it by

rote. The words, he knows, speak of a war that is mean-
ingless to him, even though they seem to evoke – in
their notes of endurance and the brave men, living and
dead, who consecrate this ground – the bleak road on
which he finds himself travelling. Still, he does not
think about the words but simply utters them. They
quiet his mind. They are comforting because they feel
stitched into the very back parts of his brain where
things are archival, peaceful, resolved.

And so he drives and fills the space with uttered
words and makes his way back into the mountains
where the sun is cresting up over the horizon when he
finds the place where the small path winds up into the
woods. He climbs out of the car and listens to the morning birdsong and draws the icy cold deep into his lungs
where it might purify him.

He climbs the path between the trees and sees the
cabin ahead of him. It is dawn, and the light casts long
shadows on the snow. He does not know what he will
find in the cabin, whether he will find his brother alive
or dead. Abraham said he could last it. It's true – he
said those words – but life can be a tricksy thing itself.
Sometimes it just runs away from out between your
grasping hands.

Moses does not know what he will find as the cabin
comes into sight. But what he does not expect to see,
sitting there on the collapsing front porch and drinking
something from a steaming mug, is a man who is not
his brother.

*

It's the doctor, Peabody, from Fletcher's caravan – the one they left tied to a tree.

Moses pulls a gun from his belt and advances on the man, his feet pounding thick and hard through the drifts of snow.

Where's my brother? he says in a loud, hoarse voice. I'll kill you if you—

Inside, the doctor says, dropping his mug and splashing hot brown liquid everywhere. Where it falls on the snow, the steam rises in sudden wisps. The doctor holds up his arms before his face, defending himself from the assault that is coming his way across the clearing.

Moses keeps the gun trained on the man's head and advances onto the bowing porch. He grabs Peabody, gets an arm around his neck and presses the barrel of the gun against his temple. Then he spins and puts his back against the logs of the cabin and, having taken his hostage, waits for the assault of Fletcher's men.

But that's when the door of the cabin opens and Abraham emerges, squinting his sleepy eyes against the morning sun.

Abraham spots his brother and yawns, scratching his ass.

Hey, brother, he says. What're you doin with the doc? You want some coffee? We found some grinds under the floor.

*

When Moses and the Vestal tied him to a tree they thought Fletcher's men couldn't fail to notice. But, instead, when Fletcher bolted in pursuit, they did not bother to count heads or look around even. Or perhaps they simply took the doctor's life for forfeit, given up to the wilderness or the wildness of man. Peabody called out, but none could hear him over the revving of the engines and the cries of the caravaners to move.

Abraham found him later, coming down out of hiding in the woods when he heard the sound of motors die away in the distance. It had been unnecessary to hide – Fletcher was not interested in what might remain at the cabin once the Vestal was no longer there. He heard the doctor's cries from down by the road. Peabody was calling crazy by then, quite sure he would freeze to death in a few hours, kissed on the lips and tied to a tree by a holy woman, abandoned without regard by his own travelling companions. No one, he was sure, would come for him. The guttural noise from his throat was a keening of grief and despair, hopeless, tuned to the pitches of nature and birdsong – a moribund bleating skyward.

Which is how Abraham found him.

I told him I'd kill him if he tried anything, Abraham says. And you know what the man did? The man laughed. I knew he was okay then. He'd gone past loyalties.

I brung you these, Moses says, giving Abraham the antibiotics. For your leg.

Look, Abraham says and shows Moses the wound in his thigh. It isn't healed, but the swelling seems to have abated, and it is less burning red at the edges.

It's gettin better, Moses says.

The doc made a poultice, Abraham says. Out of twigs and pine needles and garbage like that. It helps.

It just calms the wound, Peabody says and nods to the pills. Nothing compared to what a real antibiotic like that will do.

Moses turns to Peabody.

I apologize, he says. For the gun. For tyin you to a tree. We thought . . . Thank you greatly for helpin my brother.

Peabody shrugs it off.

It was a symbiotic relationship, he says. Fletcher kept me safe, I took care of his people. But he wasn't a good man.

But you didn't have to save Abraham's leg. That was a righteous thing for you to do. If things'd gone a shade different, we might of killed you.

Again Peabody shrugs. He runs a hand across his balding pate. Wisps of grey hair fall down nearly to his shoulders. He must be ten or even twenty years older than Moses. Here is a man who lived a good solid chunk of life before the dead started coming back and everything changed. Here is a man with memories – a man who still holds faith that things might change back, because he can hardly help but remember vividly the world before. Perhaps he even believes he could reconstruct it out of the recollections and blueprints he carries in his own aging mind.

So he shrugs, and this is what he says:

Saving or killing. I've been a doctor so long – and the world gone topsy-turvy the way it is – it's sometimes hard to tell which is called for. You have to do some of both if you would be a man in this world. And which end of the act you're on is the luck of the moment. So no hard feelings.

The three men drink weak coffee made from water heated over the fire. Abraham takes two of the pills, and Peabody looks at his wound.

How's it look, doc? Abraham asks.

It's holding, Peabody says. But the jury's still out. If there were facilities, we could do more about it.

I found a place, Moses says to Peabody. It has what you need. It's a good place. We'll drop you there.

Peabody looks first at one brother and then other. He nods and resumes his inspection of Abraham's leg.

Later, out by the pond where the surface has mended itself in ice and there is no longer any face staring up from below, Moses talks with his brother alone.

You got there? Abraham asks.

I did.

The girl?

She's there. They're lookin at her. Trying to figure her. I told her I'd come back once I got you.

You did? How come?

Moses shrugs.

It ain't exactly safety she feels bein there. She asked me to come back. I told her I would.

Is it safe?

I don't know. I think so. It's like a fortress there, Abe. Like the modern world again.

Abraham smiles.

Hot water?

Hot water.

Food?

Food.

They got something to plug this into?

Abraham tugs at the yewess bee around his neck.

I reckon they probably do.

Girls? Are there girls? I ain't had a right fuck in ages it seems like. Not a right one at least.

Moses says nothing. He looks down at the seam where he chopped open the ice days before. Then he says:

It ain't a place of brutishness, Abe.

The smile goes away from Abraham's face. He looks mean in the eyes, like he would spit on something if there was something to spit on.

You reckon me to be a monster, don't you, Mose?

Moses sighs heavily and strokes his beard. He looks away from Abraham.

Beyond bein my brother, he says, I don't give a damn what you are.

It's an ambiguous statement, but one that is just left to hang there between them. Abraham does not ask for more and Moses does not proffer it.

You know, Abraham says after a while. These two nights, I can't say as I was sure you'd come back for me.

No? Moses says and rubs his eyes against the tiredness he finds there. Then you mistake me, brother. I'm the keeper and the caliper of your life, Abraham. Some-

times it seems that's the beginning and ending of what
I am.

*

*You are already wondering, the man Moses says, what became
of him, this brother of mine. You see me, here in the dark. It's
my voice talkin the night through to all its corners. But it seems
I've swapped travellin companions.*

*He points to where the large mute sleeps on the ground, the
shape of the man like a desert stone.*

*Maury, he says, I picked him up later. A child of God, that
one – and more trouble to haul around than you might think.
But he's a wonder at keepin his business to himself – which is
more than I can say for most. No, he came later.*

*Moses scratches at his beard and brushes his hair out of his
face, exposing, barely visible in the blackness, the pale lumen
of his skin crossed diagonal by the eye patch and its strap.*

*You're wonderin – is this the story that kills Abraham,
that brings him his due which the universe in all its scaled
balance, all its holy recompense, owes to him? Is this the story
that finishes him and closes the book on the ledger of his
accounts? Is that the holiness that drives this story crash bang
to its God-spoke end? Or maybe it's some other story that
takes Abraham away from me? That's what you're wonderin,
ain't it?*

He pauses.

*There was a girl, he says. Not even a woman. A little girl.
A warrior she was, and she knew about the balance of things.
The order . . . What? The girl? She don't belong here. This
ain't her story. Forget I said anything about her.*

Moses picks something from his teeth, but his eyes look at no one – they never stray from the firelight, as though the elements of the earth themselves are his true audience. He speaks to the land, and the land is nourished by his breath.

One story or another, Moses says, it makes no difference. All men find their ends in stories told by firelight. My end, too, when it comes – it'll be spoke by someone, and my death'll persist a little while on the planet.

Then he looks again at the shape of his travelling companion.

Or, he says, it'll just keep mute.

*

They are on the road. Moses has now travelled back and forth over this same length of highway more times than he has ever done just about anything in his singular life. The road begins to have an aspect of familiarity that makes him queasy in the pit of his stomach. As though time has stopped dead – as though the progress of the earth has wound down, entropy coming to bear all over, everything gone flaccid and spent. The rote repetition of days and action. He recalls it from the time before – when it was known simply as life. The things you *might* do were shoved to the side, he recalls, in favour of the things you *could manage* to do in the brief hiatuses between doing all the same things you did the day before and all the same things you would do again tomorrow.

Yes, life. Life is what they called it.

And Moses supposes he could do worse than an exis-

tence filled with equal parts death and discovery –
when the alternative is life and listlessness.

He will be happy to be off this road at last. Happy to
be forging ahead.

They are two hours from Colorado City when they
come across a wreckage that Moses doesn't remember
from before. Perhaps he has got the roads mixed up
and they are now on a different route. Perhaps he has
become blinded to the nuances of the world now that
he is locked in the repetition of it.

Moses brings the car to a stop.

Abraham starts to complain about his leg and doesn't
mind the break from riding folded up in the passenger
seat.

The leg's stiff as hell, he says. I got to stretch it. Plus,
I need to piss.

So they climb out of the car. It is dark again already
– the days are shuffling by quickly now, as though in
the agile hands of a professional card sharp. And maybe
God is a gambler after all.

Peabody helps Abraham stand, and the two begin to
limp in circles around the car.

Moses takes the stub of a cigar out of his pocket and
lights it with a match. The road is a cut through the
hills, and he gazes around him at the trees. The road
looks familiar and unfamiliar at the same time. The
wreckage blocking their way, though, doesn't look new.
He puffs thoughtfully on his cigar.

I'm going up to that ridge, he says to the others. Take
a look around.

He climbs the slope, pulling himself up using tree branches that pop and snap in his mammoth grip. He is out of breath by the time he crests the ridge. Down below there is nothing. It's possible that they are on the cusp of the Colorado City grid, but it makes no difference. The hill on which he stands is just one rib of many on a cage of ridges that ripple the landscape. He can only see the dipping distance between one line of hills and the next – and there is only emptiness in that unlit valley.

He sits for a moment to recover from the climb. He listens to his own heavy breathing, the rasp of air in his throat. He looks at the fat cigar between his thick fingers. He is a brute, he knows, and there should be laws and cages for such as he. But sometimes he is surprised to discover that he has found a home in the wild black of what America has become. He belongs on the edges of the world – but now the world is all edges. Margins without centre for ever and ever.

Then he hears a shout from down below, indistinct and panicked, back in the direction of the car where he left Abraham and Peabody. Then other noises. The sound of scuffle and event, followed by two thunderous screeches of pain – voices Moses doesn't recognize. Then another shout – his name:

Mose!

It's his brother's voice. And then Moses is running, crashing down through the trees, an ursine monster smashing through the underbrush, calling out, Abe! Abe!

He hears the sound of an engine below – a car speeding away. And then he bursts through the scrub at the edge of the road and sees the mess in the pool of light cast by the headlights of the car they have been driving. It's a body, but not Abraham's and not the doctor's. Moses kneels over it.

It's a man, grimy-faced and ugly. He wears a leather jacket with studs on it, and there's a baseball bat still gripped tight in his dead right hand. He lies in a wide pool of jugular blood that is still pumping with weak persistence from the wound in his neck. Struck through his neck, from one side to the other like some horrible mockery of a bow tie, is a bowie knife that Moses recognizes as his brother's.

Abe! Moses calls. Abe!

There is no response, but when he hushes he can hear a guttural choke from the ditch by the side of the road. He rushes over to find the doctor, Peabody, holding his hands over a puncture wound in his chest. The blood seeps through his fingers, leaking insistently through his pathetic grip.

Who? Moses says. Fletcher?

Peabody coughs wetly. He shakes his head.

Highwaymen, he struggles to say through his gasps. Fletcher, he put a bounty on your heads. Three men. Abraham got one. Wounded another. But they took him.

Dead or no?

Peabody coughs again, cringes in his breathing.

Dead or no? Moses says again, almost angry.

No, Peabody says. Fletcher'll want to.

Okay, Moses says and begins to lift Peabody. Come on, I'll get you to help.

But Peabody coughs a spray of blood over Moses' face, shakes his head and pushes Moses away. There are reddish-brown smears all over his bald pate, the thin strands of long white hair plastered to his skull with drying blood.

I'm dead, Peabody says. It's about time, right?

The doctor's body seizes up with some internal organic fluttering, as of his organs all retching moribund against their own expiration. Then Peabody calms as Moses watches him, his breathing going slack and the grip on his chest wound loosening. He can see the man's slowing heartbeat in the weak surges of blood coming between his fingers.

It's about time for all of us, old man, says Moses.

But by that point, he is fairly certain that Peabody is already dead.

Nine

Moses does not delay. He takes a small knife from his pocket and drives it up underneath the doctor's jaw and into his brain. There is no time to give him greater service than this. Then he goes quickly to the car, but before he gets in something occurs to him. He walks around to the front where the body of the brigand is lying dead, his brain still intact. He does not want to put an end to this man who would messenger his brother to death. Instead he wants to hurt, to maim. So he raises his leg high and brings his heavy boot down onto the corpse's face. There is a brittle wet crunch as the jaw bone shatters and dislocates from the skull. When Moses raises his foot again, there is an awful gaping smile on the dead man's face. But the brain is unharmed. He will come back – he will be unable to eat.

Have a nice death, you bastard, says Moses Todd to the corpse.

Then he climbs into the car and backs it up. There is no time to finesse his way around the blockade before him, no time to search for another car on the road beyond. He will ram his way through, and it will either work or it won't. The impact will either destroy the car or it won't. But he is large with rage, he feels his brute, animal self in the very heat that rises from his skin. He will not be stopped.

He backs up far enough to get the speed he needs, locks the safety belt over his heaving torso, then accelerates quickly towards the blockade that consists of two burned-out cars positioned diagonally across the road. He draws his own car as far to the left as possible, two wheels onto the shoulder of the road.

When the collision comes, it comes hard and expected. He clips the back end of one of the cars and it spins, letting him past but also roostering his own car into a screeching spin that sends him out of control and off the road on the opposite side. The spinning car collides sidelong into the trunk of a tree – glass shatters and the passenger door crumples inward with an aching twist of metal.

When everything is still once more, Moses releases his grip on the wheel and checks himself for broken bones. There is blood all over his face and hands, but he does not know who it belongs to. Some of it could be his – but the ownership of blood is a sucker's guess in such a sanguine world. It does not hurt much to move his arms and legs, and he figures that is enough to keep going forward.

The engine is still running, which is a good sign – and even though one of the headlights has been smashed to nothing along with the whole right front of the car, the vehicle still functions well enough to scrape itself away from the tree trunk and huff its way back to the road.

Moses drives. He looks forward, grim and inexhaustible, and the night unfolds before him. He looks for tail lights in the distance but there is only black – no sign of the car that stole his brother away from him.

No matter. He will find where they took him. He will find Fletcher and his band of thieves. And then there will be a surfeit of death – and Moses does not much care whose.

*

He drives through the evening. He does not know where else to go, so he continues to the citadel in Colorado Springs where he left the Vestal. It is still hours before dawn when he arrives. But the place looks different. The front gate looks like it has been driven through with a large truck. There is a whole battalion of soldiers there who all point their guns at him when he arrives.

What happened? he says, climbing out of the car.

They shine a spotlight in his eyes.

State your name, someone calls through a bullhorn.

What happened? he says again. They got my brother.

State your name, the voice repeats.

But he doesn't have to reply this time, because there is commotion. Someone must recognize him from the night before, because he is taken and escorted onto the compound, across the wide courtyard. The lights on the jaw-bone chapel illuminate the structure violent against the blackness of night.

Inside, he is taken to a new place, a large room where people in uniforms of authority are gathered around a table in grim, controlled debate. On the side-lines, Moses spots the old man, Pastor Whitfield, who approaches him.

Marauders, Whitfield says before Moses has a chance to ask him anything. A caravan. It was led by a man in a sombrero.

Fletcher, Moses says.

You know this man?

He took my brother. Where'd he go? Which direction?

You aren't . . . affiliated with him?

I ain't affiliated. Except in the sense that I'm the man scheduled to remove the head from the rest of his body.

They broke through the fence.

They were after the girl, Moses explains. The Vestal.

Whitfield looked confused.

But they didn't take the girl, Whitfield says.

You repelled them?

We did. At some cost to our people.

He's still got my brother. Do you know where they went?

Slow down, says Whitfield. You don't understand.

He reaches a hand out to touch Moses' arm, and Moses strikes it away. There is something happened inside him. Some safety turned off – some tribal code of civility gone away in the face of his brother's abduction. He gives Whitfield a look as violent and full of murder as any on the wild plain.

Tell me now, man of God, he says. Two heads are the same as one to me. Godful or godless, it makes no difference.

The Pastor Whitfield does not flinch. He simply gives Moses a mild look and a gentle, pitying smile.

You've been on the frontier too long, my friend, he says. But so have we all. I'll give you the information you want. But you must listen to me.

Moses relents. He has no choice.

We've already sent a regiment. This man Fletcher – apparently he's allied with some local bandits. Together they levied an effective assault. They did a great deal of damage and took some valuable equipment. The fear is that they are gearing up for a larger assault. So we are going to end it. We sent a battalion.

Who? Moses asks. How many?

Whitfield shrugs.

I'm simply a pastor. My colleagues at the table there are the ones who specialize in land conflicts. I watched the soldiers go. Maybe fifty.

Where?

Apparently there's a gasworks some miles east of here. It's where the bandits call home – where your man Fletcher might be as well. But listen, my friend, this is a battle between two stubborn factions who have not yet realized that possession means nothing any more. You don't want to get in the middle of that.

What *I* want? Moses chuckles sourly. Then he repeats the words, shaking his head: What I want. Pastor, what I want is so far from what I got . . . it's all semaphores across an empty ocean. I'm gonna check on the girl. Then I'm leavin.

Wait, Whitfield says. Wait.

But Moses ignores him, walking to the door of the wide room – wanting out of the noise and commotion of miniature human strategy.

The girl, Whitfield says more loudly just as Moses reaches the door. She's not here.

Moses stops and turns. Whitfield walks quickly over to him.

That's what I was trying to tell you, he says.

You said they didn't take her.

Whitfield shakes his head.

They didn't take her, he says. She left.

With Fletcher?

Whitfield shakes his head again.

By herself, he says. Shortly after you left. She didn't even stay the night.

You didn't hold her?

We don't keep people against their will here, says Whitfield. This is not a penitentiary.

But for her own good.

One's own good – that's exactly the kind of thing

you can't define for people. As much as we might like.

Moses is silent for a moment. He looks at the floor and contemplates all the silly things in the world – all the things impossible to get your mind around.

Then, in a quiet voice, the Pastor Whitfield says:

They found something out about her.

Why she ain't attacked?

Whitfield nods.

She's got a condition, he says. A . . . genetic disorder. Related to something called Huntington's Disease.

She's sick?

In a sense. Always has been. It's something you're born with even if it doesn't have an onset until later in life. But there's something about the disease, something in her blood. The dead don't like it. Or, no, that's not right. See, they don't attack her for the same reason they don't attack each other.

Whitfield waits for the full meaning of his words to settle.

She ain't dead, Moses says. She ain't.

No, Whitfield says. But she *is* dying. Her body – it has a predetermination for death. They think that's why . . .

Moses is silent again for a moment, piecing things together. The Vestal. A tiny firebrand of a woman, chopped red hair, a catalogue of personalities, impossibly dishonest, witchy and tricksy as any cheap fraud, a calamity with translucent skin. Cursed, dying, the whole time. It is too much. Too much by any measure.

You told her? Moses asks.

We did.

And then she left.

She did.

Then they got her too. Fletcher got her too.

Maybe not.

You didn't have to tell her.

Now Whitfield is silent.

You didn't have to, Moses repeats.

Then he shakes his head and looks at the man of God eye to eye.

Jesus Christ, he says to the pastor, do we have to know the name of everything?

*

So he goes back outside where he can see his breath in the cold night wind and crosses the massive courtyard at the base of that purple nightmare cathedral – and before he reaches his car, he is accosted by a soldier on guard.

Where you headed? asks the soldier.

East, says Moses. It ain't your intent to stop me, is it?

No, it is not, says the soldier. You going after them?

I reckon so. You know what road they took?

You don't want to go there. It's bound to be a mess of destruction. Not something you want to be caught in the middle of.

Son, I ain't got the luxury of wanting things. Which road east?

The main one, says the soldier and gives him a shrug. You'll be able to follow the tracks. I'm sure there's only one army that's passed through since the last snowfall.

Moses drives. His one remaining headlight illuminates the road ahead – the palimpsest of tyre tracks in the snow. The road goes through the middle of town – which is populated only by icicles and the frozen dead. Bodies slump over against the concrete bases of buildings, many of them lost or near lost in drifts of snow. One dead woman with frosty hair sits buried in snow up to her armpits – like death in hibernation, her joints frozen until the thaw in the spring when her creaky bones will come to life again, and she will crawl, starved for a season, to the nearest meat she can find to nourish herself.

Just beyond that slug, in another deep drift of snow, Moses sees two hands poking out at the top. One is bent like a claw and the other is frozen open, like a gesture of constant waving welcome.

Here the dead wait patiently. They sit, affixed in their places, like plants and other anchored creatures of nature, biding their time, their mouths filling up with snow, their eyes filling up with snow, spectral and full of peace.

And Moses drives on, towards the indefatigable conflicts of the living, while here, in this frozen city, death is rendered petty, benign, thoughtless and allegiant to the hobbyhorse rocking of the old, tired earth.

Part Three

CRUCIBLE

Ten

*You see now? Moses Todd asks. You see? It ain't about what
you think it's about. All the wandering, all the mad pursuit,
all the spinnin cycles of life and death and death and life over
and over until you ain't but a dizzy-headed creature roamin
the plains. It ain't about anything but one thing. Drollery. You
fight and you create and you fight and you destroy – and sometimes in the middle somewhere you happen to love. But it all
comes down to ridiculousness. Dead hands waving at you from
out a bank of snow. An abducted brother who ought to of paid
for his sins in some such way long before. A dying redhead
with deceitful ways and an immunity to that which already
had a hold of her. Ridiculous. You could laugh your guts out if
you keep your brain on it too long. I challenge you. I challenge
you to look it in the face and keep from laughin.*

*

It has started to snow again by the time Moses sees the commotion in the distance. The gasworks is at the end of the road, in a mountain cul-de-sac, surrounded on all sides by ice-laden foothills. The bandits are leeching electricity from the same power grid the Airforce Academy is on, so there are bright lights shining down from tall towers and illuminating all the structures in the round valley – a giant bowl of light.

When Moses sees the military vehicles ahead, he abandons the car and climbs into the hills. He carries with him things he took from the satchel in the trunk of the car: a 9mm pistol in one hand and in the other the massive bladed truncheon crafted for him weeks before by the tinkerer Albert Wilson Jacks. He makes his way up the slope and through the trees, following the hillside that flanks the gasworks. The conflict between the soldiers and the bandits below must just have begun – because he can hear the sounds of warfare in escalation. Pistols and machine guns rattling off their rounds, explosions echoing up through the valley, orders being issued through megaphones on one side – and on the other animal screeches, the ripping calls of wild men who have for many years survived in a hostile world on nerve and simple, unadorned violence.

He climbs higher, past the mouth of the valley and around the perimeter. There is no point in fighting through the main body of the conflict. This is not his battle. He seeks two people: his brother and the Vestal Amata. Once he finds them, he will leave the rest of it behind to resolve itself.

This is how the world works: smoky blazes that burn bright for a short time and then die out again, leaving the charred quiet we are accustomed to.

Finally, he breaks through the trees and sees the whole valley spread wide before him – an abstract carnival of dread made absurd. It is a place of metal and machine, all the surfaces gone brown or green with rust and oxidation – as though the forged metals of man have reverted once again to nature and settled back into the forested landscape surrounding them. Moses does not understand the function of the structures below him – but there is something awful and gorgeous about them – like artifacts of a more ingenious time, the elegance and efficiency of human industry gone wild. In the centre of the gasworks, there are six massive tanks around which are built creaking gantries, bent scaffoldings, spiral stairs, interstitial pipes, valves and wheels. Among the six tanks are three metal smoke-stacks that climb higher out of the valley than anything else – reaching tall and rotted like the fingers of the dead from out a bank of snow. It is a mazy sight – metal twisted around metal in purposeful shapes like the bio-logical organs of industry itself, evidence of man's desire to outdo God in the creation of a complex corpus. We forge ours out of metal and spark, and it puffs itself to life like an armoured dragon in the mist-covered valley.

But this apparatus has been long dead. And, with the same impulse that causes us to make art from the detritus of other art, the bandits have painted murals and words all over the tall rusted metal structures. The graffiti is awkward and colourful, obscene and lovely. There is a pastoral scene, painted simple, as though a child had done it – a sunrise between two mountains, and someone has painted a smiling face on the sun. Next to that is a black spray-painted scrawl of male genitalia, and beyond that a woman with huge, pendulous breasts and thick, monstrous red lips. The red of her lips is striking against all the blacks, whites, greens and browns of the place. As though the painted mark of womansex is anathema to nature itself.

And Moses can make out one more graffito – a series of words painted in neat white around the top of one of the tanks. The motto says, simply:

AT DESTRUCTION AND FAMINE THOU SHALT LAUGH.

Moses recognizes the quote, for it was one he has said to himself at times over the past fifteen years of his life – usually in quiet places, under roofs with rain falling on them, or on sunless days when it seemed the road may have no end. He knows the quote, and he completes it under his breath:

Neither shalt thou be afraid of the beasts of the earth.

Moses knows it to be true – that the words are the best and the worst of everything.

Around the base of the six tanks are other structures, squat wide buildings that must contain the machinery that once processed and refined what was held in the tanks. And among and upon the structures of the gasworks, there is a war going on.

Figures run every which way, calling out or pointing their guns or hiding in some enclosed niche or collapsing to the ground with a bullet gone through them. And here is the full-blown bathos of it all. Moses can see now that there are four distinct factions at battle down in the bowl-shaped valley. There are the soldiers in their pressed uniforms, engineering precise manoeuvres around the tall metal structures, fighting with the cold confidence of a reborn civilization striking out against the filthy reminders of its own wild past. Then there are Fletcher's men, a ragged collective, a mobile army which has gathered guns from all corners of the country. They have experience on their side, for every day on the road is a battle for them. They live conflict. Then there are the bandits who have been residing at the gasworks. These are almost indistinguishable from Fletcher's men – but if one looks, one can see that they are even more ragged, embattled by stasis and starvation. They wear more the look of survivors than marauders. And they do not fight in tandem with Fletcher's men but against them as well as the soldiers – perhaps in retaliation for Fletcher having brought this battle upon them in the first place. And the final faction is the dead themselves. Some rogue has set free all of Fletcher's monstrous sideshow dead, and it seems the bandits may have had some caged dead on hand as well. Now they all roam free, feeding on the newly dead and the not quite so dead, pacing slowly through the combat, without rush, without malice – possessing the neutrality of parasites on a larger body. Some of them are struck down, and they fall with the same implacable calm with which they walked a moment before – but most are ignored since their threat is the slower one. Almost insect-like, some of these anthropophages sit cross-legged on the ground, the sounds of death and destruction coming to bear all around them, while they slowly munch away at the leg or arm of a fallen combatant and let the snow collect gently in their hair.

Good lord, Moses Todd says from his perch above the valley. As he watches, a bandit woman with a long-range rifle hunched atop one of the tanks is pierced by a bullet that sends a quick atomizer mist of blood out from her back – then she topples over and falls to the ground, crashing once over a railing that cracks her body and folds it backwards unnaturally so that when she comes to rest the heel of her foot is up by her ear. Then a slug wanders over without haste to the bent body and digs into it with unhurried and brute fingers, opening the abdomen of the woman and pulling thick ropes of viscera free from the cavity. As the slug chews on the rubbery intestines of the woman, he looks around him with patient, ruminative eyes.

Moses Todd turns his gaze away from the fray and looks behind him – into those empty mountains and the grey sky, even the misty implication of the wide country beyond. For a moment it looks as though he will turn his back on it all, as though he may give a shrugging refusal to it all. He is a mountain man, as he is other things. A nomad with many more wildernesses to explore – and it is so much easier to travel away from things than towards them.

But it's the words that are a curse – because he cannot utter a simple goodbye.

*

He remembers his daughter. His girl of the meadow – all red cheeks and powder skin, a tiara of wildflowers in her hair. How she would run to him, and he would hoist her in his arms. He would enclose her away from the world and she would cry happily to be enclosed – and his bigness was a powerful and good thing because it meant shelter for her from the world. Her tugging at his beard with her little grasping hands. His fear of crushing her, because his brute arms were not built for such delicacy as daughters offer.

And his wife, too. A woman who presented herself as beyond the knowing of any in the world but him. The way she cut his hair and trimmed his beard and made him more man than beast. He was nobody's master when he was with her – but just an overgrown child with big notions that got wobbly with her gentle smile. She did not know how she was wound around everything in him, as though his lungs and heart and stomach were gripped tight by the burning gaze of her.

And there was no goodbye for them either. Even after he stopped looking for them. Even now, years later, there is no goodbye. A farewell is a thing of the mind – and, as such, you can shut it behind doors.

*

So he turns his eyes from the empty frontier of the woods and back to the battle below. Something in him clicks, some knife switch jams into place, and he is suddenly full of purpose and movement. He scans the structures, mapping them in his mind, determining which ones would be most likely to hold his brother and the Vestal.

Then he clambers down the face of the hill, sliding much of the way on the dirty ice, controlling his fall by grappling onto the tree branches and dragging the truncheon behind as a kind of brake. He slides to the base of the hill behind one of the wide, flat buildings where piles of chopped wood are stacked against the cinderblock wall.

Before he can think what to do next, one of the foot soldiers speeds around the corner and comes to a halt three feet from where Moses stands. The soldier, little more than a boy, aims his gun instinctively at Moses' head – but there is fear and trepidation in the boy's eyes, and he does not pull the trigger immediately.

I ain't with them, Moses says.

I'm shooting you, the boy says, his voice trembling, as though a declaration of violence were the same thing as a bullet.

You ain't got to, Moses says. I ain't one of them. I'm here for my two charges is all. My brother and a redhead lady. After I got em, you can burn this place to the ground with my good wishes. You seen em?

The boy's hand shakes, the pistol remains fixed on Moses' forehead.

Hey, Moses says. You hearin me? Let go that trigger. Come on now.

Something in the boy's face twitches. He is paralysed. He could fire or not fire at any moment. Moses does not like his fate to be at the hazard of nervous chance.

Goddamnit, Moses says.

Then he raises his own pistol with practised speed and fires two shots at the boy that make charred holes in his chest and cause him to convulse as if suffocating on air that is no longer breathable. The boy's hand, in extremis, squeezes and fires too, but Moses drops in the same motion and lets the bullet fly over his head.

Then the soldier boy collapses face down on the ground. Wisps of his hair are stirred lightly by the wind.

It didn't have to go this way, Moses says to the corpse.

There is arbitrary death by nature, which Moses recognizes is everyone's equally shared hazard. And then there is arbitrary death by the foolishness of man. And this is something Moses cannot stomach.

He checks the magazine of his pistol, and he hefts the massive bladed instrument in his opposite hand – and then Moses Todd leaps out from behind the building and into the fray. And that's when he begins to fight.

*

The icy earth melts with the steam of warfare, the hot spilled blood mingling with the snowy mud in rivulets of dirty pink like the stain of old wedding roses. The ground is slippery with gory melt as Moses moves forward through the battle, swinging the cudgel this way and that, firing his pistol with the other hand. He sends the cudgel in a wide arc to his left, knocking a slug's head clean off its shoulders, while with his right hand he fires twice at a bandit wielding a sword – the first bullet thunking into his chest and the second piercing his neck, sending a plume of blood splashing to the ground. He swings the cudgel back around and catches a ragged rifle-carrying woman in the stomach. When he pulls the weapon free, most of her guts, tangled in its blades, follow. The next time he swings it upwards, it catches a massive, thick-headed slug under the chin, and a rain of shattered teeth go tip-tapping to the puddled ground.

Moses does his best to avoid the uniformed men, for he knows them to be soldier instruments of a wider order and that they would not kill him if they knew who he was. But he also knows that to them he looks like one of the bandits, one of Fletcher's men – and it is a circumstance of war that you cannot stop to palaver about the whys and wherefores of things. So when the soldiers do threaten, he kills them too. And, he supposes, this is as right as anything – because it is just as likely that, on any given day, he would be on one side as another. He is a soldier and a reprobate, a lawman and a transgressor. So it makes no difference, at any moment in time, who dies by whose hand – as long as there is some line, capricious and invisible though it may be, for the combatants to reach across.

Death is everywhere. His ears are deafened by gunfire and screaming voices. Women and children, too – for the bandits have raised their kind to be warriors. Women with throwing knives that lodge deep and true, children with sharpened teeth that have been taught to climb your body and rip out your throat as though they were feral animals. Moses slashes his way through them, digging his heels into the muck for leverage against the ugly onslaught. Everywhere is the music of slaughter, shrill swords fifing their way clean through the air, the deep baritones of surprised death cries, the airy percussives of bodies falling to the ground and giving up their final appalled breaths. And who is the conductor? And who waves the baton? And who stitches together these crescendos of grotesque majesty?

And, too, the battle is manifold – because the chaos is too thick for the combatants to end things right, to make sure the dead stay down, and so the slaughtered everywhere on the field of battle begin to rise again – and Moses finds himself killing again those he already killed once before. Death begets death, and it is no wonder that the world is overrun so. They rise slowly amidst the pandemonium, overlooked because of their calm in the middle of such frenzy. A corpse lying face down in a puddle of bloody snow melt will twitch first in the arms, a shiver will run through the torso and all the way down to the legs. Then an arm will straighten itself, find a handhold on the ground and gently leverage itself with fresh muscle to hoist the rest of the body face up. And there it might lie for minutes at a time, opening its eyes anew to the sunlight and the noisome activity going on around it. The orbs of its eyes roll lazily to and fro until, at last, it inches itself upwards, first on its hands and knees, and then rising to full height, standing tall in sudden mockery of life itself.

And so the valley quickly fills with the mangy slubberdegullions of death. They reach out pathetically for those alert bodies moving by them with the speed of survival – but when their hands grasp nothing, they drop again to the ground to feed hyena-like on the still-warm corpses of the newly dead. And if a man, along his way to other death than this, should happen to put a bullet through the slug's brain as it eats its first meal, then in a travesty of sacred stygian rites that call for dim ferrymen to cross slow between the shores of life and death, these creatures will have died twice in the space of an hour.

Now Moses confronts one of Fletcher's surgical abominations, a slug dressed up like a sasquatch, its body patched all over with the scalps of other slugs sewn on its skin – a motley of hair, some long, some short, some blond, some brunette, some curly, some straight, much of the hair crusted hard by ooze and blood. Moses dispatches the thing quickly, one bullet to the brain, because it is a sign too distressing to look upon – humanity inverted somehow.

For a moment, Moses Todd, having killed everything around him that moves, finds himself in a wide radius of stillness. The other combatants occupy themselves at a distance, and he breathes deep the stench of wasted biology that hangs cloudy in the air. He stands, a droll on an empty stage, waiting for a response from the darkened seats – laughter or applause, it makes no difference – raising his brutal weapon to examine it against the spotlight of the sun. The bladed cudgel is tangled with gore. Like a nightmare Christmas tree, its welded limbs are ornamented with human viscera, tinselled with hair and stringy offal, flaps of torn flesh that hang from the tips, sticky bile that is already beginning to crust over in the metal interstices. It is a thing that does not soften to the human condition. People explode against the weapon, undeniable. It is a force, like the abstraction of American industry itself, a machine whose gears care not what they grind.

Moses whips the weapon down and flings off some of the loose numbles that splash onto the watery ground. Then he takes a moment to reload his pistol while scanning the structures around him.

There is a series of low metal buildings, indistinguishable from one another. He walks to the first one and kicks in the door, aiming his pistol through the doorframe and waiting for his eyes to adjust to the dim light inside.

The place is mostly empty. There are the skeletons of massive refining machinery, long ago frozen and rusted into position. Atop and around this dead machinery there are strewn blankets and slop buckets and filthy mattresses. In the corner he finds three women huddled against the corrugated metal wall. They are not fighters. They are nothing but mice caught by their tails and starving to death.

You with them? Moses asks.

They respond in a language that Moses does not recognize. Their voices quaver, and their eyes are fixed on the dripping weapon he carries in his hand.

He lowers the cudgel.

You best get, Moses says. Ain't nothing to gain by stayin. Here, I'll show you.

But they won't move until Moses has put down both the cudgel and the pistol. Then they follow him to the door, and he points them in the direction of the hillside where he came into the camp.

Go there, he says. Climb. Don't come back. Everybody's dead here. You understand? Dead.

He finds his own voice not angry or sympathetic but simply flat with the ugly ungentleness of truth.

They go, and he watches them until they are safely into the trees. Then he picks up the pistol and cudgel again and moves on.

He scans the row of buildings again. The doors are all closed neatly, but none of them with very heavy locks. Then he spots a metal shed attached like a lean-to to one of the buildings. The door to the shed is held shut with a thick chain and a padlock. He moves quickly to the shed, which is on the perimeter of the valley against the base of the hills that cup the gasworks.

There is no one around – the brunt of the battle has moved to the mouth of the valley. He uses the blunt handle of the cudgel to pound on the metal door of the shed.

Abe! he calls out. You in there? Vestal?

For a moment he hears nothing, so deafened is he by the cacophonous violence around him. But then he hears it – a small, weak voice climbing to panic.

Moses? Is it you?

The voice belongs to the Vestal Amata. Holy woman. Tricksy thief. Fair beauty of the wild plain.

*

The chain and lock are too heavy to break, so Moses jams one of the blades of the cudgel down behind the hasp and yanks it free of the door. The lock and chain fall useless to the ground. The door swings wide, and there's the Vestal – dressed like a nymph of the woods. The fabric stretches and shimmers absurdly, and bright diaphanous ribbons hang off her everywhere. She has a glittering tiara in her hair, and her face is painted with glitter also.

The sight so completely baffles Moses that he cannot speak for a moment.

What— he says.

It's my costume, she says. It's what Fletcher makes me wear. Oh, Mose – I didn't know if you would come.

Then she leaps on him, her arms around his neck, her eyes squinting against the light outside the dingy shed. Then, from around the other side of the structure, a figure comes running and stops short when he sees

Moses and the Vestal. It's one of Fletcher's men – Moses recognizes him. The man raises a shotgun, but before he can pull the trigger Moses has flung the Vestal away from him and fired a hail of bullets, some of which plant themselves into the man's sternum.

Come on, he says to the Vestal. We gotta get out of sight.

Instead of going back into the shed, where there is no light, Moses takes the Vestal by the arm and leads her around to the low empty building in which he found the three women refugees. He pulls her inside and shuts the door behind them.

What're we doing? she says. Let's just get out.

Where's Abe? Moses says. They took him.

Something occurs in the Vestal's eyes – a realization, perhaps, that Moses has larger plans than simply her rescue.

But we got to go, she says. We got to go now.

He shakes his head.

My brother, he says. Do you know where they got him or do you not?

Then she approaches him, getting close, patting his bloody chest lightly with her hands as though trying to soothe a wild child.

Moses, she says. Mose, listen to me. Are you listenin good? Abe's okay. Your brother, he's okay. But we got to go *now*. They're planning—

But Abe—

He's *safe*, I'm tellin you. But you got to take me out of here, Mose. I heard em talking, the soldiers. They're planting explosives. They're gonna bring hell down. Nothing left. The whole gasworks, the whole valley. *Nothing left.*

Safe where? he says.

Moses—

My brother, he says. Safe where?

You don't believe me, she says. You think—

You left. I told you to stay. I told you I was coming back. You left.

Moses, Moses.

You went back to Fletcher.

It ain't like that. No, not back to him. He found me.

You left.

Moses. Moses, I'm *dying*. There's somethin in me like a poison. I'm already part dead. That's what they told me, the doctors. That's why the slugs don't touch me. I'm dyin from the inside out, Mose.

So's everybody – part dead.

She recoils from him, her face curling into a fierce snarl.

You ain't a man, she says.

Likely I ain't.

She spits at his feet and rushes towards the door and flings it open. Outside, the sounds of warfare continue. Someone lets loose a ripping scream. She pauses.

You best run straight for the trees, Moses says to her back, or they'll get you sure.

She hesitates a second longer, closes the door and turns back towards Moses.

Take me, Moses. Take me out of here. Please.

Abraham, he replies flatly. I ain't leavin without him.

I *told* you, she says.

You said some words all right – but I ain't sure what exactly you told me.

She comes back over and stands before him, looking up at him as though he were sitting in the very top of a tree – as though he were so high above everything that you had to squint up your eyes to see him against the shining heavens. It's all a show. She puts it on. He knows now.

I told you he's safe, says the Vestal. He's gone. They let him go.

Let him—

He was – he was headed back to you. But his leg, it was in bad shape. He wasn't movin so good. They didn't give him a car or nothing. Listen, I saw an empty garage about two miles up the road when we were comin in. He's probably there – probably he holed up for the night.

Let him go? Why? Why would Fletcher let him—

Moses, please. Please let's go – the whole place is comin down. We're gonna die, Moses. I don't want to – not here.

Why? he says, his voice booming down on her now.

She shrinks back. In her eyes there is a searching, but he does not know for what. She does not wish to say what she says – but her reluctance could mean anything or nothing.

Cause of me, is what she says.

Cause of you how?

She just looks up at him now with an expression that could be hatred or shame or simply goneness.

I acquired his release, she says. I purchased it. From Fletcher.

He looks at her. There are sounds outside the thin-walled structure, clambering echoes of moribund hordes, foolish humanity balking against its own beginnings and its own ends. Half dead. That's the phrase that throbs in Moses' brain. Half dead, half dead, half dead. He says nothing to the holy woman in front of him.

It ain't nothing, Moses, she says. It's cheap currency. It ain't a thing of meaning.

No, Moses says.

He shakes his head. He feels the handle of the cudgel in his hand, and it feels right and true and hefty and thick with the logic of order and reason and purpose and all the concrete yeses and nos that could end all the ambiguous sentences on all the pages of the world's manuscript.

No, he says. It ain't true. You're a prevaricator is what you are. You already shown it. You ain't to be believed.

It's true, Moses. I'm tellin it to you true. He's – he's in that garage. I'd bet my whole real self on it.

Your whole real self, he says with disdain.

I'm done with misdirection, Moses. I swear it. I got nothing. Nothing at all.

You just want taken out of here. You would say any-thing. You would thieve my aid with your deception.

No, Moses, no. It ain't that.

Then what? Then give me to understand why you would of purchased his life, his freedom. The life of a transgressor. A reprobate who for two decades has been only *my* obligation to keep and defend – and that only cause I'm his blooden kin. A transgressor. The world seeks to correct him and it's only *my* duty to exempt him from his rightly course – succeed or fail as I might. And succeed I have, over and over. Except I *will* fail. One day. A man, he can't hold on for ever – his fingers loosen. And who are you to intervene on this transgressor's behalf?

But it wasn't for him, Mose. Don't you see how it wasn't for him?

Then what? For the cheapness of the price? The ease of credit granted you by your sorry lot in life?

No, not that either.

Now he says nothing, because he can tell what she will say next. There is a look in the eyes that precedes some words – as though the foundation for language is laid with look. You roll it out with the eye and then you utter it with the tongue. He is already recoiling from it. The calamity of a lie so big it devastates decency itself. For in lies such as these there is the unbearable possibility of truth.

She gazes up at him. So small. Her pale skin. Her chopped red hair. Her eyes gone wet.

It was for you, Moses, she says. For you.

*

Impossible, says Moses Todd. You got to know what it is – to hear such a thing and crave for it so to be true but also know at the same time that it ain't. The more wished for some words are, the more unlikely they are to carry truth when finally uttered. Language is criminal that way. As though your wishin for something is the very thing that makes it impossible. We should none of us ever wish on anything – shootin stars or dandelions or eyelashes or pennies in wells. I say no more wishing. That's my covenant and my directive. Life comes. It comes willy-nilly. It's best to open your eyes to it and cease the buildin of lofty castles in your head – or you could blind yourself with earnest prayers.

Eleven

A Christening » Fletcher's End » The Destruction of
the Gasworks » An Identification by Boots » A Death »
The Compass of the Self » Nature » A Dream of
Dolphins » A Search » A Vision

It ain't true, he says and shakes his head in absolute
refusal. My brother's still here. I can feel it.

Then the Vestal spins on her heels and unleashes her
full fury, like a poison capsule broke into a cup of water.

Goddamn you, Moses, she says. Why don't you just
for once in your life shut up about your piss-ant
brother. You want to die here, then die here. What's
happening out in the world ain't nothing compared to
the civil war you got in you, Mose. Jesus, you'd follow
those little codes of yours straight into your grave. You
don't always have to take the bait, you know. Sometimes you can just let it go.

She walks to the door, still talking as her back is to
him.

I ain't dying here, Moses. I'm dying all right – but it

ain't gonna be here. And if it is, I want it to come from the back as I'm boltin to get the hell out. See you in heaven, Mose – I hope it's designed to your specifications.

She is nearly out the door before Moses Todd calls to her.

Hold up, he says.

She stops, but she does not turn to face him. Her back is to him, and she grips the handle of the door.

Your name, he says. What is it?

My name?

I know it ain't Amata. And I know it ain't that other name Fletcher calls you. So what is it? Your true name.

You want to know my name?

She says the words to the door in a voice so small he can barely hear. He wonders how long it has been since she has last said her own name – how long since she has been simply herself.

Yes, he says. Your name. I'd like to – I'd feel privileged to know it.

There is quiet for a moment – a brief interim in which even the sounds of the battle outside seem suspended – as though the whole world takes a breath and waits on the exhale. Everyone is heartbeats in their ears.

Then she says something, but it is so low and mumbled into the door that he can't hear it.

What? he says. I couldn't—

Mattie, she says, turning towards him and showing him her painted, sparkled face one last time. Her eyes are wet and shot through with pinpoints of brightness – as if all her fears, so many of them, bleed out like trapped light. My name's Mattie.

He opens his mouth to speak, but there are no words. He would like to take the name and affix it to his cudgel as another blade to rip and tear at the world – and then he could feel the whole true talon sharpness of it.

The only thing he can say is her name, a repetition that is just as questioning as it is confirming:

Mattie.

Do you believe me? she asks.

Is it true? he replies.

Goodbye, Moses, she says.

She goes through the door, leaving it open wide. The light reflected from the snow outside makes a portal through which it looks as though angels might spill. She said she would see him in heaven, and it was a joke. But this is something he knows deeper than all things: there are doors to heaven everywhere.

*

Outside there is no sign of the Vestal. He scans, momentarily, the tree line at the hill, but there is no trace of her. It is as if she has stepped out into the light and been spirited up – a recalled angel in gaudy ribbons.

But something is happening on the grounds of the gasworks. The uniformed men, the soldiers, seem to be retreating. They take stances behind dense stands of machinery, fire off a few shots and then fall back to other locations. They are receding from the valley with slow deliberation. It is not that they are overwhelmed – their movements are strategic.

Explosives, the Vestal said. They would bring hell down, she said.

Moses looks at the line of low buildings. There is no time. He will not be able to search them all for his brother. Something grips him, and he wonders, stilled as a philosopher in contemplation of a lakeside, if he is willing to die here for the sake of Abraham. It is a quiet, unpanicked thought, and he wishes he had more time to discover the answer, because the answer is of some vague but definite interest to him. The answer, he feels, might tell him a great deal about himself and his place in the world. His little codes, as the Vestal called them.

But there is no time for such thoughts and speculations.

He rushes forward, unsure how he will proceed. And that's when he sees Fletcher. The man in the sombrero emerges from one of the wide buildings, poking his head around the corner as if looking for an opportune moment to run. A rodent, twitchy and slick.

Moses grips the bladed cudgel tight in his hand and walks slowly to the place where Fletcher peeks around the corner. The man in the sombrero isn't aware of Moses' presence until the very last moment. Then he leaps back against the corrugated wall of the building and knocks his sombrero askew.

You, he says.

Where's my brother, says Moses.

Your brother?

Fletcher looks confused for a moment. Then he narrows his eyes at Moses.

What is it now – some kinda negotiation? You gonna spare my life if I fess up and tell you where he's hid?

No, I ain't. You brought too much abomination into the world. More than your share. You threw things off balance. I'm gonna kill you no matter what.

Then why should I tell you?

Cause it'd be one good thing you done just prior to the final reckoning of your account.

Fletcher's hand reaches up to his scabrous face and begins to pick instinctively at the little nodules of hardened skin.

You're a fuckin relic, he says in his snivelling way to Moses.

Fletcher is not looking at him when he says this. Instead, he looks down at the icy mud on the ground – as though he would like to dig himself into the very earth with his little rat nose.

Did she purchase him? Moses asks now.

Fletcher looks at him, his eyes narrowing again in the scabbed flesh of his face

Did she? Moses says again. The Vestal, did she purchase his release on her body?

Is that what she said? She told you that, eh? And now you don't know whether to believe her or not.

Did she or did she not?

Fletcher doesn't answer. Instead a smile creeps across his greasy face like slow poison. Then the smile turns into a chuckle, and the chuckle into a full-blown laugh. He laughs and laughs, Fletcher does, doubling over and slapping his thighs – as though it weren't the end of the world at this very moment. Or as though it were.

It's a goddamn shame, Fletcher says, coughing between fits of laughter, when the business of men and God is brought low by womanly wiles. Ain't it? Ain't it a goddamn shame?

Fletcher laughs and laughs.

Far as I been able to tell, he goes on, a cunt is a cunt is a cunt. But you're a romantic, ain't you?

The little man begins to do a short, hopping dance, laughing and clapping his hands, teetering as if he is on all the terrible dizzying precipices of the world.

Romantic, romantic, romantic! he cries, laughing and dancing. Romantic, romantic, ro—

Moses raises the pistol and, in the very same gesture, as though a liquid movement with no real beginning and no end, fires.

The bullet goes wide, whistles by Fletcher's ear. Fletcher, frozen in expectation, waits to see if he's dead yet. Then, a moment later, he reaches up and feels the wholeness of his intact face.

You missed, he says simply to Moses. Looks like you ain't such a good—

Moses fires again, and this time the bullet flies true and hits Fletcher in the forehead with a tiny wet crack.

Fletcher collapses in a heap on the ground, the sombrero falling and rolling a few feet before it drops like a tired top into the muck.

So quick, how some fall – so narrow the border between life and death. You could trip and stumble over it. The way Fletcher lies there in the mud, his head leaking onto the ground, as if he were simply a broken milk jug, you would never have thought such a fragile object could cause so much distress.

Moses is studying the body in the sudden quiet of the battlefield when a concussion of air knocks him backwards into the mud. It is only afterwards that he hears the raucous thunder of the explosion itself – as though sound were not a herald but an afterthought.

*

Black smoke engulfs the building at the end of the row.

Moses, his ears ringing, clambers to his feet just as the second building goes and he is knocked down once more.

And now the world is muffled near to deafness. What he can hear is his own heart beating, his teeth clacking against one another. The dead, who have no concept of self-protection, remain immobile, turning their heads slowly towards the fire to gaze with mild wonder upon the shifting colours. They will stand, mesmerized, until the flame has engulfed them – Moses has seen it. And so it happens now to one dead woman standing near the second building. She catches fire, her dress melting to her flesh as a single cinder, stumbling forward, surprised, mewling, not trying to put herself out. She collapses to a sitting position, mystified finally by the abomination of her own skin fluid with flame, raising her own arm to see the way the fire enrobes it – until at last the heat boils her brain and she falls, stinking, to the ground.

Abraham, Moses says. It could be a whisper or a shout – he does not know, because he cannot hear his own words.

Hell falls on the place and Moses has not found his brother. He does not even look behind him to the hills. Escape means nothing to him. He will die here looking for his only kin. A suitable end – it's what men wish for, finally.

There's a third explosion – not another of the low buildings this time, but one of the gargantuan metal towers. The explosion at the base causes the tower to lean, crippled, suspended for a moment at a limping angle – then, with a strain and break of metal joints that Moses can feel in his sternum more than hear, the tower crashes to the ground.

That's when he sees Abraham. At first it's just a figure, on fire, running crazy from behind one of the buildings, arms waving. Then Moses recognizes the boots. The tooled leather cowboy boots his brother has always been so proud of. He would polish them at night by firelight, bring them tenderly back to full lustre with a rag and a spit shine. A man, sometimes, is told by his boots when the rest of him has got aflame.

Then Moses is running. He tackles his burning

brother to the ground and rolls him in the mud till the flames go out.

Abe! Moses says. It's me. It's your brother. Abe!

There is no response, but Moses can see that he's still alive. He takes a fistful of mud and slathers it as a salve over the melted and charred face and neck of his brother. He does not know what else to do, and such an act feels proper to nature.

Another building explodes now, this one very near.

Moses sees his brother's lips move.

I can't hear you Abe, Moses says. I can't hear nothin. We got to get. You ready?

Moses lifts the slack body of his brother and slings it over his shoulder. Then he runs. He runs towards the tree line at the base of the hill. Another explosion shakes the earth behind him. Everything is on fire now – the heat of the valley, he can see it in the shivering air.

Then he's climbing up through the trees, the weight of his brother's body on his shoulder, pulling himself up on the slippery hillside, his breath coming short and ragged. Two more buildings explode behind him. How could there be anything left to destroy? A point must come when the forces of destruction must be stymied by their own completeness. Mustn't it?

He rests, bracing himself against the trunk of a tree, only for a moment. Something collapses in the gas-works behind him, but again he does not look to see. He keeps his eyes focused on the bright snowy rim of the hilltop. Then he shifts Abraham on his shoulder and starts forwards again.

Higher he climbs until he has crested the hilltop, well above the buildings of the valley. There he stops in a small clearing in the trees and sets down his brother gently in the snow. Moses can hardly breathe, but he falls to his hands and knees to check on Abraham. His brother's face, he sees now, is melted away – and one of the eyes is open, and he doesn't seem to be breathing.

Moses leans down and puts his ear to Abraham's mouth, and he takes the wrist to find the pulse. But there's nothing.

He can't even catch his breath long enough to curse his brother for dying.

Instead he sits back against a tree trunk and listens to the crackling inferno in the valley below – still muffled by his buffeted eardrums. The sun peers through the treetops, and he drinks in the cold air like an elixir.

He licks his lips. There are things to say and no one in the world to say them to. Not even God – who is about his business on the wonders of the world and doesn't – should not – take time for the puny sufferings of one bereft man.

So instead he talks to the charred body of his brother.

She lied, he says. She lied to me, Abe. And I almost took trust in it. Shamed to say I almost did.

There are now popping sounds down in the valley, as of a series of small tanks exploding. It will take days for the valley to burn itself out completely.

He licks his lips again.

I guess it's lucky for you you died, Abe, he says. This world, it was too easy for you to get into trouble in.

Then he gets up and crawls to his brother's body and takes the arms from where they are flailed wide and lays them neat and proper across his chest. And that's when he notices something. The index finger on the left hand is gone to the second joint. He raises the hand to look close. It seems the wound is an old one, the scar healed over clean. Then he looks more closely at the melted face, pries open one of the charred eyelids.

Moses Todd sighs heavy and sits back again against the trunk of the tree.

Goddamnit, he says. You ain't Abraham.

There is neither relief nor disappointment in his voice. It is just a statement of fact. The compass of your own self is hard to follow if the world keeps changing the direction of true north.

He sighs and squeezes his eyes shut with his grimy fingers and says:

Just when you think things're sorted.

*

Moses walks to the edge of the clearing and looks down into the bowl of fire below him. He feels the heat blustering up into his face like a summer wind – and melting the ice in the trees for an artificial kind of rainfall. The structures are all collapsed or gutted by flame – metal twisted brutal and liquid around metal. A thick grey smoke rises into the air and clings to the trees all around, causing Moses to bend double coughing. What down there was living before is now dead and gone to ashes.

When he turns back to the clearing, he sees the burnt corpse of the boot thief stirring. He walks to the slug and gazes down on it for a moment. Then he uses his pistol to put a single bullet through the forehead, and the dead man settles back into stillness.

Moses bends down and removes the boots from the dead man's feet. Then he leans against the trunk of a tree and looks up between the branches into the smoky sky. There is an exhaustion on him the like of which he has never felt before.

His hearing is still shot, so he wonders deafly what kind of complaint the birds must be making about the smoke that poisons their arboreal homes. He has an affinity for nature, he realizes, because it is governed by principles and laws that are clear and precise as anything.

It's the various and mutable nonsense of man he can't abide.

*

He follows the ridge around the valley and back to the road. There are signs of battle everywhere. Moses sees what has happened. When the explosives were detonated, the inhabitants of the valley fled by the main road, but they were met by the soldiers who cleaned up whoever was left. It looks like they were shot with mounted guns – some of the bodies perforated almost in half by a line of bullet holes.

But one thing about the military: they do things right. There is not a corpse left that hasn't been neatly brain-killed. So despite the full garden of bodies, nothing stirs in the hot breeze. Rivulets of melted ice flow down the tarmac, shifting their course around the various dams of bodies.

It is quiet, so quiet. Except now there's a ringing in Moses' ears growing louder, and he knows this to be a portent of the return of his hearing.

He finds the car he came in, but it has been pushed onto its side into a ditch and likely wouldn't run any more anyway. He searches for another vehicle, but the ones that remain have been shot to pieces or salvaged of their vital parts. So Moses sets off walking up the road. The clip of his pistol holds only three more rounds – and his bladed cudgel got left behind when he carried the boot thief out of the valley – so he is likely to be in trouble if he encounters any resistance.

But the road is clear, and the sun is bright. And soon his hearing returns. It seems to rush back all of a sudden, and for a moment the world seems unbearably loud – as if he can detect, for a brief second, the constant static that hisses there behind everything all the time. And he wonders how we are not all driven mad by it – and wonders if maybe we are.

About two miles down the road, he finds the ruin of a gas station with a garage attached. It looks secure enough. He tries the front door, but it is locked, so he goes around the back and climbs through an upper window.

It takes his eyes a moment to adjust to the dimness of the place, and then he sees the figure in the corner, wrapped in a tarp, shivering.

He walks over to the shaking man, whose eyes are closed in a sickly delirium, whose bootless feet obtrude from under the edge of the tarp. Moses leans down and wipes the sweat off the brow.

Hey, he says. Hey, wake up now.

The eyes open slowly, and they seem to take a long time to focus on anything. But then they see.

Hey, brother, Abraham says. I guess this means I ain't dead yet, huh?

Huh-uh.

It's harder to die than you think. The world, it conspires to keep you alive.

*

Moses finds a car that starts. He lifts his brother and carries him to the car and puts him in. Abe's body is shivering, and the wound on his leg stinks.

Am I gonna lose it? Abraham asks. The leg, I mean.

You might could, Moses says. But what's a leg? We still got three good ones between us.

They drive back towards the citadel. The sun is before them now, beginning its decline over the hills.

They are silent for a long time. Finally, Moses asks Abraham what happened.

You mean how I ended up at that garage? Abraham asks.

I reckon so.

Abraham shakes his head and looks abstractedly at the road unspooling ahead of them.

I don't know, truth be told. They knocked me out pretty good when they took me. I came to when they drug me out of the car at the gasworks. Didn't know where I was – or how long I'd been under. I puked on one of em.

Abraham chuckles, which sends visible shivers up and down his body.

Yeah, he goes on, I puked all over one of em. That's when they commenced to kickin me in the guts. But you know I been gut kicked before – I know how to take it. I got some bruises, but nothing in me ruptured. And I saw they had the girl, too. That Vestal. She come runnin out from somewhere towards me, yelling something or other, I couldn't hear what. But they grabbed her and drug her back. You find her too?

Moses nods.

I found her, he says.

Abraham looks into the back seat, as if to ask without out words where the girl is. But he doesn't speak it. Maybe he can see that his brother does not want to be queried on the matter.

They hauled me into one of them buildings, he goes on, laid me out on the floor. Then Fletcher came in – told me how he was gonna kill me a hundred different ways. I told him it was a shame for him he could only really kill me once – since he seemed to have a lot of brainstormed ideas on the subject. Then he told me how he was gonna kill you – and he had a hundred different ways to kill you too. That guy, he can get pretty creative on the topic of murder. He's an enthusiast. We might want to steer clear of him for a bit.

He's dead, Moses says.

He is?

Uh-huh.

You kill him?

Uh-huh.

How'd you do it?

Pistol, Moses says and points to his own forehead to illustrate where the bullet went.

Hm, says Abraham. That's on the generic side. I bet he was disappointed. Anyway, he left for a while, and I slept on the concrete – I don't know how long, could of been a week.

It wasn't.

I dreamed of the ocean. Ain't that funny? I dreamed I was ridin dolphins under the water. It felt good. I mean, it really felt okay in that dream. You know?

Moses says nothing.

I woke up and figured I'd see you there too and then he'd kill us both but I was bound determined to tell you bout the dolphins first.

I guess you got it told.

I guess I did.

And he *was* there when I woke up, but it wasn't like I thought. He'd changed his mind about killin me somehow. Hauled me to the front gates and tossed me out. Said if he saw me again he'd shoot me dead, no more palaver on the topic. How do you figure that?

Moses shrugs.

Probably it don't signify much, Moses says.

It must signify somethin.

Maybe he just spit you back out – didn't like your flavour.

Yeah, maybe.

Abraham looks at his brother with a curious gaze. His body shudders, and he wipes his nose on his sleeve and looks out at the road again.

So I walked far as I could, he says. But my leg, it wasn't cooperatin. I made it to the garage. Boxed myself in. Figured it to be as good a grave as any. Reckoned you were dead already or would be dead tryin to fetch me back. It seemed like the end comin to bear all around. All I wanted was sleep. Suck my last breath ridin a dolphin to the bottom of the ocean.

Abraham looks at Moses, and Moses nods but continues to stare straight ahead.

Anyway, Abraham says. That's the soup to nuts of what I've been up to. How bout you?

So Moses explains how there was a battle between the soldiers and the brigands, how he came down into the middle of it to find Abraham, how he saw the Vestal Amata but then lost track of her, how he killed Fletcher with a bullet to his brain, how he found someone he took to be Abraham but it turned out not to be and the man died anyway, how the whole valley got urpped into the sky by fire, how Moses got to his feet and walked away, how the world was so empty, and the sky so sooty from smoke, how he happened upon the garage and chanced to look inside.

I got your boots in the back seat, Moses says.

You do?

Uh-huh.

That bastard stole em, he said. He looked like me, huh?

I couldn't tell him – he was burned pretty bad. I was just goin by the boots.

You let him go?

Wasn't no chance to. The burns got him first.

Abraham nods. Then the shivers seize him again.

They took my pills, he tells Moses. The ones for my leg.

It don't matter. We'll get more. Anything you need.

We goin to the cathedral?

Uh-huh.

Good. I could use a rest from wanderin for a bit.

Moses nods – though he understands now that there are no rests from anything, not really.

*

Back at the citadel, Abraham is rolled away into the back rooms of the medical wing. The old pastor, Whitfield, finds Moses and claps him on the shoulder.

They'll take care of him, he says. You needn't worry.

I ain't worried, Moses says.

You were there, in the assault?

I was.

It was bad, I heard. We had some casualties, but not many.

Uh-huh.

We'll plant new growth over the burn. It's something.

It don't matter. It's just a symbol.

Don't disdain a symbol, says Whitfield. In this world, a symbol is the closest we come to magic.

This may be true. Moses is too tired to think very hard on it.

Did you find the girl? Whitfield asks.

Found her and lost her again.

She might have made it?

Could of.

We'll pray for her recovery in the chapel. But I've seen very few women as industrious as she. I have great faith that she's still out there and may find her way home.

Moses wants to ask him *What home is that, Pastor?* Instead he just nods, because it is true. The Vestal is as industrious as any. And it's also true that she's likely still out there on the wide, long roads of the country, having claimed her divorcement from Moses as just one more gorgeous escape.

*

They clean Abraham's wound and wrap his leg with sterile bandages. Then they hook him up to an IV and give him something to make him sleep. Moses stays by his bedside, watching his brother's dozing form, unable to sleep himself – exhausted though he is.

Once Abraham's eyes flutter open, and he seems to pull himself from sleep as a drowning man surfacing for a brief moment.

Mose?

Yeah. Right here, brother.

Mose, have I still got my leg?

It's still affixed. The doctors say you're gonna get restored.

Goddamn miracle baby, ain't I?

You are at that.

For a moment it looks as though Abraham will nod off again, but he revives himself once again and starts digging around with clumsy fingers on his chest.

Mose?

Yeah.

Here. Take this.

His fingers get under the cloth of the hospital gown they put him in and clutch at something. It's the yewess bee given him by Albert Wilson Jacks, Moses sees, still attached to its leather shoelace. Moses takes it from him and slips the lanyard over his head.

They got machines here can talk to it. I know they do. Plug it in somewhere and find out what kind of bee it is.

Moses says he will, and then Abraham lies back and shuts his eyes and dives under the surface of wakefulness once more.

Later Moses takes Abraham's plastic talisman and hands it to Whitfield.

What is it? Whitfield says.

Moses shrugs.

It was give to Abraham. Can you all find out what it does? I'll be back. I gotta run an errand.

*

He drives back to the valley, where the gasworks have mostly burned themselves out. The ground is charred black, and the structures that still stand are twisted and skeletal. The stink of sulphur is everywhere, and ash blows in the breeze, itself lighter than the snow that is now falling. And so there are two currents of air visible – the one that carries to the ground a speckled white to erase the destruction of man with its own destruction, and the other that blusters upwards the grey, dusty remains of people and things, like the tide that takes souls to heaven.

It is quiet, peaceful, and Moses searches the remains of the valley. He turns over the corpses one by one and looks them in their faces, searching for some sign of the Vestal Amata, dead or alive as she may be.

Some of the dead have risen again, and they struggle to move towards him over the snowy, ashy earth. But their skin is charred black and flaky, and it rustles in the breeze, the flakes of their burned flesh like the leaves on a budding tree in the springtime. A shimmying, fluid quality of death he can't remember seeing before. One of the dead, man or woman he can't tell, is a walking skeleton. Its skin has been burned away entirely, a blackened exposed skull with its wide bony grin. And, too, its eyeballs have been boiled out of the sockets, so it finds its way blindly through the wreckage, stumbling pathetically and falling face down into the mud, rising again and smelling its way forwards a few paces.

Moses puts them all down, spending his ammunition indiscriminately to make the valley an entirely quiet, entirely dead place. He puts down the ones who are still walking and examines the others. Rummaging through the wreckage, he finds the bladed cudgel he dropped in order to carry to safety the man he thought was his brother. The cudgel's handle juts straight upwards like a chiding finger, its head bent and melted into the remains of some fallen tower. He pulls once, twice, at the handle, trying to dislodge the thing, but he is obviously unworthy of this particular Excalibur, as it does not budge – and then he thinks that this is as good a resting place as any for the brutal bladed thing. He continues to look.

Finding nothing, he widens his search, stomping through the base of the tree line where the fire has wilted the evergreens and cooked them all black on one side.

He circles the valley once, and then again higher into the trees. On the third time around he sees something caught in a tree branch, dangling and whipping back and forth in the snowy air. He comes closer and takes it in his hand.

It's the Vestal's little wooden cross pendant, the one she wore around her neck, and it's a sign if it's anything. He recalls the Pastor Whitfield's warning not to disdain symbols, and he realizes he does not disdain them at all – though he wishes he knew how to read them. He is illiterate in the language of symbols.

What does the cross mean? That she is alive? That she left it as a breadcrumb for him to follow? That it fell, unknown, from her neck in her escape? Or simply that it was blown off her body in one of the explosions and that she is now part of the dusty ash he breathes into his weary lungs?

Symbols everywhere, and they refuse to be read.

He takes the cross, twining the thin silver chain around his thick, calloused fingers, holding the tiny wooden pendant tight in the meaty palm of his hand. He holds it as though he will never let it go.

Though that, too – the gripping of the cross – that too is a symbol for the speculation of those who know the language.

The night falls, and he stays among the ruins. He lies on the ground and lets the snow fall onto his beard and his eyelids and his lips. Finally, in this place of devastation, this graveyard of man and industry, this broken toe of civilization, finally, he sleeps.

*

When he wakes, it is full dark, and he realizes he has slept many hours there on the ground. He stands and sheds a thin layer of snow that has fallen and wed him to the ground on which he lay. He shakes it off, and he is not cold though he can see his breath.

The moon is out and casts mangled shadows over the valley, and in the dark he believes he sees a figure darting through the trees. A naked girl, skin pale and shimmering, almost translucent, red hair chopped short – and there she dashes from tree trunk to tree trunk, disappearing into the shadows and reappearing else-where in unexpected places, like a capricious sprite or a trick of the eye. He would call to her if he believed she would be held by his voice. Instead, he finds himself running, bursting into the trees, crashing through them in pursuit of the ghostly shape of the girl. The branches whip and slash at his face, and he can feel the blood trickling on his skin. Or it could be tears, it makes no difference – the salt and aluminium we shed as a result of our stinging contact with the world.

I'm sorry! he calls into the shadows. I'm sorry. I should of believed you. I should of. Faith and love, they ain't the same thing. Are they? Are they the same thing? I'm sorry. Come back now. You can come back!

He runs until his body collapses beneath him, his breath gone. He falls to his hands and knees, truly ursine now, a beast of the wilderness huffing and pant-ing his way through the night. His lungs are scorching, and he scoops up a handful of snow and swallows it to cool his insides. When his gasping breath slows, he looks around him. There is no sign of the naked girl anywhere.

She is a beguiling ghost.

She has ever been.

Twelve

A Map » Three Conversations about One Thing »
A Return » A Confession » Another Vision »
How Things Endure

Three days later, Abraham's fever has broken and he is
up and walking around the compound, whistling lewdly
at female passers-by.

Stow it, Abe, Moses says. Let's try to get out of here
without rilin the citizenry. I seen em riled – it ain't
pretty.

Wait, Abraham says. We can't go yet. What about
my yewess bee?

Moses has forgotten about it. He finds Whitfield, and
the two brothers are led to a room with two banks of
computers against opposite walls, facing each other like
parallel rows of guardians.

One of the operators is reminded about the yewess
bee.

Oh yeah, he says. It's around here somewhere. It

was easy – but there's nothing on it really. I was going to tell somebody, but – here it is.

The operator is a young man wearing a t-shirt. He is a poor arbiter of grand mysteries such as this, Moses thinks.

The operator plugs Abraham's talisman into a port in one of the computers and then brings up something on screen that Moses recognizes as the shape of the United States. There are red dots all over it, as though the entire country has succumbed to some kind of pox.

It's a map, Moses says.

A map! Abraham repeats.

Of what? Moses asks.

A treasure map, I bet, says Abraham.

Actually, says the operator, it's a corporate map. It shows all the locations all over the country of a particular business. I guess it was a franchise. There are, like, twelve hundred of them.

What business? Moses asks.

National Waffle or something like that? Hold on, here it is – it was something called the International House of Pancakes.

The pastor, who is the only other one present, besides Moses, old enough to remember such predominant American wonders, laughs. It is a sad laugh, full of empty spaces that used to be filled with something. Moses laughs much the same laugh, and together, unspoken, the two men try to make of the moment something less dire.

What? Abraham asks for the two chuckling men. What is it?

It's your treasure map, all right, his brother replies.

What some mysteries reveal are truths so mundane they blast wide our own ludicrous vanities.

*

They say farewell to the pastor and leave the citadel behind them. For his service against the raiders, Moses is given a good car with two extra jugs of gasoline packed in the trunk. He is also given some rifles, some ammunition. The citadel's stores are vast – they can afford such things.

They drive, first north a little ways, then south again. They are directionless as far as Abraham is concerned, though wherever he goes Moses is looking for the girl he turned his back on.

Once, Abraham discovers Moses clutching the wooden cross pendant while he drives – but he does not recognize it as the one the Vestal wore around her neck.

You got religious all the sudden? he asks.

It's a symbol, Moses replies. What it signifies ain't simple.

Who said it was simple?

Abraham has his own symbol – the yewess bee. He believes it to be more than just a map of a national chain of restaurants, but instead an elaborate code disguised as a restaurant map. He believes that if they travel to each of the locations, they will piece together some megalithic conspiracy. So every time they pass one of the pancake houses with its blue roof, Moses points it out and Abraham notates it with a pencil in his notebook. It is good for him to have something to follow.

Abraham does not very frequently bring up the topic of the Vestal, having seemed to identify it as out of bounds. The first time is while they are still at the citadel.

So the girl's lost? he says.

Yep, says Moses.

Not dead?

Could be. Moses shrugs. Dead's a kind of lost. But last I saw her she was amongst the livin.

I reckon we should look for her.

I reckon so.

I would of thought she'd come back here.

Girl like that, Moses says with a wave of his hand, you can't figure her. You can't project what she'll do.

The next time the topic arises they are on the road. It is night, and the headlights illuminate the tall trees between which they drive.

We could trace our path back, Abraham says. To look for her, the Vestal, you know.

We could do that.

Abraham does not seem to be aware that this is exactly what they are already doing.

What happened, Mose? Between the two of you, I mean.

I just lost her is all.

So it's guilty feelins that've got you all puckered up about it?

I ain't puckered. I just lost her. She was lookin to be lost anyway – you and me, we were just fightin it from the very beginning. Nature takes its course is what happens.

They drive. Abraham sleeps in the passenger seat. Moses keeps his eyes wide, his fingers clenched on the wheel.

On another occasion, Abraham raises the topic again but only indirectly. He asks Moses if he thinks much any more about his wife who went missing. He liked Moses' wife, he says. She was an okay woman. Women for the most part, he says, are a dodgy bunch – but he guesses he can't blame them what with all the men taking aim at them.

Moses says nothing. He agrees that women are dodgy, but his mind is so full of lost ones now that he wishes his memories could take refuge elsewhere than in his sleepless head. He looks deep into the tree trunks, hoping to see there another vision of the naked girl darting back and forth behind them.

But there is nothing, and they drive on. At night, when they stop to rest, Moses hears his brother's snoring and hopes he is dreaming among his dolphins.

*

They return to the town of Dolores where the whore-house is, but the inhabitants have not seen hide nor hair of the Vestal.

They drive south, out of the snow, over the mountains and down into the valley, where the arid desert lays claim to the land.

It is just after dawn when they arrive at the Mission San Xavier del Bac and ring the bell at the gate. The mute woman who opens the door recognizes the brothers from the last time they were here, and she ushers them inside. The monk Ignatius greets them in the chapel and feeds them eggs gathered from their own coops in the rear of the community.

The brothers know they must not speak, not here among the parishioners, and so they eat silently. Moses and Ignatius gaze at each other, and Moses tries to tell the man the entire story with his eyes – for maybe that mode of communication is less treacherous. But soon Moses realizes there are untruths even in looks, so he stops trying and sits meditatively at the table.

Later, while Abraham plays some version of soccer with the children of the place, the children trying to teach him without words, making wide explanatory gestures with their hands – Moses and the monk leave through the front gate and climb the hill behind the mission and sit on an outcropping of stones, squinting their eyes against the desert sun.

Did you make it to the citadel? Ignatius asks.

We did. We got her there.

Did they examine her?

They did. You ain't gonna like it, friar.

My liking it is beside the point.

She's got a disease. A hereditary one. It's in her blood. That's why the slugs don't bother with her. She's already half dead.

Ignatius nods and smiles benignly at the horizon.

So what's bestowed on her, Moses continues, it ain't a blessing.

Ignatius shrugs.

Disease or blessing, who can say? he asks. If a disease helps you survive in the world, then it's no longer a disease but an adaptation. Evolution would tell you as much.

But it's more than that, friar. The girl, she ain't a holy woman. She put on pretences.

I know that, too. I never saw her other pretences – but the one she put on here was a righteous one, so I pretended along with her. Sometimes a thing becomes true through enacting it. Sometimes you perform faith in order to gain faith. Do you believe that?

I don't know. I don't believe in nothin right now.

See, now there's a pretence you just uttered. Do you say it because you wish it were true? Because you would try to incant it?

I won't spar with you, says Moses as he raises his hands in surrender and smiles gently, on the field of philosophy.

I would be a fool, my friend, to spar with you on any other.

They are quiet for a time. Then sun is low on the horizon now, the sky lit up all shock red and streaky white.

Then Moses speaks, this time very quiet, as though his words were really meant for the wind to carry them away.

She sacrificed herself, friar. Not her life, but in another way. She said it was for me.

Do you believe her?

I didn't, not when she told me.

And now?

Now I think I do. We got separated. I thought – I thought she might be here. Now I don't know what . . .

You suspect she was in love with you?

Moses does not respond. His eyes are gone far out over the horizon.

You suspect, maybe, you are in love with her?

I'm lost, friar, Moses says, his eyes gone suddenly wet. I can't – I can't see the colours of anything any more. It used to be I was a man, but what am I now? I lost my way somewhere.

Moses Todd looks into the face of the monk Ignatius, and the holy man smiles back. It is a smile full of blustery optimism.

Look, he says to Moses and points to the sunset. Look out there. What do you see?

The desert, Moses says.

No, you have to look wider. Open your eyes more. Do you see that? It's America. No one's ever lost in

America. It's all destination. Every corner of it. Even right here, on this rock, with me. You've arrived. Do you see it?

And then, suddenly, Moses *can* see it. America. The fertile fields of the republic stretched taut from ocean to ocean, populated with ambling souls, dead or alive, it makes no difference as long as they are moving, as long as their hands still work to grasp and pull and reach and tear. A destiny manifest in every rock and ruin, a loamy soil of faith where God's work is done one way or the other – because every creation winds its way towards destruction and every destruction wipes clean a canvas for creation.

A place, indeed, poxed by calamitous treasures like Abraham's blue-roofed pancake houses – gigging itself forward in a frenzy of speed (yes, this is what Moses hasn't seen before – the country, not stopped dead, but spinning in such mazy motion the blur might be taken for stasis), galloping ahead of life and ahead of death too, and back into life, the two masquerading as each other, unable to keep up, as though time were a circuit rather than a line.

And if time is a circuit – if our paths only bring us back to where we begun, well then proclaim it holy, holy, because the friar is right – ain't nothing is ever lost but it's just on a different road, and it's all of it, the whole country, just one big road attached to itself in different ways – and so are all travellers kin, and so are all people travellers through life.

And, yes, he can see her dancing again, naked, that

white body on the sunset plain, a vision if ever there was one, holy woman and whore, never lost but she dances America to its sleep every night – and you can hear her laughter, that voice both tricksy and true, clamouring America in all its broken bells. And you are glad.

*

Was her name really Mattie? Moses says now to the caravaners, those who remain awake.

Now, in the distance, the sky is empurpled by dawn. The stars have dimmed against the lightening void, and the horizon becomes invisible as a sharp-cut silhouette – something you might trace with pencil and compass.

I like to believe Mattie was her name – that she told me it true, even if just that one time. It's passed my lips enough times, maybe more like a prayer than a rightful name. Mattie. Mattie, you out there somewhere? Mattie – where'd you get to, girl? It's just a word is all it is, a word spoke to the darkness. But so are all words. Goodness, purity, truth, God. You build somethin with your eyes closed. You speak it to life. Then you open your eyes – and what kind of tower? Where's it reach to? Maybe nowhere. Maybe all the way to heaven.

He pauses. There is rustling movement among the listeners. Perhaps some of them are waking to his voice, the same voice they fell asleep to, and are now wondering what a thing is a story with just a beginning and an end. Perhaps some of them are just antic against the dawn.

We searched her out for a long time, Moses continues, Abraham and me. Sometimes we'd hear stories that sounded like they could of been her – but we never saw her again. Ten years now. Could be I'm cursed to tail women my whole life. My wife and daughter – they got away from me. Mattie the Vestal – who ran when I sent her runnin.

He stops again and seems to consider how long he has been chasing people who refuse to be found.

It was only one girl I had any talent for huntin, he says. She – well, she cost me my eye, and the price of my brother, finally, in exchange for Maury there.

He gestures with a nod of his chin to the large mute sleeping at the perimeter of the group.

Just a young girl, that one. I bear her no grudge. One thing you could say about her, she balanced the log books like a true accountant of life. She – yeah, she got away from me too.

He pauses one last time – and this time the silence feels like a bottomless chasm everyone, all the listeners and the teller too, stands on the precipice of.

But that's a different story altogether, Moses Todd says finally. I guess this story here's found its finish.

He and his companion travel with the caravan one more day. When the night falls again, he is silent – as though his story of the previous night has exhausted him in a profound way. One of the children, a toddler, approaches him sleepily. The one-eyed man reaches out his hand as if to tousle the child's blond hair, but at the last moment he pulls his arm back – as though afraid his touch could never be light enough to keep the youngster from shattering harm.

In the morning, both men are gone.

The caravan continues its slow progress over the plain in

the direction of many Americas – more than can be counted. Three days later, it is attacked by marauders. The caravaners manage finally to repel the attack, but not without significant losses. Half the travellers are killed, but half survive.

The Reapers Are The Angels

**Set in the same bleak world as *Exit Kingdom*,
but at a different time, there was
The Reapers Are The Angels . . .**

Older than her years and completely alone, Temple is just trying to live one day at a time in a post-apocalyptic world, where the undead roam endlessly, and the remnants of mankind who have survived seem, at times, to retain little humanity themselves.

Temple has known nothing else. This is the world she was born into. Her journey takes her to far-flung places, to people struggling to maintain some semblance of civilization – and to those who have created a new world order for themselves.

When she comes across the helpless Maury, she attempts to set one thing right. If she can just get him back to his family then maybe it will bring forgiveness for some of the terrible things she's done in her past. Because Temple has had to fight to survive; along the road she's made enemies – and one vengeful man is determined that, in a world gone mad, killing her is the only thing that makes sense . . .

Read on for an extract

One

GOD IS a slick god. Temple knows. She knows because of all the crackerjack miracles still to be seen on this ruined globe.

Like those fish all disco-lit in the shallows. That was something, a marvel with no compare that she's been witness to. It was deep night when she saw it, but the moon was so bright it cast hard shadows everywhere on the island. So bright it was almost brighter than daytime because she could see things clearer, as if the sun were criminal to the truth, as if her eyes were eyes of night. She left the lighthouse and went down to the beach to look at the moon pure and straight, and she stood in the shallows and let her feet sink into the sand as the patter-waves tickled her ankles. And that's when she saw it, a school of tiny fish, all darting around like marbles in a chalk circle, and they were lit up electric, mostly silver but some gold and pink too. They came and danced around her ankles, and she could feel their little electric fish bodies, and it was like she was standing *under* the moon and *in* the moon at the same time. And that was something she hadn't seen before. A decade and a half, thereabouts, roaming the planet earth, and she's never seen that before.

And you could say the world has gone to black damnation, and you could say the children of Cain are holding sway over the good and the righteous – but here's what Temple knows: she knows that whatever hell the world went to, and whatever evil she's perpetrated her own self, and whatever series of cursed misfortunes brought her down here to this island to be harboured away from the order of mankind, well, all those things are what put her there that night to stand amid the Daylight Moon and the Miracle of the Fish, which she wouldn't of got to see otherwise.

See, God is a slick god. He makes it so you don't miss out on nothing you're supposed to witness first-hand.

*

She sleeps in an abandoned lighthouse at the top of a bluff. At the base there's a circular room with a fireplace where she cooks fish in a blackened iron pot. The first night she discovered the hatch in the floor that opens into a dank storage room. There she found candles, fishhooks, a first-aid kit and a flare gun with a box of oxidized rounds. She tried one, but it was dead.

In the mornings she digs for pignuts in the under-brush and checks her nets for fish. She leaves her sneakers in the lighthouse; she likes the feel of the hot sand on the soles of her feet, the Florida beach grass between her toes. The palm trees are like bushes in the air, their brittle, dead fronds like a skirt of bones around the tall trunks, rattling in the breeze.

At noon every day, she climbs the spiral stairs to the top of the signal tower, pausing at the middle landing to catch her breath and feel the sun on her face from the grimy window. At the top, she walks the catwalk once around, gazing out over the illimitable sea, and then, towards the mainland coast, the rocky cusp of the blight continent. Sometimes she stops to look at the inverted hemisphere of the light itself, that blind glass optic, like a cauldron turned on its side and covered with a thousand square mirrors.

She can see her reflection there, clear and multifarious. An army of her.

Afternoons, she looks through the unrotted magazines she found lining some boxes of kerosene. The words mean nothing to her, but the pictures she likes. They evoke places she has never been – crowds of the sharply dressed hailing the arrival of someone in a long black car, people in white suits reclining on couches in homes where there's no blood crusted on the walls, women in undergarments on backdrops of seamless white. Abstract heaven, that white – where could such a white exist? If she had all the white paint left in the world, what would go untouched by her brush? She closes her eyes and thinks about it.

It can be cold at night. She keeps the fire going and pulls her army jacket tighter around her torso and listens to the ocean wind whistling loud through the hollow flute of her tall home.

*

Miracle, or augury maybe – because the morning after the glowing fish, she finds the body on the beach. She sees it during her morning walk around the island to check the nets; she finds it on the north point of the teardrop land mass, near the shoal.

At first it is a black shape against the white sand, and she studies it from a distance, measures it with her fingers up to her eye.

Too small to be a person, unless it's folded double or half buried. Which it could be.

She looks around. The wind blowing through the grass above the shore makes a peaceful sound.

She sits and studies the thing and waits for movement.

The shoal is bigger today. It keeps getting bigger. When she first came the island seemed like a long way off from the mainland. She swam to it, using an empty red and white cooler to help keep her afloat in the currents. That was months ago. Since then the island has got bigger, the season pulling the water out further and further every night, drawing the island closer to the mainland. There is a spit of reefy rock extending out from the shore of the mainland and pointing towards the island, and there are large fragments of jutting coral reaching in the other direction from the island. Like the fingers of God and Adam, and each day they come closer to touching as the water retreats and gets shallower along the shoal.

But it still seems safe. The breakers on the reef are violent and thunderous. You wouldn't be able to get across the shoal without busting yourself to pieces on the rock. Not yet at least.

The shape doesn't move, so she stands and approaches it carefully.

It's a man, buried face down in the sand, the tail of his flannel shirt whipping back and forth in the wind. There's something about the way his legs are arranged, one knee up by the small of his back, that tells her his back is broken. There's sand in his hair, and his fingernails are torn and blue.

She looks around again. Then she raises her foot and pokes the man's back with her toe. Nothing happens so she pokes him again, harder.

That's when he starts squirming.

There are muffled sounds coming from his throat, strained grunts and growls – frustration and pathos rather than suffering or pain. His arms begin to sweep the sand as if to make an angel. And there's a writhing, rippling movement that goes through the muscles of his body, as of a broken toy twitching with mechanical repetition, unable to right itself.

Meatskin, she says aloud.

One of the hands catches at her ankle, but she kicks it off.

She sits down beside him, leans back on her hands and braces her feet up against the torso and pushes so that the body flips over face up, leaving a crooked, wet indentation in the sand.

One arm is still flailing, but the other is caught under his back so she stays on that side of him and kneels over his exposed face.

The jaw is missing altogether, along with one of the eyes. The face is blistered black and torn. A flap of skin on the cheekbone is pulled back and pasted with wet sand, revealing the yellow-white of bone and cartilage underneath. The place where the eye was is now a mushy soup of thick, clear fluid mixed with blood, like ketchup eggs. There's a string of kelp sticking out of the nose that makes him look almost comical – as though someone has played a practical joke on him.

But the rightness of his face is distorted by the missing mandible. Even revolting things can be made to look whole if there is a symmetry to them but with the jaw gone, the face looks squat and the neck looks absurdly equine.

She moves her fingers back and forth before his one good eye, and the eye rolls around in its socket trying to follow the movement but stuttering in its focus. Then she puts her fingers down where the mouth would be. He has a set of upper teeth, cracked and brittle, but nothing beneath to bite down against. When she puts her fingers there, she can see the tendons tucked in behind his teeth clicking away in a radial pattern. There are milky white bones jutting out where the mandible would be attached and yellow ligaments like rubber bands stretching and relaxing, stretching and relaxing, with the ghost motion of chewing.

What you gonna do? she says. Bite me? I think your biting days are gone away, mister.

She takes her hand away from his face and sits back, looking at him.

He gets his head shifted in her direction and keeps squirming.

Stop fightin against yourself, she says. Your back's broke. You ain't going nowhere. This is just about the end of your days.

She sighs and casts a gaze over the rocky shoal in the distance, the wide flat mainland beyond.

What'd you come here for anyway, meatskin? she says. Did you smell some girlblood carried on the wind? Did you just have to have some? I know you didn't swim here. Too slow and stupid for that.

There is a gurgle in his throat and a blue crab bursts out from the sandy exposed end of the windpipe and scurries away.

You know what I think? she says. I think you tried to climb across those rocks. And I think you got picked up by those waves and got bust apart pretty good. That's what I think. What do you say about that?

He has worked the arm free from underneath him and reaches towards her. But the fingers fall short by inches and dig furrows in the sand.

Well, she says, you shoulda been here last night. There was a moon so big you could just about reach up and pluck it out of the sky. And these fish, all electric like, buzzing in circles round my ankles. It was something else, mister. I'm telling you, a miracle if ever there was one.

She looks at the rolling eye and the shuddering torso.

Maybe you ain't so interested in miracles. But still and all, you can cherish a miracle without *deserving* one. We're all of us beholden to the beauty of the world, even the bad ones of us. Maybe the bad ones most of all.

She sighs, deep and long.

Anyway, she says, I guess you heard enough of my palaver. Listen to me, I'm doin enough jawing for the both of us. Enough *jawing* for the both of us – get it?

She laughs at her joke, and her laughter trails off as she stands and brushes the sand off her palms and looks out over the water to the mainland. Then she walks up to a stand of palm trees above the beach and looks in the grassy undergrowth, stomping around with her feet until she finds what she's looking for. It's a big rock, bigger than a football. It takes her half an hour to dig around it with a stick and extract it from the earth. Nature doesn't like to be tinkered with.

Then she carries the rock back down to the beach where the man is lying mostly still.

When he sees her, he comes to life again and begins squirming and shuddering and guggling his throat.

Anyway, she says to him, you're the first one that got here. That counts, I guess. It makes you like Christopher Columbus or something. But this tide and all – you wanna bet there's more of you coming? You wanna bet there's all your slug friends on their way? That's a pretty safe bet, I'd say.

She nods and looks out over the shoal again.

Okay then, she says, lifting the rock up over her head and bringing it down on his face with a thick wet crunch.

The arms are still moving, but she knows that happens for a while afterwards sometimes. She lifts the rock again and brings it down on the head twice more just to make sure.

Then she leaves the rock where it is, like a headstone, and goes down to her fishing net and finds a medium-sized fish in it and takes the fish back up to the lighthouse where she cooks it over a fire and eats it with salt and pepper.

Then she climbs the steps to the top of the tower and goes out on the catwalk and looks far off towards the mainland.

She kneels down and puts her chin against the cold metal railing and says:

I reckon it's time to move along again.

Q and A with Alden Bell

Exit Kingdom is a prequel to your last book, *The Reapers Are The Angels*. How did you come up with the idea for *The Reapers Are The Angels*? What was your inspiration?

Reapers came about because of my lifelong love of zombie movies. But many post-apocalyptic stories are too nostalgic for my taste. They are origin stories that concern themselves with how the world came to this sorry state – focusing on characters who are driven by grief and nostalgia over the lives they have lost. Instead, I've always been fascinated by what post-apocalyptia would look like once it has been around long enough to become *normalized* (like, perhaps, *Road Warrior* or *The Book of Eli* or the video game series *Fallout*). So I wanted my main character to have grown up in this new world – to have no memories whatsoever of the pre-apocalypse. I wanted her to be *comfortable* in all the situations we would find so devastating and horrific. She sees beauty where we wouldn't even think to look. I like that tension between beauty and horror – so, in *Reapers*, it was my idea to exploit it as much as possible.

Had you always planned to write a prequel to *The Reapers Are The Angels*?

No. *Reapers* was meant to be a stand-alone book. But, after I had spent some time away from it, I discovered I had a little more to say about that world. Also, I was intrigued by the idea of approaching the same landscape from a different perspective – taking a secondary character from *Reapers* and turning him into the primary character of *Exit Kingdom*. If I were to write a third book, I think I would do the same – maybe telling a story from the Vestal's perspective.

Do you miss Temple, the protagonist from *The Reapers Are The Angels*?

Definitely. But I don't believe in returning to a character or place or story just because I liked it a lot the first time around. I would imagine it's difficult for writers to do a book series without it becoming a dog and pony show, without falling back on old tricks. I would be afraid of attenuating Temple. Sometimes the best way to show respect for a character is to leave her alone.

Your characters have a very distinct style of speaking. Why was language important in *Reapers* and *Exit Kingdom*?

Both books reflect a great deal on the inspiration of southern gothic writers like William Faulkner, Cormac McCarthy, Tom Franklin and Daniel Woodrell – all of whom celebrate the epic potential of language in their writing. My characters speak in a rather hyperbolic way; they use language that's almost too big for their frames, biblical in tone, oratorical in performance – even, let's admit it, unrealistic (though realism has never really been my aim). Stories are powerful not just because of the characters they contain or the plots they outline but also because of the language used to convey them. In Conrad's *Heart of Darkness*, the protagonist Marlow tells a story that engrosses his listeners precisely because of the impossibly over-inflated language he uses. He captures his audience with oratory, and he uses language to give immense authority to his perspective. Marlow was in the back of my head the whole time I was writing Moses' campfire tale. And language is particularly important to people who are disenfranchised by the world at large. Words become not just a way to communicate but rather actions in themselves. A certain combination of words can be like an incantation: it can declare (and by declaring, create) an identity, it can be an attack more brutal than any physical assault, it can function as a gambit in a game of romance or loyalty. The characters in these books are desperately serious about language because, for them, words are all that are left to create meaning, purpose and order.

How has your outlook on life informed your writing?

I'm a sentimentalist, so my writing always borders on melodrama. On the other hand, I've always been a fan of books and movies that upset my expectations – stories that make hard left turns and go in entirely different directions than I expected them to. I love a good anticlimax – the moment where the book has built to a spectacularly dramatic peak, and then the rug is pulled out from under you and everything stumbles to a close. Stories that pander to your every readerly desire and whim are like overly loyal dogs that live for the simple glow of your approval. I'm a cat person. I like a little aloofness in my pets and my writing. I like a story that makes me work a little, a story that sneers haughtily at me from the windowsill, that nips at me if I try to get too cosy with it. It's possible that a little masochism is required to enjoy my books.

How easy do you find writing? If you had to compare yourself to a composer, would you be Mozart, who effortlessly turned out symphonies with little revision, or Beethoven, who famously agonized over each note, going back and rewriting over and over again until he was eventually happy?

I'm no Mozart – but it's true that I don't do much revision in my writing. I tend to start at the beginning of a book and write it straight through to the end in scene order – and I almost never look back more than a page or two during the process. It's not that I feel my words have any kind of holy sanctity but rather that once I've created those scenes, characters, events, it's hard for me to go back and re-imagine them. They become absolutely real to me, for better or worse. I think there's probably a flaw in my imagination that makes writing akin to glassblowing. You have to work fast and do a decent job the first time, because there's no reshaping it later – and if it's no good, you just end up with a twisted, ugly paperweight. Believe me, I've produced plenty of those paperweights.

Do you have a writing routine?

I am very ritualistic about my writing. I get up at 7.15 in the morning and start writing immediately. I write two pages and then take a break to purge the detritus from my mind with inane online searches, or Facebook, or computer games. Then I get back to the work at hand and write another two pages. My deadline for completing these four pages is 11.30 a.m. – at which time I take a walk to get a turkey sandwich for lunch. During lunch, I read twenty pages of whatever book I'm reading at the time. Then I walk back home and write another two pages in the early afternoon. That's it. Six pages a day is my quota. Of course, this kind of rigid adherence to a schedule is easier if you don't have to worry about the demands of *society*. It's possible that my constitution (like Moses Todd's) is better suited to the post-apocalypse.

What advice would you give to aspiring writers?

Write what you want. Don't try to conform to the fickle tastes of a fickle readership. The best audience you can aim for is yourself: write the book that *you* would buy, the book that *you* would have trouble putting down, the book that *you* would want to read but that nobody has written yet. That way, no matter what, whether published or un-, you will have produced a thing of value.

What was your favourite scene to write?

For all the running around and zombie-killing in this book, my favourite scenes are the quiet ones. The action in the book isn't the point for me – it's just the context. It gives a framework for all the late-night conversations between rough men and holy men and insane men and deceptive women and even the taciturn dead. All stories, in one way or another, are about people trying to puzzle through the mysteries of the world around them. The adventurous efforts of humanity to make sense of a chaotic universe, to give order and meaning to the void – those are the struggles worth writing about. And they happen mostly in the noiseless interstices between action.